Damned
by his
Angel

Samantha Barrett

DAMNED BY HIS ANGEL

GODFATHERS OF THE NIGHT

BOOK TWO

SAMANTHA BARRETT

First Edition.

Cover art by Leah

Formatting by Formatting and Design by Jaye.

Editing Elizabeth Gardner

Hey you...
Yeah, you, the one wanting to find the darkest book with all the smutty scenes that get you wet...
Slip between these pages and when you're done, slip between your sheets, ride your fingers until you scream the God of the underworld's name.
Thank me for the orgasm later like a good girl...

TRIGGERS

Note to reader, this book is a cross over from the Murdoch Mafia, Memento Mori and Re Della Strada. You DO NOT need to have read those series before starting this one.

This book contains some scenes that may be triggering, This book is not for the faint of heart, be warned.

Sexual assault
Rape
Mental abuse
Emotional abuse
Physical abuse
Sexual manipulation
Breeding Kink
Domestic Violence
Bully

Authors Note

Names of places have been changed to fit this story. Some places have been altered to fit with the storyline and the characters.

Prologue

Cronos

"I'm done!" I'm seething and vibrating with uncontrolled anger, my twin is refusing to listen to a single fucking thing I am saying! It's getting harder and harder to keep calm and not smash his fucking face in, I've never been good with controlling my temper.

"You can't just turn your fucking back on us, Cronos! This is our life now. We are in this together, I need you—"

I cut Artemis off before he can continue his fucking pity me spiel. "And what about what *I* need?" His face drops, I know that was a low blow but for years now I have put him, Apollo, Ares and Adonis first. I have never placed my own wants or needs above them but this time, I can't do that. Everything I have done is for them, I need to do this for me. "You are made for this shit, you even suit it. You got a crazy ass fucking girl that will stand by your side through all of this bloodshed. I can't keep reliving my past, Art. I need to get the fuck away and clear my head." He looks at me with sympathy, forcing me to grind my teeth or risk shouting at him again. I don't need his pity, I never asked for it or wanted it. He feels guilty for what happened and he shouldn't. I know he thinks I hate him because he's with London and found his other half but I'm not bitter. I want him to be happy, one of us should be.

"I only wanted to lead so you and the triplets would be safe. I would give it all up for you if that's what you wanted." Some of the anger drains from me as I stare at my mirror image. We are identical twins and to everyone else aside from the triplets and London, we are carbon copies but not to ourselves. Ever since Artemis took over the Godfathers Of The Night he's changed, he's grown into himself and became the man I always knew he could be. I don't envy his position being the top dog, the stress and pressure he is constantly under would get to me.

"I'm not asking you to change or give anything up for me. The triplets have their freedom, thanks to you. You freed all of us from Costa and I will always be grateful to you for that but this..." I take a deep breath and look into his eyes so he can see the truth in my own. "This isn't for me right now."

"What does that mean?" he asks quietly as he rests back in his chair behind his desk.

"It means I need to get away. I need time and space and I just need..." I clamp my mouth closed, unable to finish. I feel like a fool even saying this shit out loud. The door to his office opens and London walks in with a hard look on her beautiful face. She makes her way toward my brother and immediately his whole demeanor changes at just the sight of her. She drops into his lap and he wraps his arms around her waist, securing her to him.

They are a perfect fit.

"You need to get out of this life," she says. I narrow my eyes at her. She smirks and shrugs her shoulders. "You seriously didn't think I wasn't eavesdropping, did you?"

I roll my eyes at my best friend and shake my head. "Why didn't you just come in?" I hedge.

"You said you wanted to talk to Artemis, so I thought I would give you the illusion of privacy until I couldn't be bothered standing out there anymore," she answers without an ounce of remorse in her tone.

"Baby, you can't listen to private meetings," Artemis gently scolds. I blow out a loud exhale, he will never fucking learn!

"The fuck I can't! When these assholes want meetings held in my house, I will be involved in every single fucking one!" Artemis knows he's lost this battle and is smart enough to clamp his mouth closed and place a kiss to her temple that has her softening in his hold. Since London moved to Greece to help Artemis, they've both fallen more in love and it's been a sight to see. Longing hits me square in the chest, I've had that *twice* and both times it has been ripped away from me.

"I'm leaving tonight," I announce, drawing both their attention back to me.

"Tonight?" Artemis barks.

I open my mouth to answer him but London beats me to it. "Whatever you need, we're here." Her support means a lot to me, she knows why I need to do this and I know she will never betray me by telling my brother my reason for needing to leave this life. "You better call me twice a week and send pictures."

"Lon, I'm turning my location off." She huffs out her annoyance at my answer.

"Fine. Don't tell me where you are but I need two selfies a week and you can't reuse the same picture."

"I won't," I promise.

"Will you come back?" my brother asks.

I sigh and scrub a hand down my face. "One day... maybe."

Chapter One

Amelia

One year later...

My freedom from my family was supposed to be my redemption. I was supposed to be happy and free to live my life as I wanted. That dream was short lived when my past barged back into my life to confront me. I thought it was a sign that I was finally free to choose what I wanted out of my own life, except that wasn't the case.

He used me as leverage!

I meant nothing to him!

All these years I blamed my father for ruining the one good thing I found for myself, he chased him off and left me alone once again. I've hated my own father for what he did. I refused to hear his reasoning and chose to believe a man who said and did all the right things. He fooled me into thinking I was special, one of a kind, he manipulated me and played me. I was such an idiot for not realizing or seeing the truth sooner.

What a fucking fool I was!

"Hurry the fuck up in there!" I flinch at the cold harsh tone of his voice. I'm pathetic. I preached for years from my high horse about never being controlled or used and yet, here I fucking am. I am a puppet and he is the master who pulls my strings. He tells me what to hear, how my hair should be styled, what shifts I can and can't work at the hospital. I even let him dictate who I can and can't talk to.

"C-coming!" I call back, as I check my reflection one last time making sure my hair is parted perfectly down the center like he likes and my summer dress is wrinkle free. I grab my cardigan from the hook on the back of the door and sigh as I push my arms through the sleeves, knowing I am going to be as sweaty as a whore house on a Saturday night wearing this thing but he would flip out if I exposed my arms and chest. I button it all the way up and quickly turn the lock and pull the door open. The moment I do, I am met with those angry black eyes.

Those eyes once lulled me into a false sense of security. I found love in the depths of those black eyes—my first love. I thought I was going to spend forever with him, run away and make a new life. We were going to be happy and I would be free of the burden of my family's last name. How fucking naive I was!

He reaches forward and grips my upper arm in a punishing hold. I bite down on my lip to keep the whimper from slipping free. He pushes in close so his face is an inch from mine. I have been trained by every single person in my family to fight, endure and beat any enemy, yet here I stand, at the mercy of a man who has stripped away every ounce of my self-worth, my will to be the best doctor in my field and my will to... live.

I am a shell of the person I once was.

"You try anything funny in front of my men and it will be your funeral. Am I clear?" His words are like a whip to my battered soul. I nod my head, which seems to only anger him. His hold on my arm turns bruising and I flinch in pain, bringing a smile to his face. I hate myself for allowing him to control me like this but I don't see a way out. The one fucking time I tried to reach out to my dad, he somehow intercepted the call, broke my ribs and fractured my wrist for daring to defy him. I'm a foolish woman. "Use your fucking words," he grits out through clenched teeth.

I swallow nervously and nod. "Yes. I won't do anything to embarrass you, I swear." I hate myself a little more inside. All my life all I have ever wanted was my freedom and the right to choose how I wanted to live my own life and now here I am, being bullied daily and at the mercy of a man I decided to try and build a life with. I never realized how much safety my dad afforded me. I saw him having guards trailing me as an invasion of my privacy but now, I would give anything to have those two men back so they could help me escape this nightmare I have created for myself.

He releases my arm and interlocks his fingers with mine. To the naked eye we look like a loving couple who are displaying all the right signs of being happy, both of us smiling as he leads me down the hallway toward the restaurant where we will be dining with his *friends,* but his hold on my hand is hard and unyielding, a silent warning to not fuck up.

I keep my head down, not wanting to gaze around the crowded room, as he leads us to the table in the back. If I'm caught glancing around, he thinks I'm checking for an exit or looking at another man and it always winds up with me being in pain and crying later tonight. He always wakes the next morning and takes in the damage he inflicted on my body, then spends the next few days telling me how sorry he is and how much he loves me and will seek help. I used to eat up those lies but not anymore. I don't have the luxury of time to wait on him to change. He will never change because *he* doesn't want to.

I'm running out of time.

I need to break away and escape him before he finds out what I'm hiding. If he learns the truth, then I am as good as dead.

"About time!" I hear a man with a gruff voice say as we draw to a stop. Colson pulls me into his side but I keep my gaze down like I have been trained to do.

"Had to wait for my girl, you know what women are like," Colson says arrogantly. The others jeer and laugh while he pushes me into the booth. I peek up through my lashes and count seven men sitting around the table with beers in front of them. I sigh internally knowing this is going to be a long night. I used to enjoy long nights at the hospital, by the end of my shift I was bone tired and ready for my bed but I always felt fulfilled. Now, I'm constantly ducking out on my shifts and I've noticed how the nurses give me a wide berth, not wanting to even cross paths with me.

Sitting here listening to Colson laugh and make plans for world domination makes me sick. He thinks starting a security company where he hires tech geniuses will help him take down my father. He has no fucking idea what he is doing. If he thinks these drop kicks he calls friends are going to stand a chance against my family, he has another thing coming! Uncle Luka, Uncle Knight and Aunt Koby are the best hackers in the world. Uncle Luka is still on the FBI's most wanted list for hacking into the Pentagon when he was a boy.

"Dr. Kingsley?" I snap my head up at the sound of my name. The table falls silent and my stomach sinks at the sight of Kevin, Amara, Lisa, Devon and a nurse I have seen a few times around the hospital all standing there with smiles on their faces, they are med students. Colson's hand on my thigh snaps me out of my stupor. I plaster a smile on my face and huddle into his side to show them how in love we are.

"Hey," I say with fake enthusiasm.

"We haven't seen you lately, you're normally always on shift," Devon says with a tinge of concern in his voice. Colson's grip on my thigh tightens and I fight not to wince.

I place my hand on his chest and bat my lashes. "This one whisked me away for a few days, you know how it is," I say with a laugh and hate how the four of them smile and laugh at my lie. I just let them believe that I ran away with my boyfriend for a dirty weekend.

"Get it girl!" Lisa adds. "It was nice to see you, Dr. Kingsley," she adds before they wave and walk away, making my heart sink. I wish I could go with them. Amara hangs back and shoots me a weird look before trudging after the others, while I sit here and remain silent like a good little prop. Colson keeps his bruising hold on me as he goes back to discussing how to take down my father, like I'm not sitting right fucking here!

Men are so predictable. He thinks because he bulked up and owns a company he can take down the biggest mafia family in the world. I want to snort at the idea. I'm not even worried about what he thinks he can do because he will never get within reach of my father—

"I have the perfect thing to draw that cocksucker out, all I need to do is put her in front of King and checkmate!" I snap my head up and stare at Colson in horror, it never once occurred to me that he would use me as leverage against my dad. He smiles wickedly down at me like he knows he just flipped my world upside down. His friends begin cheering while he bends down and brushes his lips against the shell of my ear. "You play your part and I might just let that thing inside you live long enough for you to give birth to it."

I gasp loudly and reel back, tears spring to my eyes as I shake my head. "Y-you know?" I mutter.

His face blanks of all humor and that easy going persona vanishes only to be replaced by a vicious mask I know all too well. He grips the back of my neck. I shudder in pain when he pulls me in close so he can rest his head against mine.

"It was my insurance policy. Your daddy can't kill the father of his own grandchild now, can he?" Tears fall without mercy down my cheeks as he brings my worst fears to life. "Everything, and I do mean everything I have done from the moment I reentered your life eleven months ago has been planned out. You were easy prey. So desperate for love and for someone to see you as something other than a Murdoch you let a Viper into your bed." My bottom lip trembles as I shake my head, trying to deny what he says, but the truth is right there in his eyes.

"Was any of it ever real?" I choke out past the lump in my throat. I know I sound like a fool but a part of me did fall head over heels for him.

"You look like a fucking joke right now. Go clean yourself up and don't make me come and get you again." He slips out of the booth and grips my arm, yanking me out of my seat. I stumble on my feet but manage to stay upright. I keep my head down as I make my way to the bathroom, trying to stop my tears from falling but fail miserably. At the sight of the line to the women's bathroom I cringe and don't think as I shoulder past them, ignoring their protests and slipping into the disabled one. Before I can close the door, Amara is there pushing me inside and locking the door behind us. I swipe away the tears and force a smile to myself.

"Hey, what are doing in here?" I ask. Her face is stern and she eyes me warily for a beat before she reaches into her purse and pulls out a set of keys.

"Six years ago, I was you. I know what domestic abuse looks like—"

"Amara, you have it wrong—-"

"I saw the bruises at work." My face falls. "I saw how he touched you, looked at you and how you morphed into a different version of yourself earlier."

I dart my tongue out to moisten my lips. "I... I don't—"

"Your eyes tell the story you won't." She reaches out and grabs my hand placing her keys in my palm. I snap my gaze to hers and frown. "Take my car out back, it's a Kia. Leave now while he's distracted. Don't go back to your place for anything. All materialistic things can be replaced, risking your life for those things isn't worth it. Leave now, Dr. Kingsley, before you are the one we are treating in the ER." Fresh tears fall, and without thinking I grab her and pull her to me in a hug which she returns.

"Thank you, Amara."

She pushes me back and smiles knowingly. "It will be hard and you will want to give in and return. Ditch your phone and don't come back. I'll think of something to tell the hospital."

"What about your car?"

She shrugs. "Ditch it when you get far enough away and catch a bus somewhere, it has GPS so I'll pick it up in a few days. That should give you enough time to get far, far away from Chicago."

"Why are you really doing this? We don't know each other that well and here you are helping me, why?"

She inhales sharply. "You don't recognize me and that's okay but six years ago, Dr. Kingsley, you saved me when Brent beat me within an inch of my life. You saved me." I stumble back and frown at her in shock. "In recovery, you held my hand and promised me there was a better life out there for me, I just had to find the strength to go out and find it. I did that and now here I am because of *you*." I cover my mouth with my hand in utter shock at her revelation. "Now, you need to go. He'll be coming for you soon. Slip out the back and don't ever come back here unless you are ready to put that son of a bitch behind bars." I pull her in for another hug, then skirt around her to exit but stop and glance back at her over my shoulder.

"I'll never forget your kindness and what you did for me here today, Amara."

Chapter Two

Cronos

I'm cursed.

Doomed to forever live in the darkness of my past, paying for the sins of my father. I'm burdened with the knowledge that I am the reason the only woman I have ever loved is dead. I shut down and allowed the world to continue spinning without me living. I just existed until I met her.

Max Kingsley.

She breathed life back into my damned soul. She was the sunshine on the darkest of days. She was like a wave crashing against the walls I built to ward off any chance of happiness—I wanted to wallow in my misery for the remainder of my fucked up life.

She reminds me of Mother Nature, always nourishing those around her and breathing life back into strangers. She wants to heal, not maim. She broke away from the confines of what was expected of her and made a life outside of her last name, she never wanted to conform and be like the others. She carved her own path and rebuilt herself in an image that she could face in the mirror daily and respect.

When she told me to leave, I shouldn't have listened, I should have explained that I never meant to hurt her. Instead, I let the pain of her rejection consume me and abandoned her when she needed me most.

I needed time to heal after that, so left my family and everyone behind to rebuild myself and try to find my new normal. Don't get shit twisted, I am so fucking far from normal I don't even know what the real meaning of that word is—I redefined myself to fit *my* normal.

I had no idea where to go or what to do when I left my brother and Lon but I knew I couldn't stay in Greece or go to New York or Miami because London would have her family watching me, so I chose a small little place in Minnesota, Grand Marais. It has a population of 1,300 people. It's small enough to know everyone but big enough to also hide who I really am without the town folk wanting to dig into my past. I work a full time job and even went as far as to purchase the company from Bill. He was the first person with enough courage to approach me at the diner on my second week here.

I told the old man to fuck off but he just laughed and told me to follow him. Curious and bewildered by his bravery to not cower under the pressure of my glare or even heed my warning to get lost, I followed him. I was fucking rendered silent when we walked a block over and he came to a stop in front of the only mortuary in town. Bill told me I looked like the type that didn't relish being among the living and thought working with the dead might suit me better. I've been working here ever since that day. When Bill retired four months ago he offered for me to buy the business at a fair price. I paid triple what it was worth, it was the least I could do.

He will never know it but his small act of kindness that day has helped me in my journey of rediscovering who I am more than he will ever comprehend. Not only do I run and operate the morgue, I am also the undertaker of the local cemetery. My cabin is nestled in the trees behind it, I'd rather live next to the dead than the living, they don't complain or make noise.

"Morning, boy." I look up from the body I am stitching up after just completing its autopsy to see Bill standing there with two brown paper bags and a thermos that I know is filled with his wife Beth's famous chicken noodle soup.

"I'm working," I clip out before returning to my task. I may like Bill and respect the old fucker but I still haven't changed enough to enjoy the company of others.

"Tough shit, you need a break and I'm hungry." Ignoring him I continue on with my task, hoping he'll fuck off. "Well, Brady won't mind us using his body as a table since he's dead," he says as he places the bags on top of my cadaver, knowing I fucking hate any food or drinks in here. I have a fucking thing about shit being messy and he knows this. I drop the needle and snap my head up to glare at him, only to find the fucker grinning at me.

"You're going to be the next fucking body I'm stitching up if you don't watch yourself," I warn.

Bill just laughs and wags his white brows. "Boy, I am nearly eighty years young, I think I have at least another five good years in me before I'm on your table." I grumble under my breath about him being a dick as I cross the room, remove my apron and hang it on its hook, then deglove and move to the sink to scrub my hands. Bill whistles as he passes me and heads out front, feeling fucking triumphant because he got his way. I stomp after him, pissed off that he interrupted me. I hate leaving a body on the table without finishing. The dead should be treated with respect not left on a fucking slab because I'm eating.

I drop into one of the mismatched chairs in the tiny kitchen. I never use this room unless Bill stops by. I have a receptionist who works from home and handles all my books and phone calls so I don't have to deal with the people, I only want to focus on the bodies. They don't talk or judge, their presence is enough for me to fill that needy human instinct of wanting interaction with another person. It pisses me off that Becky, my receptionist, is leaving next week to get married so I need to find someone else to take over for her.

"So, Beth tells me we have a new woman in town." I scowl at the fucker as I tear into the bag and pull out my ham and cheese sandwich he brought me. "She's a looker, my wife tells me."

"Then you go fuck her," I growl, earning a laugh from the old fucker.

"Rumor has it, she isn't looking for an old washed-up man but a young twenty-five year old guy, covered in tattoos, black hair and brown eyes." I narrow my eyes.

"Good try, asshole, no one knows me and if they do, they have no idea I got inked." It's true, I decided to decorate my body with the story of my past when I left. I haven't seen anyone since then. I send London her photos, but it's never of me like she wanted. They are pictures of the landscape, a book or something trivial. We talk on the phone but rarely facetime. I don't want to see her and her knowing me as well as she does, she will see in my eyes that something is missing from my life and push me for information.

Bill shrugs and takes another bite of his sandwich as he

leans back in his chair and shrugs. "Pity. She looks like a nice girl."

"You just said you haven't seen her!" I snap.

"Oh, did I?"

I narrow my eyes. "What the fuck are you playing at old man?" I snarl.

"Take that soup and head on home, boy, I'll finish Brady off for you."

"Why the fuck would I do that?" I snarl as I toss my sandwich on the table.

"Because she asked for you by *name*." I reel back but make sure to keep the shock from splaying over my face. My guard is up now, I knew people would figure out that I left Artemis and come after me to get at my brother but I never thought they would find me here. "She didn't ask where the *Angel Of Death* lives, she asked if Beth knew where Cronos Argyros lays his head each night." My nostrils flare, all the townspeople aside from Bill and Beth call me the Angel Of Death. I hate the fucking name but it beats them knowing my real name. Bill knows who I really am and why I am here. He chose to keep my secret, which goes a long way in me trusting him, his wife Beth even calls me *Nos* sometimes.

"Was she alone?"

Bill nods as I stand to leave but his words have me halting. "I sent her to your house."

"Why?"

"She don't look like a woman who is here to kill you."

"How would you know the difference?" I snap.

"Because they wouldn't send a woman who is scared of her own fucking shadow and sporting bruises to kill someone like you, boy."

I bounce in the seat of my old beat up pickup truck as I drive along the gravel road that leads to my cabin, my gun resting on my lap. I'm poised and ready to strike. I stop the truck in front of my house and kill the engine as I climb out with my gun in hand and spin around taking in my surroundings. It's so quiet out here that I would be able to hear a gun cocking from a distance. I slowly turn in a circle scanning the trees and listening to the birds, they are my first line of defense out here. Animals are great at alerting you to something that doesn't belong, they hate their resting place being disturbed.

I pause at the sight of a shadow on the ground, whoever the fuck this woman is she isn't very smart hiding behind a fucking tree!

"You got three fucking seconds to show yourself before I start spraying led," I shout. "Three... Two..." The words die on my tongue when she steps out from the cover of the tree. My face falls and my mouth parts in surprise at the sight of her. My heart begins to pump harder in my chest, like it's trying to jump out of me to burrow itself inside hers!

"Hey, Grizz," she says nervously as she wrings her hands in front of her, she looks like a train wreck. I run my gaze over her and fight the frown from taking over my face at the sight of her rumpled clothes and the way her hair looks like it hasn't been washed in days. Her eyes have dark rings under them and she looks utterly terrified. The longer it takes for me to say something, the more nervous she becomes and it's a strange sight to see. I've never seen her like this. She is always so sure of herself and her every move yet, here she stands, looking like she might bolt if a bird chirped too loudly.

When she takes a step toward me, I instinctively take one back without thought, forcing her to stop her advance. Hurt flickers in her green eyes but I can't bring myself to care because she hurt me too!

"Grizz–"

I cut her off before she can continue. "How did you find me?"

She drops her gaze to the ground. "You told me when you sent me that... letter." I grind my teeth in annoyance. In a moment of weakness six weeks after I moved here, I sent her a fucking letter. I went old school and sent her snail mail but I never gave her my address. "The stamp on the envelope, I remembered," she mutters.

"Why are you here?" I grit out as I push my gun into my waistband and cross my arms over my chest. She slowly lifts her gaze to me and the sight of her tears has me tensing.

"I need your help," she says so quietly I would have missed it if I wasn't paying such close attention.

"That's what your father is for, Amelia." She flinches at my cold tone. I know I should stop but the words fly out of my mouth before I can stop them. "I'm just a thug for hire like them, remember?" Her bottom lip trembles, she tugs her small cardigan around her body tighter and nods.

"Yeah. You're right," she says bitterly and moves closer. I tense in preparation, waiting for her to bust a move but she stills a few steps away and now that she is closer I see the pain and fear in her eyes. "It was good to see you, Grizz," she chokes out as more tears fall. I remain strong and watch her as she leaves. This time it's not me walking away from her and it feels almost like Deja vu.

Standing here watching her walk away from me is stirring feelings I thought I had long since buried but it turns out, I still fucking care about her and I hate her for making me feel again. A whole year I have been good, fine, existing and doing everyday things like normal people. I built my own normal and made a life here, an honest fucking life. A life I am proud of. I don't have millions sitting in my account like my brother, he still sends me and the triplets money every fucking month but I don't want it.

Artemis has always been the father we never had but I'm not his problem or his child, I'm his twin. It isn't his job to look after me or shelter me from the world. I know I'm fucked up and different but I'm good with that. I don't need anyone, I'm happy being on my own. The moment Amelia disappears from my sight, anguish spurs inside me and I loathe myself for letting the past resurface.

"Motherfucker!" I roar so loud that the birds take flight from the trees to escape me.

Chapter Three

Amelia

This is my heartless era, being the big-hearted girl got me nowhere!

That's what I told myself on the bus ride here. I thought if I said it enough, I would start to believe it but it turns out two seconds of being in Cronos's presence and that shit flew out the fucking window. He has never been cold or angry toward me before, and I knew coming here to him would be hard but it's not like I could go crawling back to my family after I preached for years that I didn't need them. I bury my face in my hands and force my tears to remain at bay. The last thing I need to do is cry in the middle of this diner in front of these people who have been eyeing me weirdly since I walked in here this morning.

"A warm berry pie always solves anyone's blues." I jerk in fright at the sound of the voice. I look up to find the older woman from earlier, standing there with a large slice of pie and a warm smile on her face. My stomach grumbles and I wince in shame. My family never worries about money and yet here I am down to my last twenty dollars. I have my cards and all my accounts are loaded with money but I'm smart enough to know he would be tracking them if I was to use them. I only had the cash in my wallet with me when I left the bar that night, I guess I should have thought this out better.

"She doesn't like berries." I snap my gaze to the other side of the woman and my eyes widen at the sight of Cronos standing there looking like a dark angel. The woman smiles and pats him on the arm like they are familiar. The instant he looks at her, his anger vanishes and a warm look enters her eyes.

"Sit down, boy, I'll fix you a couple of plates and bring them out," she says.

"Thanks, Beth," he answers as she walks away and drops into the seat in front of me. That warm look from a second ago is replaced by a blank expression when he looks at me. I feel so out of sorts with him. It was never like this between us before.

"How did you find me?" I throw his words back at him, the slight narrowing of his eyes tells me he doesn't find my question amusing.

"What the hell are you doing here, Amelia?" I stiffen but don't flinch away from his harsh tone.

"I needed to... get away," I lie.

I can see it in his eyes that he knows I'm lying. If he calls me on it I don't know if I will be able to tell him the truth. I'm so ashamed of myself for what I allowed to happen and for how long I endured his cruelty.

"That *his* kid?" My jaw unhinges at his bold question, instinctively wrapping my arms around my belly. I wore this dress that night to shield my growing bump. Colson hasn't touched me in months and I have been so grateful for that because I can't hide this for much longer. When I take too long to answer he rests his forearms on the table and leans forward slightly. "Answer me," he forces out through clenched teeth.

"H-how did you know?" I rasp out.

He scoffs. "I know every inch of your body, Amelia. The fact you thought you could come here and I wouldn't notice that fucking bump is bullshit." A warmth overcomes me at his declaration. He doesn't say it to be cocky, he says it because it's true. He spent many hours studying every inch of my body as he ravished me.

You look good with the devil inside your pretty little cunt.

I shiver as the memory of his words replays in my mind. I quickly push them out of my head and force myself to focus.

"How did you know about... *him*?" I ask. Cronos's whole demeanor changed when he leans back and crosses his arms over his chest, then darts his gaze out the window of the diner.

"I came to see you six months ago." My eyes widen in surprise.

"What?"

He slowly turns his gaze back to me but remains silent when Beth places two plates in front of us, the scent of the greasy food has my mouth watering and my stomach rumbling. I thank her and throw my manners out the window as I dig in. I moan when I chew the crispy bacon. I flick my gaze up to see Cronos frowning at me.

"What?" I ask around a mouth full of food.

He shakes his head. "Nothing, eat." He doesn't have to ask me twice. I shovel everything into my mouth like a starved prisoner, I guess in a sense I was. I was never allowed to eat anything like this. Colson always said I needed to watch my weight so I only ate what he allowed—oats, boiled chicken, brown rice or fruit. I was placed on a bland food diet, and it killed me to not eat my favorite treats. I push those thoughts out of my head. I escaped, I don't ever need to think about him again.

I surprise myself when I shovel the last bit of eggs into my mouth and sigh in contentment as I sit back in my seat with a smile on my face but the moment I take in Nos's angry look, the smile slips right off and I revert back into myself and drop my gaze to my lap, sit up tall and keep my shoulders square like he taught me.

"What the fuck are you doing?" he snaps loudly. I gasp quietly and peek out the corner of my eye to see we have attracted the attention of the people eating around us. "Look at me!" I snap my head up automatically, fear takes a hold of me. I know rationally that Nos would never hurt me but I also thought the same thing about Colson and look how that fucking turned out for me! He flicks his eyes between mine and I see the moment he begins to piece things together, horror fills me.

I jump to my feet and rush out the door, needing to escape him and his prying eyes. I look left and right, trying to gauge which direction to go in. I dart left but I don't make it more than two steps before he grips my arm and yanks me back. A shrill scream escapes me without consent. Nos immediately releases me and raises his hands. Both of us stand here panting and staring at the other in terror.

He knows!

"Angel." I slam my eyes closed at his pet name for me. It's been so long since I heard it and I never knew how much I missed it until now. I slowly blink my eyes open and the sight of the anguish and anger warring in his brown eyes spears me.

"Don't ask me what happened," I clip out. His jaw locks and his nostrils flare.

"That why you won't go back to your dad?" I turn my head not wanting to see the judgment on his face.

"I don't want him to know about *any* of this," I spit. I take a second to gather myself before facing him again. "This is my business, not his."

He eyes me for a beat before nodding. "Get in the truck," he says as he walks past me and opens the door to a beaten up old Ford pickup with peeling paint. I don't question his request as I follow after him and slide into the cab, he follows after me. The ride back to his place is quiet. I guess neither of us know what to say to the other, the silence is awkward and filled with tension. There is so much that was left unsaid between us, but what I can't stop thinking about is him saying he came to see me six months ago.

He puts the truck in park out in front of his house but neither of us move to get out. "Why didn't you ever come to me when you came to Chicago six months ago?" I see his shoulders hunch out of the corner of my eye.

"Let's go," he says, not bothering to answer my question as he climbs out. I sigh and follow after him, not having much other choice. I shiver and pull my thin cardigan around me and rub my hands up and down my arms. Nos opens the wooden door and steps aside to allow me to enter first. I forget what it is like being around him. He always made sure to open doors for me like earlier and right now. I step inside and gasp.

It's like a hunting cabin from the movies, a small kitchen off to the left with a tiny two-seater wooden table, a cozy living room with one three-seater sofa that looks like it has been around for longer than I've been alive. But my focus is drawn to the large open fireplace with a recliner in front of it. A pile of books is stacked beside it. With a mind of their own, my legs carry me across the room and suddenly I'm kneeling down beside the pile and going through the stack. He says nothing as I open a book and flick through the pages, smiling at the sight of some of the pages being dog eared.

"You like to read?" I ask as I thumb through the pages of the book in my hands, his only answer is to grunt. I don't know if I'm shocked that he's reading or because of what the content of the books are. I place the books back in the stack and slowly push to my feet to face him. He assesses me with those all too knowing eyes. A shiver works its way down my spine, he's always looked at me like he can see beneath the layers of clothing I wear. "Why do you have so many autopsies and mortuary books?"

A single brow hikes up as if in challenge. "Why does it matter to you what I read?" Hurt unfurls inside me, I know he's angry and hurt but I never expected him to act this cold toward me.

I shrug trying to brush off my hurt as I answer. "I guess it doesn't, I was trying to..."

"Trying to what?" he pushes. "Get to know me? Find out if I'm reading that shit so I know how to dispose of bodies easier for your family?" I drop my gaze to the ground in shame. I said some horrible things to him out of fear, I never meant for them to hurt him as deeply as they clearly have.

"That wasn't what I meant," I mutter.

"Whatever. Take the room at the end of the hall, I'll be back later." Fear rushes to the surface inside me and without thinking I dart forward and grip the front of his shirt in my hands.

"Don't leave!" His eyes widen and realization slams into me. I release him quickly before hastily rushing down the tiny hallway to escape his questions. I dart inside the bedroom at the end of the hallway and freeze in the entryway. I look around bewildered at the sight. This room is... unoccupied. The bed is bare of sheets and blankets, the dressers are dusty and clearly untouched, the only foot traffic I can see is through to the adjoining bathroom.

Where does he sleep?

A thought hits me and my stomach sinks, what if he has a girlfriend and stays at her place? Was that where he was about to go? Searing pain burns inside me at the thought of another woman seeing him smile lazily when she runs her fingers through his hair, or when you scrape your nails along his side, he would burst out laughing. He may be dark and broody and give off I'll kill you vibes but the big Grizzly bear is ticklish.

Grow the hell up, Amelia!

I have no right to be standing here feeling hurt over him moving on with his life when I tried to do the same thing but... with the wrong person. I place my hand against my growing bump and smile. It's not huge or anything and I'm only roughly about twenty-two weeks pregnant—I tried to track my periods but they are so irregular. I also know that women can still get them throughout their pregnancies, which is why so many women don't even know they are pregnant.

I may hate him but I could never hate my little angel.

Warmth spreads throughout my body as I rub my belly. I always wanted to be a mother but I wanted to be married, have a home and be more established in my career before bringing a life into this world. A whoosh of air escapes me, that's not true. I always dreamed of children but I didn't want to bring them into the world knowing they could be used as a pawn or taken from me to get at my dad or uncle's. When I first realized I was pregnant, the first person I wanted to call was my mom. I slam my eyes closed and force my emotions to remain in check as I force my legs to move and carry me to the bathroom where I can cry privately.

The instant I close the door behind myself and turn the shower on my tears fall. I let the fear, worry and pain pour out of me. I have never felt so terrified in my life, except for the night my mom hid me under her bed when I was a child to keep me safe from the men who came to take me as leverage against my father. Colson inspired that amount of fear inside me now and I fucking let him, I let him hurt me. I allowed him to destroy the life I had built on my own. I was weak and couldn't handle never being enough for my father to renounce his place at my uncle's side. I pushed away a man I was in love with because I was terrified loving him would cost me, like it cost my mom loving my dad.

Allison Murdoch isn't like me, she doesn't need a man to hold her or make her feel complete. She was a single fucking mother. I may not be biologically hers but that woman is my mom and if any bastard tries to tell me otherwise, I will claw their fucking eyes out. Mom gave me everything I ever needed, kept me safe and raised me right. I will do the same for my child. I have to because I will not let the world I was born into harm my baby.

Now, I just need to figure out how to escape my past.

Chapter Four

Cronos

By the time I get back to my place it's a little after midnight. I needed to get out of here earlier and clear my fucking head, seeing her brought back memories and feelings I thought I had long since buried but it turns out, I was fucking wrong. Leaning against the door jam, I just stand here and stare at her sleeping on the bed I've never used. She's left the bathroom light on, which is a clear sign she's afraid of the dark. She chose the wrong person to run to because I am the fucking shadows. I normally fall asleep in my chair in front of the fire, but most nights I spend outside in my swing so I can stare up at the stars.

I thought I would never see Amelia again after the day I left her in Chicago. I had come to terms with the fact I was destined to never open my heart to another. I vowed after I lost Aida that I would never allow another person to have me at their mercy again. Turns out I was full of shit because I was powerless to stop my own heart from claiming Amelia. She didn't need to do anything, she was just herself, but the time we spent away together bonded us in a way neither of us expected and I can vouch for the fact that neither of us meant to end up in bed together, but I couldn't regret it because she fit me perfectly.

I lost Aida years ago and the loss of her still burns deeply inside me, I've never been able to let her go fully. Hand on the fucking bible, I never once prayed for the pain of her loss to lessen because that was my penance for loving her when I had no fucking right. She was too perfect for this world. Much like Amelia, I have struggled with accepting my place in my family because of the loss of Aida. Artemis still blames himself for her death and I guess a part of me does blame him for it too, but I know why he never completed that trial and I understand it, but it doesn't mean I agree with his choices.

She rolls over, pulling me from my thoughts. The blanket falls away, the sight of her sleeping in one of my shirts has my brows raising. It's not the fact she's wearing my shirt that has me shook, it's the sight of the bump. My legs carrying me across the room without consent. I stand over her, just staring down at the growing bump, and a pang of longing hits me in the chest.

That should have been my baby in there!

I push the thought away, not wanting to dwell on it. I've never wanted to be a father. I never exactly had a great example of one and I know for a fact I would never do a good job raising a kid. I would fuck that kid up beyond repair so it's better not to curse the world with another mini me. But then out of nowhere an image of me and Amelia sitting out on the back porch watching a dark-haired, green-eyed little girl running across the lawn slams into me with such force, I stumble back a step knocking into the dresser. She jolts awake and screams as she scurries to the other side of the bed.

"I'm sorry! I didn't mean to do it, I'll clean it. I swear!" I can see her trembling, tears are gathered in her eyes, but what surprises me most is how her motherly instincts have already kicked in. Rather than shielding herself she has her arms wrapped around her stomach, protecting her child without thought. It takes her a second to realize it's me standing in here with her before the tension drains out of her weary bones and she slumps forward, taking some deep breaths.

"He beat you, didn't he?" Her head snaps up, her mouth parts but no words come out. I don't need to hear the words, I can see it in her eyes.

That cunt hurt her!

I clench my fists at my sides and try with all my might to tamper my anger and remind myself that she isn't mine to care for, isn't my family to avenge. She isn't my anything, but my mind and body can't seem to agree because in the next second I'm flying out of the room and heading for the coat closet near the front door to retrieve my guns. I yank the door open with enough force that it breaks one of the hinges. I reach forward to grab my case but Amelia is there pulling me back. I shake her off, not paying her any mind as I pull the two black cases out. I haven't needed to use these things since I moved here. I always carry my Glock—force of habit—but I've never needed to use it.

"Cronos, please." I ignore her as I slam the cases on the counter and press my thumb on the scanner to unlock them. The moment the first case is open I move on to the next one but when the lock clicks open, I freeze at the sound of a gun cocking. I slowly turn my head to see her standing there with my Smith and Wesson 9mm aimed at my chest. Her hands are shaking. "Please, just... stop—"

"Stop what?" I roar. She flinches and takes an involuntary step backward as she shakes her head. "Look at you, Amelia. You're a fucking shell of your old self. You preached to me for months about never being controlled by your family and wanting freedom and now look at you!" I regret the words the moment they fly out of my mouth, but it doesn't mean they aren't true. She's lost weight and looks like a strong gust of wind would blow her away.

Her bottom lip trembles as the first tear falls. She angrily swipes it away but still doesn't lower her gun. "You don't know shit!" she screams.

"And whose fucking fault is that?" I snap, making pain flash in her eyes before she masks it.

"Is this what this is? You want to go back to Chicago and murder in my name because you got your feelings hurt?"

I grind my teeth and clench my hands into fists so I don't reach out and wrap one around her neck. She may not say it out loud, but I can tell a move like that wouldn't be seen as me trying to subdue her, she would think I was trying to hurt her like he clearly did.

"Are you worried about my feelings or the fact you would be grateful that I killed the cocksucker that hurt you and knocked you up?" Her jaw unhinges but I'm not done. Ignoring the gun, I press in closer until the muzzle is pressed against my chest. She takes a step back but I follow her until she is backed against the wall with nowhere to go. "Wasn't it you who preached to me about safe sex and making sure to always wear a condom and yet here you are, pregnant by some motherfucker that you're clearly on the run from."

Tears cascade down her cheeks unchecked. Having had

enough of her little display of power, I snatch the gun out of her hands, then push in closer until I'm flush against her. A gasp escapes her and the hint of fear I see in her eyes angers me but I refuse to backdown. She isn't this scared little meek woman, she is a fireball and if she plans to survive in this fucked up world she's going to have to dig down deep and find that version of herself again, because no one else can do that for her.

"I didn't know," she says barely above a whisper.

I keep my face blank of all emotion as I grip her chin and force her head up so she has to look me in the eyes. "Know what?"

A whoosh of air escapes her. "I never changed my stance on safe sex. He poked holes in the condom. He wanted me pregnant." I'm smart enough to read between the lines and know there is more to it than what she is saying but before I can push her further, my phone rings. There is only one person who would call this late. I pull it out of my pocket without taking my eyes off Amelia as I answer and bring it to my ear.

"What?"

"Sally Johnson just passed," Becky says.

"I'm on it," I bite out.

"Cronos?"

"What Becky?" Amelia's eyes widen at the sound of my receptionist's name. I fight the smirk from breaking free when I see that green-eyed monster enter her gaze, finally, some other emotion instead of fear!

"Reggie is distraught over the loss of his wife so... be nice." She ends the call before I can bite her head off. She fucking knows I hate dealing with grieving spouses. Normally on jobs like this one she will meet me there to deal with that while I tend to the body, but since she is out of state preparing for her wedding, I'm stuck doing this shit on my own!

"I gotta go," I grit out as I shove my phone back in my pocket, relock the cases and stash them back in the closet.

"Oh, so you had me pinned to a wall a second ago and now you're about to leave to go see your booty call?" I shut the closet door as best I can, then slowly turn to face Amelia who looks like she is about to do bodily harm to Becky.

"Grow up, Meelz." Her face reddens in anger. "You and I both know if I wanted you pinned to that wall, you wouldn't say no because you love it when I take control so you don't have to think." Before I can get my mouth to shut the fuck up more words pour out. "I guess being a thug for hire taught me about being a brute as well, huh?" Shame colors her cheeks as I pass by to grab some fresh clothes from my room. I hear her stomping down the hallway after me and sigh quietly knowing the tiny thing I thought of as an angel is about to turn into the she-devil. Amelia has the worst fucking temper and it's no surprise considering her who her father is. King also has a short fuse. I pull a pair of black jeans out of the dresser as she enters the room.

"You don't get to pass fucking judgment on me then leave!" I slam the drawer closed and spin around to face her. She looks wild and crazed and this is the version of her that I fucking frothed at, even now my cock is growing hard at the sight of the fire in her eyes. Her temper matches my own. Shit, it could probably rival mine.

"Why the fuck not? You did. You checked out on me weeks before I finally gave in and left. I fucking left because that is what *you* wanted and now here you are, trying to fuck up what I built because you were too fucking stubborn to see what was right fucking in front of you!" I don't realize I'm yelling until I have to clear my throat.

"What the fuck did you want me to do?"

"Fuck off with that bullshit, Amelia!" I snarl as I push my sweats down my legs. Her eyes immediately drop to the bulge in my briefs. Her throat bobs as she swallows, I don't have time for her shit or this argument, I pull my jeans on and yank my shirt over my head and the moment a strangled gasp escapes her I realize my fucking error.

Fuck!

"Grizz—"

"Shut up, Amelia."

"Fuck you! That's my name across your abs!" she snaps back. I pull another shirt out of the drawer and pull it over my head before brushing past her and rushing out of the cabin. What I don't expect is for her to follow me. I grip the door handle of my truck and open it only for it to be ripped out of my grasp and shoved backward. I glare down at the little shit as she stands there blocking my door. "Why do you have *Kingsley* tattooed across your abs, Cronos?"

I scrub a hand down my face, utterly spent after spending a small fucking amount of time with her! She was always like this, a dog to a bone whenever she wanted information. I try a different approach needing to get the fuck out of here so I can get to the morgue and grab the hearse, before heading to Reggie's to collect Sally. Because it's such a small town I am the undertaker and the medical examiner, I love what I do.

"Amelia, I don't have time for your meltdown right now. Go inside, get some sleep and I'll be back as soon as I get Sally set up."

"Who the fuck is Sally? What happened to Becky?" she sneers.

"Jesus fucking Christ, woman! Becky is my receptionist and Sally is the dead body I have to collect. Now can you fucking move so I can go do my goddamn job?"

Her face falls. "The books..." she whispers.

"Yes. I read those fucking books because it's my job, now for the love of my barely there fucking sanity, *move!*" She steps aside without another word allowing me to escape. I climb inside my truck and don't glance back at her as I drive away. Unlike my twin, I won't chase after Amelia if she decides to run while I'm out. I tried that once, I listened to him and put my pride aside and went after her but that didn't turn out well for me.

Chapter Five

Amelia

I couldn't sleep after Cronos left, my mind was too wired and I was far too angry at him and myself for my mind to shut off and allow me the reprieve of sleep. The fact that his house is nestled in the trees behind a cemetery doesn't exactly set my anxiety at ease. It's creepy but also... so him. I've looked around the entire cabin and found no personal touches of his own, no pictures or photos on the fridge. Instead of hiding out in his bedroom, I decided to light a fire and get comfortable in his recliner while I waited for him to return home.

I have no clue what the fuck I am doing or why I even chose to come to him. I do know without a doubt, if I sought out my family they would protect me and help me but I couldn't bring myself to do it. I have preached for years about not needing anything from them or wanting their type of help. I am many things but I don't want to be labeled as a hypocrite.

I hear Cronos's truck grumble down the gravel drive just as

the sun begins to crest, marking the dawn of a new day. I suddenly feel foolish about our earlier disagreement and mortified that I dared to pull a gun on him. I know how to shoot and how to fight but that doesn't make what I did okay. I built a career on saving lives and there I was holding a gun to his chest, mentally prepared to pull the trigger, but emotionally... I could never have harmed him. Not again.

When he enters the cabin his gaze lands on me instantly. I don't know what he sees as he looks at me but his muscles relax and the tension in his shoulders eases at the sight of me. Spending months alone with him in South America as we delivered aid to sick children gave me a chance to get to know him and read him. He never says much to anyone but he never seemed to have that problem with *me*.

"You're still here." It's not a question, just a fact. Unsure of what to say to that I just nod and drop my gaze to my lap as he ambles over to me lazily. "You're in my seat." Without thought I jump to my feet, prepared to flee to the solitude of the bedroom but when he drops into the chair, he snakes an arm gently around my waist and pulls me into his lap. I tense on instinct. He says nothing as I calm myself. Months of Colson's false kindness has hardened me, I have grown to fear kindness, knowing that from him it was just an act and later on I would pay for his niceness.

"Grizz—"

He cuts me off as he pulls me in closer. He grips my legs with his other arm and pulls them up so I'm sitting across his lap. He then places a throw blanket that was on the back of the seat over me.

"I don't want to talk, Meelz," he says tiredly. I sigh and melt into him, soaking up the feeling of being safe and protected in his arms.

"Okay," I whisper as I rest my head on his shoulders and close my eyes in contentment. It has been a long time since I felt safe and relaxed enough to actually let my mind wonder and let sleep fully consume me. I've always been too fearful that if I fell into a deep sleep it would give Colson a chance to attack me while I was incapacitated. Within seconds my body is relaxed and I feel myself drifting off, but then his hand lands on my bump and panic flares inside me. I snap my eyes open, expecting to see a look of anger on his face but to my utter disbelief, he's fast asleep, his large hand resting protectively across my stomach and my stupid hormones get the better of me. A lump forms in my throat. I close my eyes and will my tears to remain at bay.

I wish more than anything that I could turn back time.

I was a fucking fool, he was right earlier. I was a fucking idiot to not see exactly what was right in front of me.

The scent of biscuits and gravy hits my nose and I slowly blink my eyes open as my stomach protests its need for food. My brows furrow as I register that I'm no longer on Cronos's lap in the living room but instead laying on the bed in his bedroom. I stretch out and still, my heart beats over time as I wait with bated breath to see if I'll feel it again. I squeal in delight when I feel my baby move again. I sit up and place my hands on my belly with the broadest smile. The bedroom door bangs open and I jolt in fright. Cronos stands there in only a pair of jeans. My eyes drink in the sight of his naked inked skin.

"What happened?"

I drag my eyes up his chest and meet his worried look. "Huh?"

"You screamed!" he snaps in annoyance. I frown until I feel the baby move again and smile causing his frown to deepen.

"Come here." He crosses the room and drops down onto the edge of the bed beside me. I grab his hand and place it on my stomach. His muscles coil in anticipation, a flicker of fear flashing in his brown eyes, but the moment he feels the little flutter of a kick against his palm, his eyes widen in wonder. Without being prompted, he knocks my hand away and places his other on my bump staring at it like it's the most fascinating thing he has ever seen in his life.

"Holy shit!" he breathes out when he feels another kick.

"It's the first time I've felt movement, that's why I squealed. Sorry I alarmed you." He doesn't pull his gaze from my belly as he answers.

"Is that normal?"

My brows furrow. "To feel a baby kick at around twenty-two weeks?"

He lifts his eyes to mine and nods. "I don't know shit about kids, Amelia."

My heart warms at his honesty. "Yes, Grizz, it's perfectly normal to feel a baby move and kick inside the womb. It's when they don't move you have to worry."

Alarm clouds his features. "Why the fuck didn't you say anything?" he snaps as he removes his hands and stands, towering over me. I instantly shift away from him in fear.

"W-what do you mean?"

"You just said this is the first time you felt it move!"

It takes me a second to understand why he is so panicked. I rise onto my knees and close the space between us, I tentatively reach out and place my hand flat against his chest.

"The baby was too small to feel anything before. It's the right size now to feel it move and kick. The baby is perfectly fine, Nos."

The unease flees his body as a whoosh of air escapes him. "Yeah, right. Come on, I made food." He pulls away and leaves me here, feeling lost and lonely. Sighing I decide to worry about my fucked up predicament after breakfast. I stumble to a stop in the center of the living room, he has a picnic rug on the floor in front of the fire with an array of food set out in the center.

"Nos..." Words escape me at this amazing act of kindness, no one has ever done something like this for me before.

"What? You don't like the food?" I can hear the apprehension in his tone and I quickly rush forward and drop down onto the blanket so he doesn't storm off.

"I love the food, this was really... nice of you to do." He huffs and grumbles under his breath before sitting opposite me and handing me an empty plate. I smile my thanks and begin loading it sky high with bacon, biscuits, gravy, eggs, sausages and few other meats. I don't wait for him to begin, I can't seem to get enough food into my mouth fast enough. I stop eating like a starved woman long enough to see him sit down and stare at me like I have grown two heads. "What?" I ask around a mouth full of food.

His face contorts in amusement. "You look like a fucking chipmunk, swallow." Heat unfurls inside me at his last word as a memory of me on my knees in front of him with his cock down my throat assaults me—he loved it when I swallowed every drop of his cum and licked his shaft clean. Cronos has a dark side in the bedroom and I never realized how kinky I was until he and I explored it and fuck, sex with him was the hottest thing I have ever experienced in my life. I swallow audibly and don't miss the way his eyes blaze with heat. The air suddenly seems to charge between us, my breaths growing ragged the longer we remain here in silence.

Cronos breaks the moment when he tears his gaze from mine and returns to eating. I scold myself internally, here I am pregnant with another man's child and on the run from said man, hiding from my own family and trying to jump my exes bones—I need serious fucking help!

"You gonna be sticking around for a while?" His question snaps me out of my inner turmoil. Too ashamed to meet his gaze, I keep my own on my plate as I answer.

"I don't know where else to go," I say quietly, feeling like a weak mouse admitting that out loud, but he deserves better than me lying to him. I gasp when he reaches out and grips my chin, forcing my head up. I stare at him in surprise.

"Then don't go." I sense there is a double meaning to his words but I can't decipher what it is.

"I'm not a freeloader, Grizz, you know I earn my own way and always have since I left college."

"Then earn your way."

I reel back and scoff. "That might take some time since I don't think a lot of people want to hire a pregnant chick." I can hear the bitterness in my own voice. Back in Chicago, the hospital would have been elated for me and helped me however they could but because of Colson, I can't go back to the job I love.

"You have a job and will start Monday."

My eyes widen at his response. "Say what now?"

"You'll work Monday to Friday as my receptionist. Becky is leaving and I need someone to take over. It's not a glamorous job like you are used to, but until we can... sort things out it's the best one you're gonna get."

"I'll take it!" I say excitedly. He purses his lips but says nothing else. I feel giddy at the prospect of getting to see him in action at his job. "So, who do you work for?"

He chuckles. "No one. I own the mortuary and I'm also the medical examiner." My jaw unhinges at his response.

"I never knew you wanted to get into that line of work."

He shrugs. "I didn't until I moved here and met a guy who offered me a chance, no one has ever taken the time to teach me anything except Bill." I can hear the respect and love he has for the man in his tone, it's clear he means a lot to him.

"So, you work and live here?"

"Yes, Amelia, was that not clear?"

I shoot him a scathing look. "I was just trying to be polite!"

"You being polite would mean you are not lying to me and telling me the truth as to why you are really here." My face falls but he isn't finished. "We both know you aren't going to spill the truth so let's just pretend we don't have a past. You go about your life while I try to do the same with mine."

"It's not that easy," I bite out.

"It really is. It's like an addict coming off the drugs, you just need to trust the process but you don't, which is why you came here. You knew I'm too fucked up to push you for the truth when I can barely handle living with the truth of my own life."

Chapter Six

Cronos

Sitting out here on my back porch, I watch the sun set, bathing us in darkness again, this is the time I feel most alive. There is something about the darkness that calls to me, there is no light to show your imperfections, just the never ending abyss of nothing in the distance.

"Are you going to keep ignoring me?" I don't even bother to acknowledge Amelia as she claims the seat beside me. I have ignored her for the past two days. I was hoping I wouldn't have to speak to her until tomorrow when we head into work but I guess the darkness didn't hide me well enough.

"I chose Grand Marais because it was small. I didn't need to know anyone or vice versa for them to become familiar enough that I had to keep checking over my shoulder. The day you arrived here everyone knew you were from out of town."

"What are you trying to say, Nos?" I take a swig of my beer then let the bottle dangle between my fingers as I turn to face her. Her beauty still astounds me. She is a fucking angel living amongst mere mortals, yet she was so stupid and lowered herself to the level of a piece shit because she wouldn't allow herself to see what I saw whenever I looked at her. Light.

"You don't belong here." She reels back as if I slapped her, her mouth hangs open in shock. "You aren't meant to hide out in a town like this. You have dreams and goals and none of them center around this place. Call your father and make amends, Meelz. He will eradicate that vermin that lives in Chicago trying to find you." Her bottom lip quivers but I refuse to allow her tears to sway me from my decision.

"I can't go back," she chokes out through her tears. I scrub a hand down my face, utterly frustrated with this fucking situation.

"What the fuck do you want from me, Amelia?" I shout. She flinches but I can't control my anger any longer.

"I don't know!" she snaps.

"You ended shit between us a year ago and now here you are in my fucking house. Why?"

She shakes her head trying to deny what I'm saying. "I was scared!"

I scoff. "Not scared enough to move on with the cock-sucker from your past, how did that shit turn out for you?"

The instant the words flee my mouth I regret them. "Wow. You sure know how the fuck to kick someone when they are down, don't you?"

"You taught me well," I bite back.

She pushes to her feet and stares down at me with disdain in her eyes. "You also taught me how to hide from pain and how to endure a miserable existence. I guess we were a good pair then, huh?" I jump to my feet, seething in anger as I glare down at the spitfire that brought me back to life. I hate her for making me feel! She reaches out and grips my left arm, lifting it between us so Aida's portrait is on display. " I couldn't compete with a fucking ghost! It was never just us, Cronos, Aida was always in the middle and I could never compete with her."

My nostrils flare. I yank my arm free and grip the back of her neck, pulling her in close until she is forced to stand on her tiptoes.

"There was never a fucking competition, Amelia. She's dead and you're not!" I'm yelling now and can't seem to stop myself from spewing more words. "She isn't some ex or someone I left, she died for Christ's sake! I loved her—I still love her and always will because there was never any closure for us. My family killed the love of my life and set my life on the current course it is on now. You foolish fucking woman–" I spit out as I release her abruptly and step back shaking my head. "You never needed to compete with Aida, you were in a league of your own."

"You didn't see me when you looked at me, you saw her," she defends weakly.

I look her up and down in disappointment. "All I ever saw when we were together was *you*, I never saw anyone or anything else, it was always just you, Amelia." I can hear the pain in my own voice. "Unlike you, I will never get closure from my first love, but you can if you stop being stubborn and make a fucking call... but you won't, because you think you are too good and above this mafia life. News fucking flash, Meelz, this mafia life paid for your upbringing, your private school, college, med school and everything you have ever needed. You may hate me and your family for being killers but it's because of us you were protected and never harmed until you chose to turn your back on family."

Having had enough of this bullshit argument with her, I turn my back, ready to flee but her words have me halting and my shoulders tensing.

"You have her face on your arm but also have my name. Why would you do that if you thought so fucking little of me and my choices to build a life of my own away from my family?"

I keep my back to her as I answer the question, I knew she wouldn't let this go from the moment she saw the tattoo.

"I have Kingsley tattooed on me because she was the version of you that loved me first." I slowly turn to face her and note the shock etched into her features. "I fell in love with Max Kingsley." Tears gather in her eyes at my declaration. "Amelia Murdoch is the heartless bitch that hates everything about me and my choices in life." I leave her standing there with her mouth agape and remorse plastered across her face, she wanted the truth and she got it. Amelia is the version of her that sabotaged what we shared, Max is kind and loving and never judges, that is the person I fell in love with, not the jaded bitch that thinks she is above us all because she has a degree.

I only manage to make it three steps inside the cabin before I'm shoved from behind. I stumble forward a step before whirling around on her. The tears from a moment ago are long forgotten, in their place is unfiltered rage and hatred. Good, she is finally dropping her woe is fucking me act!

"I wanted you to fight for me, Cronos. You just walked out and never once tried to fight for me or come after me!"

The last tendrils of control I had on my anger slips through my fingers as I release all my pent up pain and anger.

"I fucking fought for you!" I roar. This time she doesn't cower away from me, she stands tall and weathers my outburst. "I did come after you!"

"When?" she screams.

"Six months ago I came for you! I wanted to drop to my fucking knees and profess my love for you but then I saw that cunt with you. You looked happy and he fit the image for the type of guy you should be with."

"You profiled him?"

I scoff. "Get the fuck off your high horse, Amelia! You and I both know I don't fit the stereotype for a girl like you."

"Why didn't you come to me?" I grind my teeth, fighting to keep my mouth shut so the words don't pour out of me. "Tell me!" she screams.

"Because it fucking hurt!" I scream.

"What?"

I stab my hand through my hair and tug on the strands as a memory of the words London spoke to me long ago replays in my mind.

"All the greatest loves in history are designed to be painful, Nos. Most people think love should be easy and comfortable but that isn't the type of love people like us crave. We want painful, soul-shattering, groundbreaking love that consumes us and drives us insane. What you shared with Aida is something that can never be replaced. She was your first love and don't you dare push me in the fucking lake for saying this but... she wasn't your greatest love, your soul-breaking, death-craving love."

"How do you know that?"

"Because you're still here—" she whispers. *"Romeo couldn't live without Juliet and vice versa. Your Juliet is out there, Nos, you just need to find her and let her break down your walls and destroy the fuck out of your heart until she owns every goddamn fucking piece of it. If it doesn't hurt then it isn't worth it."*

"You walked out on me and I thought the pain I felt was because I was just sad to see you go, I thought I would be okay after a few weeks, but I wasn't. When I saw you with him, I felt like my chest was breaking open, my heart wanted out of my own body so it could live inside yours." Her mouth parts on a gasp but now that I've started I can't stop the words from spilling out of me. "I rang London, she wanted to claw your fucking eyes out and torture that cocksucker but I said no."

"Why?" she whispers brokenly.

"I knew who he was the moment I saw him. I knew he was the one that got away and I couldn't hurt you like that, Amelia. If that was Aida, I would have taken the chance to rekindle that love as well." My subconscious is screaming at me to stop lying but I shut that fucker up really quick, I've said enough as it is. Tears slowly cascade down her cheeks as she stares up at me. I see so much pain and regret in her eyes that it spears me. I do the only thing I can think of, I close the space between us and grip the back of her head pulling her forward, so I can place a kiss on her forehead.

She clutches the front of my shirt in her tiny hands, trying to keep me here but she knows as well as I do that we can't turn back time. Our time has come and gone. Too much has happened and I don't think I could ever open up to anyone again—I tried that shit twice and got burned, badly.

"Grizz," she chokes out. I close my eyes briefly, then pull back to stare down at her.

"Don't do it, angel." She gasps at the use of my nickname for her. "Whatever you say now will be just words spoken in the heat of the moment—"

"I came here because I knew you would protect me, I knew you wouldn't turn me away no matter how upset you are with me. I chose you over my family because you wouldn't judge me for my choices and call me a stupid girl for falling into the trap with Colson like I did."

I cup her face between my hands and force a smile to my face. "No, angel. You came here because you thought I could fix the pain you are in and change the outcome of what already happened. I'm not your savior, Meelz. You and I are the same, we're both broken by our pasts and the only one who can find the old you and bring her back is *you*." She opens her mouth to argue but I push on. "Find her and let her guide you because she was fucking magnificent and she is the person who will be able to save you. When you find her, let me know." I release her and walk out the front door without a single glance back, knowing she will be waiting for it. I climb in my truck and head out. I have no idea where the fuck I am going but I just need to get out and away from her for a while so I can clear my head.

I pull up to the pier and kill the engine. The best part about a small town is no one is out late so I can be left alone with my own thoughts and not have to worry about some fucker sneaking up on me. I climb out and hop on the hood, leaning back against the windscreen as I stare out over the water and try to calm myself and all the emotions swirling inside me. I don't do these types of fucking feelings. My phone vibrating in my pocket pulls me from my thoughts. I pray it's work and someone died but when I see the caller ID, I sigh.

"Do you have ESP or some shit?" I ask instead of a greeting.

"Of course I do, bestie, I could feel it in my soul that you needed me and I was powerless to control the urge to call you." I snort out a laugh, London is a lot of things but caring and attentive isn't fucking one of them.

"You sound like an idiot."

"Kiss my ass, dickhead!" I laugh, now she sounds like the Lon I know and love. "Why do you sound wounded?" The fact she can read me so well should scare me but it never has. She doesn't have to ask what's wrong, she just knows from the tone of my voice or from a look.

"You gonna rat me out to your man if I tell you?" I may be angry and confused about all this shit with Amelia but I would never betray her trust by outing her to her father and the others. I know if London gives me her word she will never betray me.

"I would never fuck you over like that! You want this conversation to stay between us, then it will. The only time I would ever break my promise to you is if your life was endangered and I knew Artemis could save you."

I don't beat around the bush. "Amelia found me," I blurt out.

"How?" she asks without missing a beat.

"I wrote her a letter months ago and she saw the post stamp."

"Why is she there?" The anger in her tone is clear and I love her for being angry on my behalf but she shouldn't be. Her and Meelz used to be close but ever since she found out about what happened between us, she pulled away from Meelz. The final straw for London to cut all contact was when we spoke six months ago after I went to Chicago.

"Shit went south and she needed to run, she thought coming to me was better than asking her father for help."

"You turned that trifling bitch away... right?" I bite down on my lip and close my eyes. "Your answer should be, *of course I did, Lon, she broke my heart and I sent her ass packing as payback!*"

I chuckle but there is no humor to it. "Yeah, that is not what happened."

London exhales loudly. "You saw her and then all your anger went straight the fuck out the window, didn't it?"

I sigh and nod. "Yeah."

"Cronos, she fucked you up and left you high and dry. She didn't wait around, she moved on with that cunt and forgot about you. Don't you dare fucking let her do that shit to you again."

"I won't."

"Bullshit. Unlike her you never fell out of love with that ungrateful bitch. I give you two days before you're fingering her next to a corpse."

"Like how you fucked my brother next to a dead body?" She bursts out laughing and I can't help but smile.

"To-fucking-ché!" We both remain silent a while until she speaks again. "Don't let her break you again, Nos." Her tone is light but I can hear the edge of her anger in there as well. London is fucking loyal to her core and would go to war against her own aunt for me if I asked her to.

"I think it's too late for that, Lon. The king's men never put me back together the first time when she broke me and I don't think they will repair Humpty this time when she leaves again either."

"I let her get away unscathed the first time but if she does it again, not even you will save her from me. No one fucking hurts my bestie without paying for it, am I clear?"

"Crystal."

"Nos?"

"Yeah?"

"Can't you just fuck her and get it out of your system, then move on?"

I shake my head, this girl has no fucking boundaries. "Goodbye, London."

"Cronos, don't you dare hang up—" I end the call and pocket my phone, ignoring it ringing again, knowing it's just London. Talking to her has made me feel lighter and more clear headed.

Could I fuck her and feel nothing?

I push away the thought but it keeps resurfacing. My cock is growing hard in my pants at the thought of sinking inside her tight little cunt again.

Maybe I need to remind her what it's like being fucked by the Devil again.

Chapter Seven

Amelia

It's been over two hours since Cronos left, I waited out on the porch for him but gave up after an hour. I've showered and stole another one of his shirts to sleep in. I can't stop replaying our disagreement over and over again in my head. I had no idea he felt so deeply for me, the fact he came to Chicago to confess how he felt about me rendered me speechless. If only he had looked deeper he would have seen there was no real happiness, it was all a mask, a show for everyone else. He had no idea the horrors I was facing behind closed doors and I have no one else to blame but myself.

I snuggle down lower in the bed and pull the covers up to my chin. This freaking cabin is freezing and I don't want to sleep in front of the fire and have him thinking that I was waiting for him this whole time, when in truth I have been but he doesn't need to know that. I close my eyes and try to force myself to sleep but the instant that I do, I hear the sound of his truck pulling up. I swallow and clench my eyes shut, trying to fake sleep, my breaths labored as anticipation of his arrival builds.

Will he come find me?

Does he still want me to go?

Those thoughts plague me as I hear the front door open and his heavy footfalls on the wooden floor. I slip one hand lower and place it over my growing bump, I was selfish coming here but he wasn't wrong. I knew he wouldn't turn me away or judge me for being pregnant to someone I don't love. I hear him coming down the hallway and stiffen. I try to relax and even out my breathing but the moment he enters the room my breath hitches giving me away. I can feel his gaze boring into the back of my head but I'm too much of a coward to roll over and face him.

"Tell me to get the fuck out and to not touch you and I will." His words have my breaths quickening. I try to control them as I slowly sit up and turn to face him. The dim lighting from the moon doesn't illuminate his features but I know him well enough to know those brown eyes have turned dark with lust.

"I don't want you to go," I say boldly. Some may think this is wrong, wanting another man while I am carrying another's child but fuck them because the truth is, I never stopped wanting Cronos—I just didn't know how to admit that shit.

"This is purely physical, Meelz." Pain slices through me but I get it, we both need this release but neither of us wants more and I respect that. A relationship is the last thing I need right now, the last one was enough to put me off for life.

"Okay," I whisper. He glides across the room, only stopping when he stands before me at the edge of the bed. I know what he likes and how he likes it. He may be a lot younger than me but when it comes to what happens in our sex life, he is the one who is more skilled and dominant, he knows exactly what he is doing and how to do it. Given what I have lived through the past year, I need that type of control. I need him to fix what someone else broke inside of me.

"Same rules as before." The husky lilt to his voice sends a shiver down my spine. He reaches out and grips my arms, forcing me to my knees. "I need the words, angel," he rasps out as he buries his face in the crook of my neck. The instant his tongue touches my skin I moan.

"Any discomfort, I tell you. If you push a hard limit, I stop you. You may be the one giving the orders but I'm the one in control, always." I recite his rules aloud, knowing he needs to hear them. I don't know why he always needs me to say them but I know if I don't he won't touch me.

He sucks the lobe of my ear into his mouth, drawing a sharp gasp from me as he releases it. "Good girl, angel." His whispered words have me clenching my thighs together in anticipation. "Lose the shirt," he demands as he pulls back and crosses his arms over his chest. I shakily grip the hem of my shirt and slowly pull it over my head, a hiss escaping him when he takes in the sight of my nakedness. When Cronos looks at you, it's like the sun is kissing your skin. The heat of his gaze scorches my skin, sending delicious shivers down my spine. "Next time, we're doing this how I like." His promise of what is to come has me reaching out and gripping his shirt. He helps me lift it over his head.

The moment that tattoo with my name comes into view I pause. I never felt like I meant enough to anyone to warrant them wanting something so permanent etched into their skin. I trace the lines of the ink, relishing in the way he trembles beneath my touch. He doesn't stop me when I trail my fingers lower. When I reach the button of his jeans, I flick my gaze to his and hold it as I pop the button and slowly lower the zipper. I push his pants down but leave his boxers on. Cronos likes aspects of control in the bedroom and me making a move without his consent means he will punish me by not allowing me to come.

"Remove them." I eagerly obey his order and push the boxers down his legs. The moment his cock springs free, my vision is laser focused on it, I forgot how big he is. Having him inside me again is going to sting, but knowing the pleasure he can wring out of me has my thighs clenching.

"Can I taste you?" His nostrils flare as he peers down at me.

"On your knees before me, now." I scramble to get off the bed and obey but the instant I try to lower to my knees he grips my arm stopping me. I snap my gaze to his, worrying that he has changed his mind. My worries are put to rest when he grabs a pillow and drops it to the floor. Normally he would have his fingers tangled in my hair and shoving me to the ground. He helps me lower to my knees and this tender side of him in the bedroom shocks me. Until it dawns on me, he is being gentle because of the baby, my heart fucking melts inside my chest. "Hands behind your back."

I do as he demands and interlock my fingers behind my back, keeping my gaze on his as I open my mouth. I feign for his taste, before him I never liked blow jobs or even enjoyed them but Cronos flipped a switch inside me. I not only love giving them to him, I get off on it. Just the taste of him makes me wet, I can already feel how slick I am between my thighs.

Gripping his shaft, he pumps it once exhaling a loud hiss. Rather than slipping his cock inside my mouth, he rubs it on my cheek, smearing his pre-cum across both sides. I turn my head, trying to capture him but he uses his other hand to tangle in my hair and keep me still.

"Please!" I beg, making his eyes blaze.

"Tell me how much you want it."

"I want it so bad, I need to taste you on my tongue and down my throat." My tone is needy to my own ears but I can't find it within myself to care. With him I have never had to pretend, I can just be me without fear of him judging me for my darker tastes.

"This time you get only my cock but next time, you'll be sucking someone else's while I watch, am I clear?" A wanton moan escapes me. Rather than waiting for my answer, he rewards me by finally pushing his cock inside my mouth. My jaw aches with the effort of opening wide enough to fit him without scraping his shaft with my teeth. The instant my lips wrap around him, he throws his head back and groans. "Fuck, angel, suck me!"

I do just that. His hold on my hair loosens enough for me to find my rhythm as I bob up and down on his cock. I know he's waiting to disrupt my tempo and I long for that moment, for the beast inside him to takeover and fuck my face. I swirl my tongue along his shaft as I pull back, relishing in the sound that rips out of him.

"Fuck, you're such a dirty girl aren't you, angel?" he growls as he begins to thrust his hips, forcing me to gag—the sound and sight of me gagging on his dick always gets him off. He loves it when spit trails down my chin and tears leak from my eyes. He continues to fuck my face. I breathe through my nose trying to take him as deep as I can but I've never been able to master that talent, he's too big. My throat is growing hoarse from gagging so much, but the sight of my tears only feeds the demon inside him.

It's crazy how I can trust him so easily. Even after everything I have endured, I know without an ounce of doubt that Cronos would never hurt me physically. As if sensing my mind has wandered elsewhere he pulls his cock free, kneels in front of me and uses the strands of my hair to tug my head back, his other hand gripping my chin, forcing my mouth open. He spits in my mouth then shoves three fingers inside. I gag around his digits.

"When my cock is in your mouth, that is all you think about!" he snarls, then yanks his fingers free. I suck in lungfuls of air. He pushes back to his feet and tugs me to mine by my hair. "Bend over the side of the bed and spread your fucking legs." I place my hands flat on the edge and spread my legs like he orders, his hands gripping the globes of my ass. "I miss watching you get fucked, Meelz."

I turn and peer back at him over my shoulder, the sight of him lowering to his knees behind me has heat spreading throughout my body. He uses his hold on my cheeks to part them. I tense in anticipation. He spits and I moan the instant I feel it sliding down my ass. He catches it with his tongue and prods my hole, my fingertips grip the sheets.

"Cronos!" I plead, needing him to tend to the ache he's caused between my thighs, my clit throbbing, needing attention. I squeal in surprise when he lands a swift smack to my ass. When he repeats the move, a moan tumbles free this time. The second his tongue slides through my folds and touches my clit I scream out, a shudder working its way through my body when he sucks it into his mouth. I press back against him. He grips my hips and holds me in place as he eats my pussy like a man on a mission.

Chapter Eight

Cronos

The taste of her pussy has me growling from deep within my throat. I feel her body shudder at the sound. I swipe my tongue over her clit loving the cries that tear from her. She's backing her ass up like a pro as she rubs that pussy up and down my tongue. I feel her body grow tense and know she is close, so I pull back. She whimpers but she knows better than to question my motives or her orgasm won't happen until I say. I run a hand down her back, loving the way she melts at feeling my touch.

"You gonna take my dick like a good girl, angel?" I ask as I line my cock up with her entrance.

"Yes. I'll take it so fucking good, Nos," she promises as I press the head of my cock inside her tight little cunt. I may be ruthless and downright nasty in the bedroom, but I also take into account her current condition. I don't know much about babies but the last thing I want to do is fuck her too hard and leave the imprint of my dick on the baby's forehead. I press further inside her and still, giving her a chance to adjust to my size. She's breathing hard and clutching the sheets in a vice-like grip.

"Breathe, angel," I grit out through clenched teeth as I ease further inside her, her cunt so fucking wet I glide inside her with ease. It's taking every ounce of self-control I possess to not just slam all the way inside her. I begin to lose the battle when her pussy starts fluttering, finally losing it and thrust the remainder of the way inside her. She cries out and I bite down on my lip to keep my groan from slipping free.

"Fuck, you feel so good," she rasps out. I give us both a minute to adjust before drawing almost all the way out of her, leaving just the tip inside her tight wet heat, then slam back inside her. She screams out her pleasure and lurches forward, but I pull her back to me. I reach around and grip the front of her throat, pulling her until she is flush against me. I lean down and capture her lips in a kiss of ownership as I begin to move inside her, swallowing her moans.

Fucking her at this angle feels so good, I can feel the tip of my cock brushing against her G-spot. She starts to quake in my hold, I break the kiss and stare into her eyes, loving the blissed-out look I see in them.

"You want to come on this dick, baby?"

She whimpers and nods. "Yes, please let me come!"

My hold on her throat tightens. "I want you to scream my fucking name when you break apart." I slam inside her ruth-lessly twice more. She slams her eyes closed and arches forward as much as my hold will allow.

"Cronos, I'm coming," she screams out, her cunt strangling the fucking life out of my cock as her orgasm rips through her.

This, this sight right here is everything to me.

I love watching her come, it's a sight unmatched by anything in this world. The way her eyes turn glassy and the red hue that covers her body drives the beast inside me mad. The cage I keep him in inside me bursts open. I shift my hold and grip the back of her neck, forcing her forward so her face is buried in the mattress. I grip her hip in my other hand, my hold is punishing and will leave bruises. I can't control the monster, he overshadows my rational thought and fucks her like a possessed man.

I feel my balls tightening and know I am seconds away from blowing my load deep inside her pussy, then the sounds of her muffled cries penetrates the fog. I want her to swallow every drop of my cum but the need to stamp my mark— coming inside her wins the battle raging inside me. I throw my head back and roar her name as I come. The shudders are still rolling through me when I pull out and force her to her knees before me, she knows what I want.

She locks her arms behind her back and opens her mouth. Pressing forward, I groan the moment her wet little mouth wraps around me. "Lick it fucking clean," I snarl. She obeys without complaint and bobs up and down on my shaft, moaning at the taste of both our releases mixed together. She pulls back and releases me with a pop, licks her lips and moans, knowing that shit gets to me. I reach down and cup her cheek, loving the way she presses it into my touch. "Next time, I want to watch you on your hands and knees while you get fucked." A shudder rolls through her at my promise.

I have a fetish for cucking and I am so fucking pleased that she enjoys it as much as I do. The sight of another man's cock sliding in and out of her pussy gets me so fucking hard, and the thought of his cum inside her cunt as I fuck her, sets my beast roaring inside me. The only man that gets to come inside that sweet little cunt is me.

Reaching down, I stroke her cheek and shoot her a thankful smile before heading into the bathroom and closing the door behind myself. I know this is probably a dickhead move but the truth is, I went into things with her with my guard down and I got burned... badly. This time, my guard will be up always, this way there will be no chance of her getting under my skin again. I know that the child inside her will change things, I'm not the father of her baby and I know because of her history that she will want her family back together again. That is the only reason I didn't go after the cunt the other night and kill him, she would never forgive me for hurting the father of her unborn baby.

She won't admit it out loud but I know she is going to walk away again and take the kid with her. I can't allow myself to fall into the trap of thinking that she and I can be more than just fuck buddies. Losing her will kill me, but if I allow myself to care for that kid and she takes it from me... I don't think I will ever recover from a loss like that.

The tension between me and Amelia is so thick, it's practically suffocating and the short ride from my house to the morgue feels like hours. She hasn't spoken a word since I left her on her knees last night, it's better this way and if she can't see that, then that shit is on her. I park the truck out front and climb out, not bothering to wait for her. I won't hold her hand and baby her through this shit, if she is going to make it on her own in this world without her family, then she needs to start relying on herself and not someone else.

I unlock the front door and head inside, flicking the lights on as I head toward the back where I feel most at home—*in the chiller*. The moment I push through the swinging doors, I inhale the scent and sigh in contentment. Nothing beats the scent of this room. Most people hate the smell but I don't. I find it calming. I move across the room and double check the name tags on the chiller doors. Unlike most funeral homes, I only have one chiller room here because of the small size. I would like another one but it wouldn't be used that often, because sadly we don't have enough death around here.

I slide the door open and pass by Jack and Connor to retrieve Sally. I saw her around town a couple of times and she seemed like a nice old lady. I pull the zipper down on the body bag and shoot her a smile—she looks peaceful.

Lucky lady, I wish I knew what peace felt like.

"I'm gonna fix you up real good, Miss Sally, and then send you back to your husband, kids and grandbabies." I wheel her trolley out and close the door behind me. I come to a stop next to the metal slab where Amelia stands eyeing me cautiously as she looks from me to the body bag.

"You talk to the dead?" she asks.

I shake my head, of course she wouldn't get it. She's so used to saving lives that she doesn't spare the dead a second thought. I lift Sally off the gurney and place her gently on the metal slab, so she can be prepared for embalming.

"The dead deserve the same amount of respect as the living, if not more," I bite out as I begin to unzip the bag, Amelia averts her gaze which just serves to rile me up. "Does Miss Sally's appearance offend you?"

She turns back to me and glowers. "I wonder if *Miss Sally's* husband left her on her knees after she sucked his cock?" I purse my lips and tear my gaze from hers to look at Sally.

"Did Reggie leave you on your knees, Sally?" I ask. When she doesn't reply, I turn my head to the side and bring my ear down closer to her mouth.

"You're a real dick, you know that?" Amelia snaps. I stand to my full height and shoot her a wink.

"And that is why I prefer to work with the dead, because they don't speak, they don't harm and they sure as fuck don't stab you in the back."

Her mouth pops open but no words come out, I can see the regret in her eyes but it's too late for that shit. She needs to learn to live with the choices she made and make the most of this shitty situation she has found herself in. If she thinks for a second I am going to help guide her or make things easier for her, then she has another thing coming.

"Head out front. If the phone rings, answer it. Don't come back here unless someone has died and needs to be collected." I dismiss her as I turn and head to the storage room where all the chemicals for embalming are kept under lock and key. This may be a small town and with that, kids get bored and can't get their hands on normal coke or weed so they used to break in here when Bill owned the place and steal the chemicals to get high.

Idiots!

I'm still learning how to embalm, so I always have someone come in and help me out when it needs to be done. I never liked school or paid any attention to that boring shit but the moment I worked with Bill, suddenly I couldn't absorb enough information. I set all the chemicals we will need out. Sally will be done first then Connor, Jack will be last as he has no family and no one to pay for my services. Unlike other funeral homes, I don't treat him differently. I cover the costs and give them the funeral they deserve.

I give back to the dead because I couldn't save the living.

Chapter Nine

Amelia

I've been sitting behind this desk for an hour and I am bored out of my mind!

I'm used to the rush of the ER and never getting a chance to sit down. This is the polar opposite, I've even resorted to naming the two fucking fly's that keep buzzing past me. It doesn't help that Cronos is being distant. Last night I thought we crossed a bridge. Clearly I was wrong, he just wanted to use me and get off. Okay, I admit I definitely got off as well but that isn't the point. He left me on my fucking knees while he escaped to the bathroom. Even when he was finished he didn't climb into bed beside me, he stalked out of the room and slept on his recliner in front of the fireplace!

I'm pulled from my thoughts when the front door opens. I climb to my feet with a smile on my face but the moment I drink in the sight of the woman, the smile slowly slides off my face. She is beautiful. Natural blonde hair that is just past her shoulders, blue eyes that hold so much innocence and a body that rivals swimsuit models. She smiles kindly and it takes great effort on my part to return that smile.

"Hey, you must be Becky's replacement?" she says cheerfully and extends her hand to me. "I'm Tracey."

My arm feels like it weighs a ton as I lift it and shake her hand. "Max," I reply in an even tone but her smile never falters.

"Nice to meet you," she says as she pulls her hand back and tries to step around my desk to head toward the back. I cut in front of her.

"Sorry, it's staff only back there," I clip out. I'm lying through my teeth as I have no idea what the rules are here, but the thought of this beautiful blonde who is clearly Cronos's age heading back there *alone* with him has my stomach churning.

"Oh, I know. I am staff." Her smile is nowhere to be seen as she sidesteps me and heads into the back while I stand here watching like a broken hearted puppy.

"Thanks for coming." I hear Nos say when she enters the room. I feel tears pricking the backs of my eyes. I want to find a cleaning closet and hide in there as pictures of him fucking her next to Sally's body play on a loop inside my head. Unable to handle the pain searing my chest, I turn to flee but stop short at the sight of an elderly man standing there with the broadest smile on his face.

"My lord, my Bethy wasn't telling tales, you really are beautiful." I reel back and frown at the old man. He shakes his head and takes a step forward only for me to back up one. He freezes instantly. A look of understanding washes over his face and I cringe when the smile he was sporting vanishes. "I mean you no harm, my dear, my name is Bill and my wife Beth served you and the boy at the diner."

I swallow and nod even though I can't recall much about that day, but keep nodding anyway and go along with it. I never used to fear being alone in a room with a man before but now, I feel like the walls are closing in on me. Bill must see something on my face because he takes a step back and tries to smile reassuringly, but my heart won't stop beating into overdrive.

"How about we go find the boy?" I can't help the laughter that breaks free, this old timer referring to Cronos as a *boy* is just... I have no words. I nod my head and wave for him to follow me, appreciating the fact he keeps a good distance of space between us. I pause outside the swinging doors when I remember that Tracey is in there. Rather than asking me what's wrong, Bill just pushes through the doors, leaving me no choice but to follow after him. I freeze when I find the space empty and the slab that held Sally vacant. "Boy?" Bill calls out.

"Back room!" Cronos calls back. I tense and drop my gaze to the floor feeling a tinge of pain in my chest.

"Give us a minute!" Tracey adds, her reply has my breath hitching.

Did we just interrupt their fuckfest?

When I hear footsteps approaching, I can't even bring myself to lift my head, I don't want to see him with just fucked hair, knowing she would have been running her fingers through the strands and tugging on it as she came on his cock. I close my eyes and will my tears to remain at bay, I won't let him see them fall. I have no right to feel this way but I can't seem to stop myself from feeling jealous.

"You look rough, boy, did she take longer than you bargained for?" Bill's question has me cringing and biting down on my lip to keep from screaming at him to shut the fuck up!

"It's getting easier. I still feel bad for draining her but it's dressing her after we finish that I struggle with." My anger peaks, how can he speak about fucking her and then dressing her after they finish in front of me like it means nothing when he left me naked and on my knees last night!

"Are you fucking serious?" I snap as I finally lift my head to look at him, only to frown at the sight of him in a... hazmat suit thing. Cronos looks pissed while Bill just looks confused. Before another word can be spoken, Tracey enters the room pushing Sally on the gurney. Tracey wears a suit similar to Cronos.

"Watch your mouth, *Max*," Cronos spits the name at me like it burns his tongue. I look between the three of them before focusing on Sally and that's when I notice she is dressed in a silk blouse and black slacks with a pair of ballerina shoes on her feet.

Oh my God!

Shame washes over me. I open my mouth to speak but Cronos crosses the room, grips my arm and drags me back out into the hallway. I can feel his anger radiating off him in waves —I fucked up badly. He doesn't stop pulling me after him until we are next to my desk. I look up at him ready to apologize but the dark look in his eyes has me clamping my mouth shut.

"You want to explain what the fuck that was?" he snarls in a deathly low tone.

"I–I... I thought—"

"You thought what?" He sneers as he bends so we are eye level. I clamp my mouth closed, knowing now isn't the time to push him. "You thought I was sinking my cock into Tracey in the back room?" I recoil but he doesn't let me move away, he grips the front of my shirt and pulls me in close so our noses touch. "Unlike you, angel, I don't sleep with every person who bats their lashes at me." My jaw unhinges at his cruel words. "Sit your ass down and do your job—"

"Boy, that's enough!" I see Bill out of the corner of my eye glaring at Cronos. The latter ignores the old man as he continues to glare at me.

"Do your job and stay the hell out of my business, *Max*." He releases me with a slight shove and I catch myself on the edge of my desk. I watch as Cronos turns to face Bill, who looks at Nos like a disapproving father.

"You know better than to handle a woman like that," Bill scolds.

"She isn't a woman, she's a siren that lures men in only to kill them slowly from the inside out." I gasp at his description of me. Is that really how he views me now?

"Head on out back and help Tracey finish up with Sally."

"You don't tell me what to do, old man," Nos seethes.

"Boy, now isn't the time for one of your power trips. Head on out back now, before you do more damage here." Nos snarls but does as he is told, making sure to shoulder check Bill on his way past. The moment the Devil himself disappears through the swinging doors, my legs give out and I drop into my chair, gasping for air. Bill is before me in an instant and resting his hands on top of my shoulders. "Breathe for me, darling." I nod and try to do as he asked. Bill is patient and doesn't hurry me, he just keeps smiling and offering me words of reassurance.

"Thank you," I rasp out when I finally manage to get my breathing under control. Bill shakily rises to his feet and smiles down at me as he takes a step back.

"That boy has a temper but I've never seen him be so harsh to someone other than me," he admits. I inhale sharply and nod.

"We have a... complicated history."

Bill nods but I can see a shadow fall over his features. "The baby you carry, is it... his?" I blow out a loud exhale, clearly my hiding period is over now.

I smile sadly and shake my head. "No."

"Hmmm."

I furrow my brow. "What does, *hmmm* mean?"

He shoots me a boyish grin. "He clearly feels for you, darling, and he must just be messed up that the wee one inside ya isn't his."

I shake my head. "Cronos doesn't—"

"Denials are a waste of good air." I balk at the old man. "Working and living together without fixing past issues isn't a good mix." I drop my gaze to my lap and wring my hands together.

"I don't have any another choice," I admit shamefully.

"Come on, darling, let's give the brute his space. I think I have an idea that will benefit everyone."

Chapter Ten

Cronos

I've stayed in the back all day avoiding Amelia. I was fucking livid with her earlier and the fact that she would think that I would seriously be fucking another woman with her sitting out front. I know she has issues after the shit she went through but she had no fucking right to project that shit onto me! Tracey kept as much space between us as possible as we embalmed the other two bodies. She couldn't get out of here fast enough and honestly, I couldn't fucking blame her.

I double check the lock on the chemical room before switching the lights off and heading out front to deal with Amelia but when I reach the front she is nowhere to be found.

"Amelia?" I call out thinking she may be in the small kitchen or bathroom. When she doesn't reply I check both places and still can't find her. Worry begins to gnaw inside me. I exit the building and look around the parking lot that is empty except for my truck and the hearse. I lock up and jump in my truck, pushing it to its limits as I head straight home.

She wouldn't have walked home, would she?

A pit begins to form in my gut when I pull up out front of my house and see there are no lights on inside. I rush through the small cabin and check for her, only to find the place empty. My worry starts to turn into panic as I rush back outside and climb into my truck, heading for the diner. Maybe she stopped there and grabbed something to eat? I double park out front, not giving a fuck. I scan the diner and curse beneath my breath when I don't see her.

Did he track her down?

I rush back to my truck and smack my hand against the steering wheel before putting it in drive and driving to the local park. When I don't find her there, I check the pier and still find no sign of her. I wrack my brain trying to think of what could have happened, then it hits me. I pull my phone out of my pocket and scroll my contacts until I find his fucking number. It rings five times before he answers.

"Boy?"

"Where the fuck is she, old man?" I snarl, not bothering to hide the anger in my tone.

"Safe and resting." A part of me is relieved to know she is safe and didn't get taken or worse, run back to that cunt who hurt her and knocked her up. But, the other half of me, the part that thirsts for carnage and death, wants to snap the old fuck's neck for daring to interfere in my business.

I white knuckle the steering wheel with my free hand so I don't crush my phone. "She isn't yours to care for!" I roar.

"From what she has said, she isn't *yours* either!" Before I can scream at him he pushes on. "She's pregnant, Cronos, and the added stress of what you did to her today isn't good for her or the baby. You have my word that she will be looked after and kept safe here with me and Beth."

"She doesn't belong with you!"

"And from what I witnessed today, neither of you two are good together for more than a few seconds. Working and living together while you both are so angry at the other isn't good for anyone, let alone the wee bub she carries."

"I don't give a fuck! She belongs with me—"

"Then you need to find a way to forgive her, boy. I saw the anger and blame in your eyes today when you looked at her. If she is someone important to you, then you need to show her that." I take a shuddering breath. "I know your past wasn't easy but I also know she hasn't been treated kindly either. I know the signs of abuse, boy. I won't watch another woman suffer, I can't." Shame washes over me, I forgot all about what he and Beth went through.

"She can stay but I'm coming over." I don't wait for a reply, I end the call and swing the truck around to head to Bill and Beth's place. The whole ride there all I can think about is how hard this must be for both of them, having Amelia in their house. They are good people and Bill doesn't deserve the way I treat him, but I can't seem to change that shit. He is the only person here that isn't intimidated by me or scared to look me in the eye. Everyone else gives the Angel of Death a wide berth or crosses the street to get as far from me as they can.

I put the truck in park out front of their place and sigh when I see Bill sitting on the steps out front with two beers in his hands. I scrub a hand down my face before climbing out and making my way toward him. He nods his head to the spot beside him. I choose to ignore his request and snatch a beer from his hand, then lean against the railing.

"You hold so much anger inside you, boy."

I snort before taking a sip of my beer. "Yeah, well, you would be angry all the time too if you lived through what I did."

"We are the authors of our own destinies. You can rewrite your future anytime you want to, but you don't seem to want to change your own outcome."

"How the fuck would you know that, old man?"

He smiles sadly. "Because I've seen it all before. I was angry for a long time, Cronos. I wanted everyone to be just as furious as I was but they all kept on living while I died more and more inside with each passing day."

"Our stories aren't the same."

"Not the same but similar."

"What are you getting at, old man?" I've just about reached my quota for talking today so he better make his point fast.

"I see your anger and pain but I see her anxiety and fear. Together you both are a volatile mix until you each overcome the demons of your past."

I scoff. "This isn't some fucking movie, Bill, this is real life and people like me and her don't get do overs. We have to live with the hand we have been dealt and accept what is."

He shakes his head and looks at me with... pity. "You don't have to live with shit! You just need to find a reason to fight, find something that gives you the strength you need for change and I promise you, boy, it will be the most frightening and exhilarating feeling in this world." Our conversation is cut short when the front door opens and Amelia walks out. She's wearing a pair of Yoga pants and some white fluffy socks but it's the form fitting long sleeved shirt she wears that captures my attention—her growing bump is on display. Bitterness of that bump not being because of my seed seeps into me and I quickly push that feeling away.

"Bill?" He peers over his shoulder at her and smiles kindly as he pushes to his feet and arches his back.

"I'll give you kids some time alone," he says as he walks back inside. Amelia shoots him a thankful smile as he passes. When she approaches me, I can see that her eyes are red and bloodshot. She was crying. She motions for me to join her on the love swing on the corner of the porch. If it wasn't for the fact I could tell she was crying I would have denied her. The chair creaks under my weight, she rolls her lips over her teeth to keep from smiling which earns her a scowl from me.

Silence stretches between us for a while. I sip my beer and slowly swing us. She gets comfortable, tucking her legs under her and pulling the sleeves of her shirt down so they cover her hands. I lean forward and place my beer on the ground, then grip the back of my hoodie and yank it off. I toss it to her without another word as I retrieve my beer and start swinging us again. I spy her out of the corner of my eye pulling the collar of my hoodie to her nose and inhaling, it shouldn't but that sight has my chest swelling with pride.

"You staying here then?" She jerks at the sound of my voice. I feel her gaze boring into the side of my head but refuse to look at her.

"I think it's probably for the best, don't you?"

I fight not to scoff. "Since when does my opinion matter to you?"

"I guess it shouldn't but contrary to what you think, Cronos, I don't want to cause problems for you."

"If that were true, then you wouldn't have judged me for a past I had no control over."

"Like how you're judging me now?"

I turn my head to the side and look at her. "What do I have to judge you for? You made it clear the day you kicked my ass to the curb, I either choose you or my brothers. The worst part was you didn't give me a chance to answer the question before you went off ranting about how I was no better than your family, a 'thug for hire' were your words, I believe."

"You knew how I felt about the lifestyle my family leads—"

"So you just thought you would chuck me in the same basket you put them in?"

"No—"

"You gave me a choice to go back to my brothers or run away from this life with *you*, want to know what my answer was?" Her bottom lip begins to tremble and I see her eyes turn glassy with unshed tears. "If you had given me a chance to answer before you self-sabotaged what we shared, I would have told you that this lifestyle has taken everything from me and I owe it nothing." Her mouth parts on a gasp as I stand and face her. "For me there was no choice, Amelia. I saw my redemption from the darkness in you. You were never a second choice for me, you were always my first thought in the morning and the last before I slept." I reach into my pocket and retrieve the roll of cash and phone I got for her. I toss them next to her but she doesn't take her tear filled gaze off me. "I. Would. Have. Chosen. You."

I turn my back to her, ready to leave but her words have me pausing. "I saw the world through your eyes and I got scared that you would never see me as more than a fleeting moment. My entire family always chooses this life over me and I couldn't handle you doing the same."

I keep my back to her unable to look at her or I'd risk my anger getting the better of me again. "Look how well that shit turned out for you, Meelz. Maybe if you had chosen me and the family you claim to hate so much, you wouldn't be on the run from the bastard that knocked you up and ruined your life." I attempt to leave but she grabs my arm and spins me around to face her. I keep my gaze focused above her head.

"I did fuck up. I am woman enough to admit that. I'm so sorry I hurt you, Cronos. If I could go back and change what happened, I would." I lazily drop my gaze to hers and make sure to keep my emotions closed off.

"You're a liar. If given the choice to go back you wouldn't, you may hate him but you already love the kid growing inside you." Her face falls. Despite my anger, I reach out and cup her cheek in my hand. "Take it from someone who wasn't wanted by either of his parents, you loving your kid is nothing to be ashamed of. That baby has no idea how lucky it is to be loved already by you." I lean forward and place a kiss against her forehead, my lips stay pressed against her longer than they should. Pulling away from her is harder than it should be but walking away from her again... that shit stings worse than taking a bullet to the chest.

Chapter Eleven

Amelia

Two weeks later...

Despite how things ended on the porch two weeks ago between me and Cronos, I still turned up to work the next day. The look of shock on his face when he pulled into the parking lot and saw me standing there was comical. The first few days were awkward and filled with tension. He even chose to eat his lunch in the chiller room rather than sit with me in the kitchen. A cold shiver runs down my spine at the memory of walking in to check on him, only to find his half eaten sandwich resting on Mr. Connelly's chest. I nearly threw up right there when he picked it up and took another bite.

"Max." The sound of him calling my name draws me from my thoughts. I push back from my desk and head for the back. The moment I enter, he is nowhere to be found.

"Grizz?" I hear him groan from the back room and fight

back my smile, he still doesn't like it when I call him that. The nickname came about when he wouldn't let me out of bed for four days unless it was to eat or use the bathroom. I told him he couldn't hibernate like a grizzly bear forever but the truth is, the name really stuck because he's always protected me fiercely like a Grizzly would their home.

"Back here." I follow the sound of his voice around the corner to the embalming room. I poke my head and scrunch my nose at the smell.

"Why are you embalming without Tracey?" He shoots me a loaded look.

"She's sick and the dead wait for no one."

"Okay..." I let my sentence trail off.

"I need you to help me."

My brows jump to my hairline. "I'm a doctor, Cronos, not an embalmer!" I grit out. For someone who is quite smart, he doesn't seem to grasp that I have no experience with the dead.

"Gretchen needs to be dressed and I..." I flick my gaze from him to the woman on the slab and it dawns on me when I see the white towel draped across her breasts and another is placed on top of her vagina. My mouth pops open in shock.

"You don't need Tracey's help for embalming, do you?" His eyes narrow in warning but seeing him so uncomfortable is fucking priceless, so I push on. "You keep her coming back so she can dress the females."

His jaw locks and his eyes spit fire, laughter bursts out of me which just serves to piss him off further. "Shut the fuck up and help me."

"Nuh-uh. You have to ask me nicely and take me to dinner or you're on your own, buddy."

"Amelia!" he snaps angrily.

I kick the door open wider and lean against the door jam, crossing my arms over my chest. "Cronos," I taunt.

His nostrils flaring is the first sign I get that he is at his wits end with me. I expect him to argue some more but to my surprise, he yanks his gloves off and tosses them on top of Gretchen, then grips the front of his disposable hazmat suit and rips it off in one swift move. He stands there in his black shirt and dark jeans, the angry look in his eyes vanishes as he moves toward me, it shifts into a look of... lust.

My breath hitches when he stops before me and cages me in, then places his hands on either side of my head. I swallow audibly as I try to calm my racing heart and plead with my hormones to remain in check. I lose the battle when he dips his head and buries his nose in the crook of my neck, inhaling. I gasp when he sucks the tender flesh into his mouth. I grip the front of his shirt instinctively. He licks a trail to my ear. I'm panting and unable to control myself as my fingers find their way into his hair and tug on the strands when he sucks my lobe into his mouth.

"My cock is rock-fucking-hard for you, angel." I moan at the promise in his tone. I press forward so I'm flush against him. He removes his hands from the wall, grips the globes of my ass and lifts me. I lock my legs around his waist as he moves us toward Gretchen. The moment he places me on the edge of the slab I squeal in horror and try to shove him back but he uses his size against me and keeps me in place.

"Nos, I am not fucking you next to a—"

"Dead body?"

I glower at the smug prick. "You said the dead need to be respected," I remind him.

"I'm fucking you, not her." I balk at him. "Just don't touch her tits or pussy, no harm no foul." Before I can tear into him, he silences me with a kiss that robs me of breath. The dead body behind me is long forgotten as his tongue tangles with mine and the taste of him overcomes my senses. Before I can deepen the kiss, he pulls back and smirks at me. "Lift up." I brace my hands on the edge of the metal slab while he peels my leggings and panties off. The second his eyes land on my bare pussy he bites his bottom lip. "Fuck, I want to take my time with you but I have a viewing in ten minutes so this has to be fast."

I nod eagerly, too turned on to comprehend what he is saying, I open my legs wider to accommodate him when he steps forward. I expect him to drop his pants and slip inside me but to my surprise he doesn't, he runs his fingers through my slit causing me to buck off the table.

"If there was more time I would be sinking my cock into you," he growls as he slides two fingers inside my greedy little cunt. I moan shamelessly. "My fingers are going to have to do it until tonight."

"Grizz," I whimper when he begins to thrust his fingers in and out of me, hooking them at the perfect angle, stroking that spot inside me that only he has been able to reach. "Fuck, I need your cock," I plead a second before I smash my lips to his and cup his hard length through his jeans. He breaks our kiss with a groan.

"Fuck, angel. You want me to fuck you?"

"Yes!" I practically scream when he hits the spot inside me but it's not enough, I need his cock. He yanks his fingers free and bends down to retrieve my panties from the floor. I frown but he says nothing.

"Open." I open my mouth, he slips my panties inside, then lifts me off the table and spins me around so I am now facing Gretchen! I try to push away from her but he grips the back of my neck and forces me forward, I am an inch away from the side of her face. "You're going to remain quiet and not make a fucking sound. I would hate for Gretchen's children to hear you coming on my cock while their mother is beside you." Horror fills me and I want to protest but the moment the head of his cock prods at my entrance, all rational thought flees. "This is going to be hard and fast, baby. Hang on." I do as he says and grip the edge of the table to make sure my stomach doesn't come into contact with it.

A heady moan tumbles from my lips when he slides inside my pussy. I can feel him stretching me out and the slight burn mixed with pleasure is fucking intoxicating. My eyes roll backward as he bottoms out inside me. Fuck, I have been dreaming about feeling him move inside me since the last time we fucked. I don't know if it's pregnancy hormones or not, but I am always horny and seeing him every day has me instantly wet. Each night, when Bill picks me up after work, I go home and finger myself while thinking about Cronos.

"Fuck, this pussy is perfect!"

"Hmmm," I moan around my panties. He draws back and slams inside me. I expect him to drag it out and make me work for my orgasm but he must have meant what he said. He fucks me at a punishing pace. I grip the edge of the slab for dear life, feeling my knees getting weak as my orgasm begins to build inside me. "Arghhh." He pulls me back by my hair so my back is to his chest. He covers my mouth with one of hands and trails the other down my body, pinching my clit between his fingers and I detonate. His hand and my panties muffle my cries of pleasure.

"I love knowing my cum will be inside you all day," he growls in my ear a second before he bites down on the tender flesh of my neck to mute his own cries as he comes, buried deep inside me. He moves his hand and plucks my panties from my mouth. I gulp in lungfuls of air, melting into him as I try to control my breathing. He wraps his arm around me and splays his hand flat against my stomach. My eyes widen but I force myself not to tense. "Is... Is the baby okay?"

I turn my head to the side and peer up at him, the look of worry in his brown eyes has me melting further into him. "Yeah, Grizz." He nods and slowly eases out of me. I expect him to disappear like last time and brace myself for the pain of his rejection, but when I turn around he is kneeling before me with my leggings in his hands, ready to help me dress. "Where's my panties?" He flicks his gaze to me and smirks.

"Help me dress Gretchen and I'll give them back to you." My jaw unhinges, the bastard just laughs as he helps me into my pants and pulls them up. When he stands before me, I shove him in the chest and spin away, but he grips the back of my neck and yanks me back to him. Before I can utter a single word, he slams his lips against mine, robbing me not just of air but of rational thought. Before either of us can get too lost in the kiss, the bell on the front door rings, signaling the arrival of Gretchen's family. "Help me get her ready and I promise I'll make it worth your while tonight."

I run my gaze over him trying to decipher his meaning. "What do I get out of this deal?"

A dark look enters his eyes. "The feeling of another man's cock inside you tonight while I watch."

Chapter Twelve

Cronos

I'm leaning against my truck waiting for Amelia, she's talking to Bill and I can see from the look on the old man's face he knows I'm not taking her out for dinner and being a gentleman. The shit I have planned tonight is sure as fuck going to get me locked out of those pearly gates and sent down south on a one-way ticket to fire town. Meelz steps back and waves to Bill as he drives out, I shoot the old man a wink just to be a prick, he needs to learn that he doesn't own her.

I do.

She makes her way over to me with her head down. I can feel the nerves rolling off her as we climb in the truck. The silence stretches between us, unlike her I'm not filled with nerves, I'm excited for the first time in a really long fucking time. The moment we pull up to my place, I spot his car parked out front. Before she can get out, I grip her arm, halting her escape. She meets my stare with a worried look in her eyes.

"You call the shots." She darts her tongue out and licks her lips, my mind blanks as I picture her using that tongue on me.

"Nos, I... I'm scared." Her honesty astounds me for a moment.

"Why?"

"I trust *you* and I know you will always make sure I am protected but things are different now."

I reach out and cup her cheeks. "Say the word and this ends now, I'll never force you to do anything—"

"My body has changed, not my desires," she admits.

The tension flees as I smile at her, the sight has her breath hitching. "You know you have never looked more beautiful than you do now. Being pregnant only enhances your natural beauty, angel."

She melts into my touch. "You may feel that way but I don't know how... whoever that is will feel."

I drop my hold and reel back. "The fuck do you mean?"

Her brows furrow. "The guy in the car—"

"The guy in the car is Vance." Her eyes widen in surprise. "I may have a kink, Amelia, but make no fucking mistake, I would never allow just anyone to touch you. I called him yesterday and told him to come out." Vance is the only guy I have ever let touch Amelia. I vetted the guy thoroughly before even considering letting him touch her. The fact she thought I would just allow some cocksucker to touch her pisses me off.

"Well, that changes things."

"You're going to pay for that shit," I vow.

"Pay for what?" She balks.

"For thinking I would let some fucking random cunt touch you!"

Her jaw unhinges. "How was I supposed to know you would call him—wait, you called him yesterday?" I nod. "Well, wasn't that very presumptuous of you!" The little minx slips out of the truck before I can reply. I follow after her and eliminate the space between us in a few strides, slinging my arm over her shoulders as Vance steps out of his car. We don't do pleasantries, there is no need for it. He is here for a job, provides his service and then leaves. Any more than that and it complicates shit and I hate complications.

Vance nods his greetings and follows us inside the cabin. I have a set of rules that I will never deviate from. Ever since Amelia agreed to embrace this side of me I made sure there were rules from the start, if there are no rules then shit gets blurred and I won't have that. She may be the one who has the final say about this going ahead or not, but make no mistake, I am the one in control and I call all the shots. He can fuck her but I am the one who dictates when and if she gets to come.

I turn to face Vance, the thing that settled my unease when I first met him is the fact he didn't fidget or act nervous, he knows why he is here and what his job is.

"You remember the rules?" I ask him.

"Yes," he answers without hesitation.

"It's been a minute, Vance, I'm gonna need you to say them for me." My tone is firm and unyielding.

"No kissing, always have my dick wrapped, only do as you say, she says stop at any time and it ends there and then, no questions asked." He's bang on the money. I also won't allow him to ever fuck her in our bed, that place is sacred and for her and I only. I refuse to allow his lips on hers, that shit is too intimate and reserved only for me. You can fuck someone without kissing them. In my mind, if you kiss someone then you must feel something for them. I pull my attention from him to look at Amelia, only to find her gaze already on me. Before I can utter a single word, she grips the front of my shirt and pulls me down to her so she can kiss me. I grip her hips and pull her forward so she can feel how hard I am already.

She breaks the kiss before I can deepen it, the sinister look in her eyes has a fire surging in my veins. She pushes me back and I fall into my recliner. A sultry smirk graces her stunning face as she grips the hem of her shirt and slowly pulls it over her head, then tosses it to the side. My mouth waters at the sight of her lacey bra, her tits are growing along with her bump and fuck me if I'm not loving the sight of her pregnant. I send a silent thank you to Beth for taking her shopping. Vance presses forward and plasters himself against her back, she leans back into him and tilts her head to the side offering him her neck. He obliges her silent request and bites down gently on the tender flesh, he knows better than to leave any marks on her flawless skin.

He bats her hands away and cups her tits, drawing a lust-filled moan from her parted lips. My cock is rock-fucking-hard. "Get rid of your pants, angel." Vance continues to nip at her neck as she rids herself of her pants and kicks them to the side. My eyes zero in on her bare pussy, knowing my cum still coats the walls of her addictive cunt brings a smile to my face. "Touch her pussy."

Vance skates his hand down her body slowly. As his fingertips graze her hip, she begins to tremble in anticipation. The sight of his hands near her bump gives me pause for a second, as a surge of protectiveness rises inside me until he shifts lower. Vance knows how she likes it and needs it but won't do shit until I give the order. He cups her pussy and Amelia rises to her tiptoes, moaning.

"Nos, I need him to finger me," she pleads.

"You get what I tell him to give you." She whimpers but clamps her mouth closed. "Play with her but don't let her come on your hand." Vance slides a finger through her folds and she cries out, arching forward. He wraps his other arm around her chest, holding her in place as he begins to circle her clit. She widens her legs to give him better access. "Eyes on me!" I snap, instantly she meets my heated stare. She knows I have to have her eyes on me the entire time or this stops. Her face contorts in pleasure when Vance inserts two fingers inside her tight little cunt.

"Oh, fuck," she grits out when he presses the pad of his thumb against her clit, her eyes grow glassy as she tries to fuck his fingers and wring an orgasm out of them but Vance is aware of her dirty little tricks and yanks his fingers free, causing her to pout.

"Punish her," I bark,

He takes a step back and nods. "Face me," he orders. She eagerly obeys his command. "Undress me." With shaky fingers she does as he says and begins to unbutton his shirt. She trails her fingers down his chest, then peers over her shoulder at me as she lowers herself to her knees. I sit forward, watching her every move as she grips his hips and positions him so they are sideways and I get a better view. Her gaze remains on me as she pops the button on his pants and slowly lowers the zipper—my mouth begins to water, forcing me to swallow continuously. When his cock is freed she pulls her stare from me to look up at him, I smirk. The little she-devil still hasn't learned, I call the shots, not Vance.

He looks to me waiting for the next instruction. Amelia flicks her head toward me and glares. She knows I'm purposely dragging this out just to keep her on edge. She pretends to hate that I constantly edge her but the truth is, she is fucking thirsty for it and is just too shy to admit it.

"Make her choke." Vance doesn't need to be told twice, his fingers tangle in her hair forcing her face back to him.

"Open that pretty little mouth of yours." Amelia does as he asks. Fisting his cock in his free hand, he lines it up with her mouth and pushes inside without mercy. Tears instantly spring to her eyes as she gags around him. Vance doesn't relent or allow her to pull back. I palm my own dick through my pants. "Suck it!" The sight of her lips wrapping around his length has a groan coming from me. Vance allows her to release him—she gasps and drags in lungfuls of air. I nod for him to continue, this time when he slips back inside her mouth he is gentler. Vance allows her to set the rhythm. Watching her bob up and down on his cock has me shifting in my seat. I free myself from the confines of my pants and palm my dick. When she sees me out of the corner of her eye, she whimpers around him, the vibration has Vance throwing his head back and groaning.

"Enough!" Vance pulls free of her mouth instantly and faces me. "Angel, get over here." She rushes to obey me. When she is within reach, I position her so her hands are on either side of me. "You keep your eyes on me as he fucks you, understood?"

Her eyes blaze with heat. "Yes!" I lean forward and unclip her bra. I wrap it around the back of her neck and pull her forward so I can kiss her, as Vance gets into position behind her and rolls a condom on. I feel it in her kiss the moment he pushes inside her. I swallow her moan and tighten my hold on the bra as I pull back. True to her word, she keeps her gaze on me as he grips her hips and fucks her. The sounds she makes and skin slapping skin fills the cabin. She locks her arms and tightens her hold on the arms of the chair as Vance increases the pace. "Nos, I need to come."

I lean forward and press my forehead against hers. "I think

you can wait a bit longer," I growl. She whimpers and bites down on her bottom lip. Releasing the bra, I toss it to the side as I grip her hair and yank her down. The second she wraps her lips around my cock, I slam my eyes closed and growl. Fuck, the feeling of her tight wet mouth wrapped around me is the closest I will ever get to being in heaven.

Chapter Thirteen

Amelia

I choke on Cronos's cock when he hits the back of my throat. Vance's thrusts are hard and unyielding, my orgasm right there, on the cusp of tearing through me but I know what he is doing. I may not be able to see him but I can feel every time I try to clamp down on Vance's cock, he slows his pace and I know it's because Cronos is giving him a look. I try to pull back but he fists my hair and forces my head back down. The instant I gag he chuckles.

"Choke on that dick, angel."

"Hmmmm," I moan out when Vance strokes that sweet spot inside me. Fuck, the need to come is so strong and each time he denies me I want to scream out and cry. Just when I think I can't take it any longer, Nos rips my head up by my hair, and grips my chin so my gaze is on him.

"Come all over his fucking cock and scream *my* name so he knows that cunt belongs to me!" His sinful words and Vance's relentless thrusts send me spiraling. My pussy clamps down on his cock as my orgasm tears through me like a cyclone, my eyes remaining locked on Nos's.

"Grizz!" I scream out. His eyes darken and Vance roars out his release behind me. Before I can ride out the high of my climax, Cronos orders Vance to pull out. I stare at him in shock, he robbed me of finishing! "Nos."

"Lock the door on your way out, Vance." He grunts and goes about collecting his clothes while Nos's hold on my jaw turns punishing. "I told you to scream my name!"

My eyes widen. "I did."

"No the fuck you didn't. You called me Grizz." I balk at him. "Now, you will be punished."

"But—"

"Turn the fuck around now and put that pussy on this cock." Heat surges through me, I do as I'm told and hover above him. I reach back and grip his cock, lining it up with my entrance. Nos always gets off watching me fuck someone else, he likes to envision their cum inside my pussy when he fucks me after, but he's way too possessive to actually allow anyone to fuck me bare. He and I are okay to do it but no one else. I was on the pill and made him get checked before we slept together without the protection of a condom.

"Oh my God!" I cry out as I lower myself onto him, his grip on my waist bruising, but the slight tinge of pain mixed with the pleasure of having him inside me again is fucking potent.

"Bounce up and down on that dick, baby." I open my legs wider and lean forward so I can rest my hands on his knees and bounce. "Did you like fucking him?"

"Yes!" I moan as he thrusts upward.

"Did you love knowing you made him cum, angel?" he

growls. My reply is cut off by a sharp cry when he slams me down onto his waiting cock. He gave me the illusion of control by allowing me to be on top but I'm not deluded enough to fool myself into thinking for a second he was never the one pulling the strings. He begins to set the pace and I am nothing but a passenger on this ride to see who gets off the quickest. My nails dig into his legs as I hold on for dear life, I don't even feel my orgasm cresting until it shatters me from the inside out.

"Cronos!" I scream out as I fall over the edge and into the sweet abyss of ecstasy as pleasure surges through me. This climax is so strong and potent that I don't even realize he's come until he stops moving beneath me. Utterly spent and boneless, I slouch back against his chest. He instantly wraps his arms around me. Just when I think I can't possibly feel anything other than exhaustion, he splays his hands across my stomach and nuzzles into the side of my neck.

"Is little Kingsley, okay?" he mutters against my neck.

Be still my breathing heart!

I swallow a couple of times and force my tone to remain neutral. "Y-yeah." I curse myself for stuttering.

"Good."

"Kingsley?" I ask after a moment of silence.

"Beats calling it an *it*," he answers as he gently lifts me off his lap and I wince slightly when I stand. His all seeing eyes don't miss it, and without another word, he grasps my hand and leads me toward the bathroom.

All I can do is stand there while Nos washes me, dries me off and dresses me in one of his shirts before tucking me into bed. I thought he would leave and go to sleep in his chair but to my shock, he climbs in behind me and spoons me from behind.

I spend the rest of the night fighting back tears, how the fuck could I have been so stupid and let him go?

Three days later...

Ever since the night with Vance things have been different. Cronos can't seem to get enough of me. Even at work, he finds the stupidest excuse to get me in the back room only for him to rip my clothes off and fuck me. I drew the line at him trying to fuck me on one of the metal slabs, I know I will be on one of those some day but it sure as fuck wasn't that day! As punishment, he fucked me on the gurney next to Claudette's body in the chiller room. There is something so taboo about orgasming next to a dead body.

Ever since Beth sent me a text message this morning, I have been filled with nerves. I finally returned to her and Bill's house last night. Neither of them brought up me staying with Cronos and I appreciated that. I did ask her for a favor but I didn't think it would happen so soon and now I am nervous as fuck to tell Nos I have to leave an hour early before clock-out time. I finally pluck up the courage twenty minutes before I have to leave to face him. As I enter the back, I find him sanitizing the slabs. Wringing my hands in front of me, I gnaw on my bottom lip.

"Angel, you coming in here for round three?" My cheeks heat but I shake my head. He searches my gaze for a second before he drops his cloth and eliminates the space between us in an instant. He grips my face between his hands and bends at the knees so we are eye level. "What's wrong?"

"I..." I take a deep breath and force the words out. "I have to leave early and get an ultrasound!" I blurt out.

His brows raise and his mouth parts on an exhale. "Oh."

I cringe and brace for his anger, but to my surprise he just leans forward, places a chaste kiss to my lips, then steps back. "Let me lock up and I'll drive you to the clinic." I stand here gawking at him like he is a two headed snake. I manage to get myself under control after a minute and rush out the front. I snap my phone off my desk and quickly fire off a text to Beth to let her know Cronos is going to drive me and to just meet me there. Call me clingy or whatever you want but since my mom can't be here I wanted someone there. I never thought Nos would want to come so I asked Beth to come with me.

Five minutes later, I'm sitting beside Cronos in his truck, nerves are riding me hard the closer we get to the clinic. I haven't been able to even look at him. I know it's childish and wrong but I'm scared for him to come inside the clinic with me because this will make it real. He will see my baby and know that I created the life inside me with another man.

It's getting harder and harder to keep my secrets. I know there is a wall between us and it's because of the truths we refuse to tell the other. Maybe if things hadn't ended like they did he would have trusted me enough to tell me what really happened to Aida. I need to come clean about Colson and tell him why I ran but I'm petrified that he will hate me and think I'm worthless for not knowing my worth sooner. If it wasn't for what I read on Colson's phone that night before we left for the pub I don't know if I would have even thought to flee.

"Angel?" I snap my head toward him and frown at the sight of the worried look on his face.

"Yeah?"

"You good?"

"Of course," I say in false bravado, he sees right through my bullshit but can't say more because Beth is there knocking on his window with a bright smile on her face. Her and Bill are amazing and truly great people. I know he wants to press me more but I don't give him a chance. I hop out of the truck and rush around to hug Beth. I link my arm through hers and drag her toward the clinic without waiting to see if Cronos follows.

Chapter Fourteen

Cronos

She's acting fucking weird!

She chose to seat Beth between us as we waited to be seen, she won't even look in my direction. When a woman calls her name she drags Beth to her feet and drags her along while I follow, I know she is using the old woman as a shield and I don't fucking know why. As we enter the room, the woman hands her a gown and tells her to change then hop on the table and the doctor will be in soon to us.

Beth and I claim the two seats beside the bed while Meelz disappears into the bathroom and changes. When she returns, she looks more nervous than a minute ago. Her sudden mood change is starting to piss me off. When I stand to help her onto the bed she flinches away, causing me to frown. Beth pats me on the arm and tells me to take a seat as she helps Amelia get situated on the bed. I'm too wound up to sit down now so I remain standing while Beth fusses over her and makes sure she is comfortable.

The tension in the room is thick—when the doctor enters, it doesn't lessen. She looks between the three of us and purses her lips but doesn't comment.

"Hi, my name is Jenny," she says as she comes to a stop at the side of the bed where the ultrasound machine is.

"Hi," Meelz squeaks out.

"So..." Jenny peaks down at the clipboard she carries before continuing. "Max, I see here you haven't had a scan before. Can I ask why?"

Amelia nibbles on her lips and drops her gaze, Beth being the saint she is, answers for her. "The pregnancy was a surprise and she only just learned she was with child." The lie rolls off her tongue easily and Jenny seems to buy it.

"Oh, well in that case congratulations to you both," she says as she looks from her to me. My face is stoic and gives nothing away. Amelia doesn't correct her either and I don't know why but a part of me is happy she didn't say I wasn't the father. "Let's get you set up so we can take a look at the wee one." Meelz nods and Beth shifts away and waves me over. I shake my head, trying to deny her but she hardens her features and narrows her eyes. This is the first time I have ever seen her look so angry so I do as she instructed and step forward. She grabs my hand and then places Amelia's tiny hand in mine as Jenny lifts her gown and squirts some gel shit on her bump.

Jenny presses a button on the remote and the TV at the end of the bed turns on. I start to feel... nervous and I have no idea why I am suddenly feeling... fuck, am I excited to see the baby?

"We are going to check bubs heartbeat, size and make sure everything is traveling along as it should. If you are as far along as you have guessed then we can even reveal the gender today if you like?"

At Jenny's question, Amelia darts her gaze to me and I answer for the both of us without hesitation. "Yeah," I croak out. Meelz seems to relax at my answer and it must have been the right thing to say because even Beth pats me on the shoulder. Jenny squirts some blue gel on her belly, then grabs a wand-looking thing and begins moving it over Meelz stomach. Out of nowhere the sound of a strong steady heartbeat fills the room a second before an image of a baby appears on the screen. My mouth drops open in awe and everything around me becomes white noise as I stare at the screen.

Kingsley.

Giving the baby a nickname without seeing it was one thing but now being gifted with such a treasured sight is something else. Amelia squeezes my hand drawing my attention back to her, tears fall from her eyes as she stares at the ultrasound of her baby on the screen.

"Well, from the size of this wee one I would say you are about twenty five weeks along." Amelia's mouth parts but no words come out. "Would you like to know the gender?"

"Yes," I answer before Meelz can. Jenny shoots me a smile before shifting her wand thing around some more. "Congratulations, dad, you're having a baby girl." Those are the last words I hear before everything around me silences.

Dad.

Baby girl.

Those three words play on a loop in my head as Jenny continues to do her checks while I stand here staring at the miracle growing inside of my girl. I feel so protective over this baby and it doesn't even have a single drop on my DNA inside her.

Amelia is still acting strange as we leave the doctor's office, I don't know if it's because she misses her old job or if she is just overwhelmed about seeing her daughter for the first time, but something is definitely up with her. I walk Beth to her car and thank her for coming. I'm ready to get Meelz home and celebrate or something but when I look at her, her gaze is on the ground and she's scuffing her foot along the pavement.

"Angel?"

My eyes narrow when she cringes at my pet name for her. "I'm gonna head home with Beth, I'll see you Monday," she rushes to say before beelining for the passenger side of the car and climbing in. I stare at her at a loss for words.

"Let me talk to her and I'll give you a call later. You go on home now." Beth tries to placate me but it does nothing, I stand here and watch them driveaway.

What the fuck just happened?

I climb in my truck battling internally as I try to understand what the fuck changed within her. She was fine this morning and happy to see me. Fuck, she couldn't get my clothes off fast enough after I dressed Pete. I get she was nervous to see her baby for the first time but to run from me...

Fuck!

She's doing it again, she's about to push me the fuck away and force me to leave her. I don't know if her abandonment issues stem from her bio mom dying and leaving her to be raised by her chosen mother but she has some fucking trauma she needs to deal with. I yank the steering wheel and pull over to the side. I fish my phone out of my pocket and dial his number.

It rings for so long I don't think he will answer until he does. "If you're ringing me because you can't get a hold of my girl, I'll shoot you with your own fucking gun!"

A smirk tugs at the corners of my lips, this fucker has been salty ever since Lon and I got close. "You gotta let that shit go, brother."

"Yeah, easier said than done when she runs to you every time I fuck up or she reminds me that she should have gone for the other twin first." I can't stop the laughter from bubbling out of me, he and I both know she doesn't mean what she says. She just knows it works his last nerve when she says that shit. Truth is, London is just as madly in love with my brother as he is with her, those two are a match made in hell.

"Artemis?"

"What's wrong, Nos?" The edge to his voice tells me he knows something is wrong.

"I don't know what to do."

"What happened? Say the word and I'm on the first flight out." Hearing that shit has me feeling some type of way but I shut that feeling down, now isn't the time to get all caught up in that shit.

"Nah, stay where you are. I just need..." I put my pride to the side and seek advice from the person I never thought I would ask. "Amelia is here." The sound of him whistling through the phone has me pulling mine away from my ear.

"So, is this where you finally admit that there is something going on between the two of you?" I scrub a hand down my face and exhale loudly.

"Yeah. There has been something going on since I left and traveled with her. When I came back, I didn't go touring or anything, I was in Chicago with her."

"Fuck. That whole time you were with *her?*"

"Yes," I grit out.

"Does her dad know you were with her?"

"No."

"Wait. Is she the reason you left me and wanted to be alone?" There is a slight hint of anger to his tone and that shit has my hackles rising. I get to be pissed at her, not him.

"Careful, brother," I warn.

"Holy fuck!" He breathes out. "You went and fell for the heiress that repaired the Murdoch family." I scrunch my face in confusion.

"What?"

"Nos, what I'm about to tell you stays between us." He doesn't give me a chance to answer. "When King found out about Amelia, it was a rough time for her family. They had enemies coming at them from all sides. That woman is the reason why her family fought harder to secure a safe future for *her*. She healed her family without even knowing. All those brothers were pulling away from each other but because of her, they worked shit out because no one wanted to leave her side. They all have children of their own now but that girl will always hold a special place in each of their lives because every single one of them loved Amelia like she was their own child."

"Fuck," I mutter.

"Bishop let her go and freed her of the burden of being a Murdoch because he loves her like he loves Royal."

"That just makes this shit so much more fucked up," I force out.

"What do you mean?"

"She sought me out, Artemis. After she ended shit with us in Chicago, I had to get away and clear my head. She got under my skin, brother. I hadn't seen her since she kicked me out until the night with Taylan and Destiny at Bishop's. Seeing her again fucked me up. It felt like my heart beat again just at the sight of her but what blew me the fuck away was her strength.

She didn't give up on her dream of freedom, she fought her family."

"Is that what you want?"

"Huh?"

He sighs and I can picture him closing his eyes and leaning back in his chair. "Do you want your freedom from being in this life?"

I mull over his words for a minute. Is that what I want, to be done with this mafia life and live life as I am now? Have I not been content this past year to live in this small town and earn an honest living?

"I don't know," I answer honestly.

"Then let me help you. Cronos Argyros, as Don of the Godfathers Of The Night, I hereby release you from your vow and grant you your freedom from this lifestyle." I suck in a sharp intake of air.

"Artemis—"

"This life has taken everything from you, Cronos. I won't let you lose someone else you care about because of the choices our father made. If you feel for her even half of what you felt for... Aida." I slam my eyes closed at the mention of her name, pain still ripples through me at the thought of her. "Then you go after her and fight for what you deserve, brother, because you do deserve happiness. You and I both know Aida would not want you to punish yourself. Be free of the burdens of your past, brother, and build the life you have always wanted."

"I can't just leave you—"

"You can and you will. It's not every day that you get a second chance at life or love, brother, so you get the fuck off this phone and go after your girl."

"Artemis..." I let my sentence trail off, unable to say the words I need to.

"I once overheard a conversation between you and my girl. She once told you Aida wasn't your greatest love. She said all the greatest loves are designed to be painful, love isn't easy or comfortable. You need a love that is painful, soul destroying and consumes you whilst driving you insane. Aida will always be your first love, brother, and she will never be replaced, but I believe London was right."

"How so?" I croak out.

"Aida wasn't your final love. London is my greatest victory and always will be. If anything happened to her, Cronos, I would die. Every time I look at her, I see my own heart beating inside her chest. Loving London hurts so bad but fuck it also feels so good. You survived losing Aida. Amelia has forced you out of the shadows you have hidden in since you lost Aida. Let her break down those fucking walls you hide behind and give her your heart. Hold nothing back, because if it doesn't hurt, brother, then she isn't worth it."

Chapter Fifteen

Amelia

The sun has set and I still haven't moved from this spot since Beth and I got home. I refused to go inside and stayed out on the porch on the swing Nos and I sat on, with the ultrasound picture in my hand. I can't believe it.

I'm having a little girl.

Tears prick the backs of my eyes. None of this felt real until I saw her on the screen. Hearing her little heartbeat for the first time robbed me of breath. I've experienced love and know what it feels like, but the instant I heard that heartbeat and saw her, my heart was no longer my own. It belongs to my daughter.

Daughter.

God. It feels so weird thinking that. I close my eyes and will my tears to remain where they are. I have cried enough these past few months and now that shit has to stop. It's not just about me anymore, this is about my little girl and keeping her safe. She needs me to be strong and that is exactly what I'll do, starting now.

"You're gonna catch a chill sitting out here, little missy." I turn my head to see Bill strolling toward me with a warm smile on his face and a throw blanket in his hand. I smile my thanks when he places it on my lap and sits down beside me, swinging us. We remain in comfortable silence for a while as we stare off into the distance, lost in our own thoughts. "Can I see that?" I jolt and frown at him. He flicks his gaze to the picture in my hand. I hand it over and watch as a smile so wide scratches across his weathered face. "Beautiful," he whispers.

"I may be biased but I sure think so."

"My Bethy tells me you're having a little girl."

I nod. "I am."

He hands me back the picture, smiling. "She is lucky to have a strong woman as a mother."

I snort. "I'm not strong," I mutter bitterly.

He places a hand on mine, his eyes take on a hard edge and I stiffen. He immediately withdraws his hand as if sensing my unwarranted fear. I curse myself internally for allowing my past trauma to intrude on this moment. I open my mouth to say sorry but Bill beats me to it.

"Bernice was the light of mine and Bethy's life." My brows draw in and I cock my head to the side, slightly confused. "She only answered to Berry, God, I wish I could have had more time with her but time can't be borrowed." He sounds so bitter.

"Who was she?" I ask.

His watery gaze meets mine and I suck in a sharp inhale. "She was our only child." My jaw slackens in horror.

"*Was*?"

He nods. "Berry was a force, so strong and courageous like

her mother. She wanted out of this town as soon as she could and she did, she got out." He sighs and drops his gaze to his lap. "Six months after she left and moved to Texas we got a call saying she was in love and pregnant." A gnawing feeling begins to stir inside my stomach, I already know this isn't going to be a happy story.

"What happened to Berry?" I whisper.

His shoulders droop. "Bethy said she could feel something wasn't right so we went to her. When we got there she was battered and bruised, scared of her own shadow and any loud noises." I drop my own gaze, knowing exactly how that poor girl felt. "We packed her things and brought her home. She was a mess. So timid and easily frightened by a gust of wind. She was always looking over her shoulder. We did our best to try and reassure her that the father to her unborn baby would never get near her. We filed police reports but they couldn't find that son of a bitch."

Anger thrums through me at the injustice this beautiful girl suffered through. "What happened to her, Bill?"

"She was here for five months and finally started to heal. Her belly was so big and round, she was due in four weeks. Beth and I had everything set up and ready for our grandbaby to be born. Berry started to act like her old self and was even smiling. She didn't look over her shoulder as often, but we knew she still had a long way to go."

A strangled sob tears from him. I slide closer to him and grip his hand in mine as I rest my head against his shoulder, offering my comfort.

"There was an accident, five bodies, it was late and raining that night. Beth came with me to help retrieve the bodies. Berry assured us she would be fine. I could see it in her eyes, she was scared but she was trying so hard to be strong. I remember being so proud of her for not allowing that bastard to win and continue to hold her in fear. Beth and I were just placing the last body in the chiller when we got a call." My stomach sinks. "Berry was screaming for me to help her."

"Oh my God," I choke out as my own tears cascade down my cheeks.

"Beth and I raced out of the morgue and drove as fast as we could in the rain to save our little girl. As we got out of the car we heard a gunshot." A shiver runs down my spine. "Every molecule in my body knew at that moment that my baby had just taken her last breath." I cover my mouth to muffle my sob. "When we got inside, we saw that bastard running out the back door. I wanted to run after him but the sight of my girl laying on the floor in our living room staring up at the ceiling with no life in her eyes stopped me."

"Bill, I am so sorry," I choke out.

"Hearing her fight for her life and not being able to save her broke me. Seeing the man that fathered the grandchild my wife and I will never get to know kill our daughter, destroyed me. Having to complete the autopsy on my daughter and remove her child from her womb and place it in her arms to be buried, obliterated any chance of me ever overcoming her death." My heart breaks into a million pieces for Bill and Beth and all they have suffered through.

"Bill—"

"I see the same fear I saw in my daughter's eyes in yours, Max." I reel back in shock and begin to shake my head, trying to deny what he says. "She denied it as well, told me she fell and gave me the run around for weeks until she finally didn't. I know you and the boy have a history, I also know that boy would never raise a hand to you."

"Bill, I don't—"

"Max, he isn't the type of man to stand in a living room and watch a killer run out the back door. He is the type of man to hunt a son of a bitch down and make them bleed. I care a lot about that boy and I don't want to see him hurt by you or the events of your past." Guilt churns inside me. I turn away from Bill, knowing everything he is saying is true. Me coming here has turned what Cronos built for himself upside down, I've brought an evil to his doorstep and I had no right to do that. I know it with every fiber of my being that Colson will be hunting me down. He'll be using his security and tech company to track me and it's not a matter of *if* but *when* he finds me, what he will do.

"Kill a demon today and face the devil tomorrow." Both Bill and I snap our gazes up to see Cronos standing on the porch steps. "It's my battle to fight, old man. If I want to hunt the cunt down then I will." Oh God, he overheard the conversation!

"Boy, you need to be smart about this. You have made a good honest life for yourself here and I don't want to see that getting messed up by secrets from Max's past." Nos grinds his teeth and clenches his fists at his sides at Bill's words.

"That's my cross to bear, not yours," he grits out.

Before they can continue, I climb to my feet and meet my dark angel's gaze for the first time since this morning. Some of the anger seems to flee him as he stares into my eyes and I hate that I can calm him. He shouldn't find my presence comforting.

"I don't want anyone getting hurt because of me." Nos opens his mouth to argue but I push on. "I've made my mind up. I'm leaving." He moves so fast I don't have a chance to back up, he stands before me with my face clasped between his hands and a look on his face I can't decipher but it almost resembles panic.

"If you choose to walk away and end this *thing* between us, I won't stop you but I also won't write, text or ever let you know where I am again in the hopes that you will find me."

"Nos—"

He cuts me off before I can continue. "Angel, I am standing here trying. I'm showing you I want this to work. I want a future with you and that baby. I want sleepless nights as we just stare at that little girl. I want it all, Amelia, every single fucking second of your future and hers. I want to be a part of it. I don't want to miss a single fucking thing. You told me to choose last time and this is me making that choice."

Tears burn the backs of my eyes as I stare up at him and see the truth in those brown eyes that hold so much love in them. I grip the front of his shirt and offer him one last chance to turn around and walk away from me and the mess I have made of my life.

"It's not just me anymore. I have this little girl to think about, Nos. Can you handle always being second because she is and will always be my first priority?"

A slow smile spreads across his face as he bends down and rests his forehead against mine. "As long as I'm the runner up to her, I'll always be good with that." Relief washes over me, never in my life have I ever felt so cared for until this moment.

"Max, huh?" Nos and I pull a part to stare at Bill, who is standing there with a cunning smirk on his face.

"Old man—"

Bill raises his hand stopping Cronos. "I wasn't born yesterday, boy. I knew a beautiful thing like her wouldn't be named *Max* but so you can rest easy tonight, I will forget all about hearing your real name but just know, little missy, I want your full story when you are ready to tell it." Gratefulness surges inside me as I nod, I've never met someone so genuine and understanding before. "I'm assuming you two have a lot to discuss?" Nos and I share a look. I exhale and nod, it's time he knew the truth.

"Yeah, we do," I answer.

"Good. Now both of you go on, this old man needs to get his rest." Bill waves us both off as he makes his way inside, patting Cronos on the shoulder as he passes by.

"Old man?" Bill stops and peers over his shoulder at Nos. "Thank you... For everything."

Bill's eyes turn misty for a second before he clears his throat and nods in a manly way. "Thank you for waking me up from a dark and lonely slumber." His dark ominous words hang in the air as he disappears inside.

"Come on, angel, let's go home and... Talk." He seems just as nervous about this as I am.

Chapter Sixteen

Cronos

The drive to my house is silent. It isn't... awkward, it's just quiet. We are both lost in our own thoughts. I won't lie and say I'm not hesitant to tell her about Aida. I know keeping that to myself before was hard for her but I guess I wasn't ready to... let go of that part of my life. I put the truck in park out the front and climb out. She follows behind me, keeping space between us. I don't like the distance she is keeping between us but I say nothing as I open the door and head inside.

"Have you eaten?" I ask her as I enter the kitchen.

"N-no." I turn and scowl at her.

"Sit, I'll cook while we... talk." A whoosh of air escapes her as she climbs onto one of the stools at the breakfast bar while I sort us some dinner. I'm no Gordan Ramsey but I can make a decent meal. I grab the fixings to make some chicken fettuccine. I can feel her gaze on me and just know without her having to utter a word that she is waiting for me to open up.

Fuck!

This shit is going to be a lot harder than I thought. I focus on the garlic I am chopping while I tell her the story of my past that broke me and shaped me into who I am today.

"I'm the second born twin. Artemis is older by ten minutes but what most people don't know is that we were actually born on separate days. He was born a minute before midnight and I was born nine minutes later. Costa was happy about that, he never wanted twins."

"Why?"

I close my eyes and take a deep breath, forcing my emotions to remain in check as I continue to prepare dinner. "Because it meant he had double the chance of losing his place as the head of the family when it came time for us to complete the trials. The elders didn't care that we were born on separate days, as far as they were concerned we were twins. Costa argued that we weren't because of our technically different birthdays but all you had to do was look at me and Artemis and see we are identical. He was out voted by the elders, both his sons would trial together against the other heirs. Artemis and I knew we could win—those heirs never trained a day in their life or had to fight for everything they had like we did. Nothing was ever given to us, we had to fight to earn our meals, our clothing, anything we had, we earned."

"I'm so sorry," she whispers but I ignore it as I push on.

"We were never allowed anything of our own. Costa made sure we always knew anything we had could be taken from us at a second's notice. Artemis was always stronger, smarter and wiser. I fell into line and did as I was told, he could control me but never Artemis. Even when the triplets were born, Artemis never cowered to our father. He fought to protect not only Adonis, Apollo and Ares but... me as well. We never knew that he was being beaten if we ever stepped out of line. He took beating after beating just so we wouldn't have to. My brother wanted us to try and lead a normal life. I was selfish and listened to him," I growl.

"Aida," she mumbles. I turn my head to the side and hold her gaze as I nod.

"I found something of my own and I ruined her," I admit as I return to my task. "She was everything to me, my entire fucking world. It wasn't my brothers keeping me alive anymore, it was *her*. She showed me there was more to life than darkness and misery, she broke down all my walls and made my heart beat again. She was perfect." I slam my eyes closed and grip the edge of the counter in a vice-like hold as I try to calm myself and not allow my anger to take control. "Costa could see I was losing my edge, I didn't want to kill anymore. I wanted something different from my life. I tried to drop out of the trials and be free. I thought he would be happy that he would only have Artemis fighting for the win, but he wasn't. He forced me into the trials saying that if I won he would grant me my freedom and allow me to leave The Godfathers, I just had to hand everything back to him at the end. Simple. Easy." I scoff at my own stupidity.

"Nothing was ever simple or easy where Costa was concerned but I was blinded by love and believed what he was selling. Artemis tried to warn me but I refused to listen. He didn't know what it was like to love someone, he refused to allow himself to care for anyone who wasn't his brother and now, I understand why. Costa used my weakness against me and... Artemis."

"How?"

"If he succeeded in saving one brother, three would die. Art

had no idea what that shit meant until we entered that room."
I turn away from the stove and face Amelia. She looks like she is
on the verge of tears, pain evident in her beautiful eyes. But the
pain she feels is for me and what I suffered through, not herself.
"The last trial is designed to separate the boys from the men as
they say, but the truth is, that trial is designed to destroy any
ounce of humanity you have inside yourself. That trial will
break you beyond repair and it did."

"What happened to Aida, Nos?"

"They had her tied to the bed inside that room. They had
cut away her clothing and left her bare for all to see. All
Artemis had to do was rape her and he would have won, sealing
the triplets fate. But he knew winning would cost him the
triplets and me. What we both didn't know at the time was
that his refusal meant that Costa, his men and the elders would
all have her—one by one, the next more ruthless than the last.
We were forced to stand there and watch as the men took their
turns, her gaze remained on me the whole time. She begged and
pleaded for me to save her. I tried with everything I had to get
to her but they all held me back. When it was over, I took her
out of that room but I knew deep down inside that her soul
died in there. Two days later, Aida took her own life and left
me behind. I went into her room to bring her breakfast, she
wasn't in her bed or in the bathroom. When I turned and saw
the closed door on her wardrobe, I knew. It took everything
inside me to open that door and face my worst fear—the girl
that I loved more than anything had hung herself. Her eyes
were open and bloodshot, she was looking right at me with
vacant eyes. That is the final memory I will have of her for the
rest of my life." I drop my chin to my chest, unable to look at
her any longer. "You see, angel, being loved by me is a death

sentence and that is why I could never commit fully to you because the fear of my past still had control of me."

"What's changed?" she whispers. I don't answer as I begin to plate her food and then place it in front of her. After reliving the horrors of my past, I'm no longer hungry so I choose to watch her eat instead.

I mull her words over for a moment before I answer. "The old saying, *you don't know what you have until it's gone.* I didn't realize what I had with you until you kicked my ass to the curb." She drops her gaze to her plate in shame. "You were right to get rid of me." She snaps her head up in shock. "It forced me to deal with the past and I don't think I would have ever done that if you didn't force me out. I see a future with you, Amelia, and I will fight through my demons to get the chance to have that life with you and that little girl." Tears shine in her eyes but she blinks them away. "I will never not love Aida, she will always be a part of me." To drive my point home I raise my left arm that has her face inked there. "But I can't keep living in the past with her. I thought I died the day she did but I can see now I didn't, because I was meant to live on so I could find *you.*"

She pushes back and hops off her stool to come around and stand before me. Her eyes glisten with her tears and when one finally falls, I reach out and brush it away with my thumb.

"Being loved by you is like being loved by the Devil." My face falls and I drop my hand. She smiles and steps in closer, craning her head back so she can meet my gaze. "The Devil fell from heaven and made a world of his own. You remade your world like he did and here you stand, stronger than ever and willing to live again."

I search her gaze trying to detect a hint of a lie but get nothing. "Meelz, I'm not the type of guy that buys flowers and drops to his knees and tells you that he loves you." Her eyes widen.

"Is this you telling me you love me for the first time?" I narrow my eyes and snap my arm to grip the back of her neck forcing her onto her tiptoes.

"Was me not letting you push me away a second time, not enough to show you that I do?"

A devilish glint enters her eyes. "Do, what?"

I bend until my lips ghost over hers. "I do love you, angel," I whisper. She gasps and inhales sharply before I seal my lips to hers in a kiss that says more than words could ever. I never thought my heart would belong to another after losing Aida, but I was wrong. She trampled over my walls and forced me to wake up, now my heart not only beats for her but for that little girl growing inside her womb. Before I get a chance to deepen the kiss she pulls back and stares up at me through her lashes.

"If I don't tell you now, I don't think I ever will," she admits. I reluctantly release her when she steps back and reclaims her seat. My stomach is in knots as I wait for her to tell her story. I know hearing about what she went through is going to hurt but I need to know what happened so I can deal with it. Because, regardless of what she wants or what she thinks is right, the cunt won't get away with hurting her.

"You sure you want to hear this, it's a long story?" I pin her with a bored look, there is no way she is getting out of this.

"Start talking."

She purses her lips and nods, then takes a deep breath as she squares her shoulders. I see her begin to wall off her emotions and shut down everything she feels so she can dive into her own past. I understand that and resonate with how fucking hard it is to relive those moments that tore you apart and set you on the course you're on now.

"After we ended, I dove into work and started to focus more on my career again. I wanted to prove to myself that I could be happy on my own and didn't need a man. I wanted to show not only myself but I guess a part of me wanted to stick it to my dad and show him that I could be okay without his constant pestering and interfering in my life. I stopped checking in with Uncle Bishop and told him I was fine. He backed off but I knew he was always there watching somehow. Then suddenly out of nowhere when I was leaving work, I bumped head first into someone. I was utterly shocked to see it was Colson."

Colson is soon to be fucking dead!

"I won't bore you with all the details but we agreed to meet up. One thing led to another and I stupidly thought that this was the universe telling me that I was meant to let you go so I could find Colson again." I grind my teeth so fucking hard they begin to ache, but I remain silent. "It started off small. He would pout and beg for me to take days off so we could spend more time together. I was foolish, I thought if I poured my focus into him I would stop thinking about... *you*." My brows raise at her admission, I never knew she still thought of me. "Then it changed from me taking days off to what I wore, who I spoke to, who I hung out with, my weight and when I rebelled, he got angry. He would scream and shout but never laid a hand on me, until he did."

I hold a hand up, stopping her as I try to rein in control over my anger and thirst for blood. I'm not in the right head-space to hear this. I am going to flip out and drive to Chicago to kill this cock sucking cunt. "Carry on," I grit out.

"The first time he hit me, he acted like it was an accident and he never meant to actually do it. I was a fool, I believed him. The days after, he was so sweet and kind and always apologizing. I decided to move on and let go of that but then he came into work and saw me talking to Conrad—my coworker—and lost it. I left work early and in the car on the way home he... he... punched me."

"Motherfucker!" I roar and spin away from her, my breaths are coming in rapid pants as I fight for control.

"I tried to leave, I fought back like Uncle Knight had trained me to do but it was useless. He overpowered me and forced me into submission. He told me I was his and I would never get away. I retreated inside myself. Everything my dad had told me about the world was true. Men aren't princes and treat women like prizes, they use them for their advantage." I hear the bitterness lacing each of her words. "Colson showed his true intentions not long after that."

I spin around and face her to see tears cascading down her cheeks. I want to go to her and wrap my arms around her and vow to protect her, but I'm too wound up and don't want to scare her further so I remain where I am. "How?"

"He admitted that he targeted me at college. He thought bagging the heir to the Murdoch Mafia would cement his place as one of the most powerful men in the world. What he didn't know was that I didn't want any part of my family's business. I thought my dad sent him away because he didn't want me to have a semblance of happiness unless he decided I could have it. I blamed my dad for everything after that. I pushed him away and the truth is... I was wrong. He was just protecting me because they found evidence of Colson plotting to use me against my family and Dad chose not to tell me because he didn't want me to feel like I was a fool. He allowed me to blame him and... hate him because he would rather that, than let me feel like an idiot for falling for the wrong boy."

"You aren't a fool. He used and manipulated you, angel."

"He did more than use me, Cronos. The night I fled, he admitted to tampering with the condoms we used so I would get pregnant. He wanted to make sure I could never escape him. He knew birth control was a huge thing for me and I was always safe, so he tampered with the condoms."

I swear on my life this cunt will die slowly!

Chapter Seventeen

Amelia

I've never been a leader, never had a thing for fairy tales. I'm not really a believer in happy endings. I thought I was doomed and destined to live a life of pain and injustice until I fled. I didn't expect Cronos and I to end up here. I gave up hope on second chances after being with Colson again.

"It doesn't matter how that baby came to be, she is here now and a fucking testament to the strength her mother possesses. Never forget that, angel." A lump begins to form in my throat at his words.

"I thought you would be mad after seeing her today."

He reels back. "Why the fuck would you think that?"

"Cronos, she shares *his* DNA not yours. I don't expect you to care for my daughter or be happy about it—"

"Shut the fuck up, Amelia!" I snap my mouth closed instantly and stiffen. "If you think for a second I wouldn't fall in love with that little girl because she has another's eyes, someone else's smile, then you clearly don't know me as well as I thought. She is part you and that means, I love her already. Which is why I am asking you to be sure you want this with me, because if shit goes south with us now, I'll walk away but five years from now, if you decide I'm not the man for you, then be ready to fight, baby, because I will go to fucking war with your entire family for that little girl."

My jaw unhinges. Love for this man surges hot inside me, that he is here and willing to raise another man's child and love her like she is his own, means more than he could ever imagine. I can't let myself get sidetracked by his words so I push on.

"Cronos, he will come for me."

"Let the cunt try and see what the fuck I do to him." His conviction sends a shiver down my spine.

"He wants to ruin my father for ruining him. He has a tech company and a security firm that he operates under different names so my dad won't know he is back in the States. I was just a tool for him to use to get to my father. I proved useless to him, which sparked his anger because I had left my family behind. He won't stop until he has ruined my dad."

He scoffs and shakes his head. "This little fuck has no idea who he is messing with. Your father is untouchable, Meelz. He is the underboss to the biggest mafia family in the entire fucking world. You have a better chance of getting a meeting with the King of England than you do with your dad."

I shake my head and drop my gaze to my untouched plate as shame washes over me. "I let some things slip, I didn't mean to and I thought I could trust him."

"What details, Amelia?" The hard edge to his tone has me slowly lifting my head and meeting his gaze. "What. Details?"

"Meeting times, stash houses, shipments that rotate from each port."

"Fuck!" Panic enters his eyes and now I am worried. Cronos isn't the type of guy who gets ruffled easily.

"You need to call him, they could be going into an ambush!"

"You said it was easier to see the King than it was my father."

"That was before I knew that the cunt had any idea about their shipments. Your father and uncles handle those drops on their own, their men don't do the pickups."

My eyes widen and fear grips me. "Cronos, I didn't know—"

"It doesn't matter, you need to call him and warn him, now." He pushes away from the counter and moves toward the living room where a calendar is tacked onto the wall. "Fuck! Call him now, the shipment comes in tonight." I shakily pull the phone Nos gave me out of my pocket and scroll the contacts, only to realize I don't have my dad's number. I flick my gaze back to him.

"I don't have his number." I admit. He sighs and pulls his phone from his back pocket and tosses it to me. "What's the passcode?"

"263542." I input the numbers and then freeze as I snap my head back to him in shock.

"263542 is your passcode?"

He grits his teeth. "Yes."

"My name is your passcode?"

He rolls his eyes. "Yes, now call your fucking father, Amelia!" I shake my head and push all those warm fuzzy feelings away as I scroll for my dad's number. Nerves thrum through me as I press dial and bring the phone to my ear. I can feel Cronos's gaze boring into the side of my head as I wait with bated breath for my dad to answer.

"What do you want, Cronos?" The sound of my father's voice reduces me to a puddle of shame. I open my mouth to answer but no words come out. "Cronos?" he bites out. I dart my gaze to my dark angel who nods encouragingly, I find my strength in his eyes.

"Dad?" I rasp out.

He stays silent for a long moment and I have to check to make sure he didn't end the call. "Meelz?" My name sounds like a prayer, almost like he is hoping that he isn't imagining this moment.

"It's me."

"Are... are you okay?" I hate that he sounds scared to even speak to me in case I lose my shit at him again. I deserve for him to hate after everything I have put him through.

"Dad, I screwed up," I admit.

"It's okay, baby. Just tell me where you are and I'll come to you... if you want." After everything I have put him through, he is still willing to come rescue me. I close my eyes so the tears don't fall.

"You can't go to the pickup." I force the words out before I lose my nerves.

"Why?" I can hear the hard edge in his tone.

"It's a trap, please don't go, Dad," I beg.

"Bishop, turn the fuck around it's a trap!" he shouts.

"What?" I hear Uncle B yell in the background.

"Turn the fuck back, it's a trap," Dad snaps, then I hear the sound of tires squealing. "Amelia, what's going on?" I dart my gaze to Cronos, pleading with him to help me. He steps forward and takes the phone from me and wraps his arm around my shoulder as he places the call on speakerphone.

"King?"

"Cronos?"

"Yeah, it's me."

"What the fuck is going on and why the fuck are *you* with my daughter?"

Nos doesn't falter in his response. "We'll explain everything when we get there. We'll be on the next flight out to New York in the morning."

"I want to know what the fuck my daughter—"

"She will explain everything to you when we get there and you better listen or I will take her from you and I promise you that you will never see her again." The threat in his tone is clear. The fact he is willing to go against my family for me shows me he means what he says, he really does love me.

"Threaten me again, kid, and I'll slit your fucking throat."

"It's not a threat, it's a promise." Nos ends the call and then smashes his phone on the counter. I scream in fright. "Sorry, I can't risk them tracing my cell here. This is my slice of paradise and I don't want anything from that life touching this place." I swoon, reach out and wrap my arms around his waist and rest my cheek against his chest.

"Thank you for letting me invade your paradise."

He returns my embrace and places a kiss on the top of my head. "You are my paradise but I want this place to be our home, angel. I want to raise *our* little girl here, away from that life and everything it entails."

I pull back and stare up at him, shocked to see the conviction in his eyes. "You really want to do this with me?"

He cups my cheeks in his large hands and nods. "I'm always gonna want you, Meelz, the real question is, do you want me to do it with you? I meant what I said, if you say yes and then change your mind, I won't turn my back on that little girl, blood or not she will be raised as mine and I will protect her with my life."

Gripping the front of his shirt, I pull him down until I can capture his lips with my own, he tries to push his tongue inside my mouth but I pull back, earning a growl that has a smile tugging at the edges of my mouth. "I love you too much to not do this with you." His eyes blaze with heat, and before I have a second to comprehend what is happening, he lifts me from my chair. I squeal in surprise.

"I want you to scream how much you love me as you come all over my cock, angel." Heat surges inside me at his promise. Rather than using words, I show him. I mesh my lips to his as he walks us down the small hallway to his bedroom, his fingers digging into my ass and I moan at the feeling. I love when he gets rough like this but Cronos never pushes me to do more than I am comfortable with. I thought I would never heal after the abuse I suffered at the hands of Colson, but I was wrong. Cronos knew without me saying a word that something had happened and never once did he treat me like I was made of glass and could break at a moment's notice. Instead, he silently offered me his strength and showed me that there is more than fear in this world and you can trust a man, but he has to be the right one.

He gently lays me down on the bed, then breaks the kiss as he pulls back. I press up onto my elbows and watch him remove his shirt, the sight of his inked skin has butterflies erupting inside me but it's the sight of my name etched into his flawless skin that steals my breath. I'm pulled from my thoughts when he pops the button on his jeans, my mouth beginning to water when he peels the zipper down. The cocky bastard knows exactly what he is doing to me with this little show. He winks, then pushes his pants down, exposing his hard length. I dart my tongue out to moisten my lips, sit up and grip his cock in my hand. A strangled groan escapes him.

"Tease me and you will be punished, angel."

I peer up at him through my lashes as I dart my tongue out and lick along his shaft, loving the dazed look that enters his eyes. I hold his gaze as I wrap my lips around him and suck him in as far as I can.

"Fuck, that mouth of yours is perfect, baby," he growls as he tangles his fingers in my hair. He doesn't stop me or change my tempo when I begin to bob up and down on his dick. The taste of him hits the back of my throat, pulling a muffled moan from me. His fingers tighten in my hair a second before he thrusts forward, forcing me to gag. A dark chuckle escapes him at the sound, he loves knowing I can't take him all the way. I grip the base of his shaft with my free hand, stroking him while I suck as much of him as I can. "Fuck, baby, you're coming straight to hell with me."

I release him with a wet pop, his eyes narrowing in contempt. I bat his hand out of my hair and grip his waist as I stand and reverse our positions so I'm now standing between his legs.

"Hands by your sides, Grizz, it's my turn." He leans backward and rests on his elbows, his cock resting proudly against his abs. I don't let the sight of it deter me from my mission. I grip the hem of my shirt and slowly lift it over me, exposing the black lacy bra I chose to wear today. Next to go is my skirt, leaving me in a pair of lacy boy shorts and my bra. His eyes burn with hunger as they roam my body, the way he looks at me with such love and longing makes me feel stunning, like I am the center of his orbit.

"Show me my pussy, baby, I'm done playing." I quirk a brow at his heavy-handed comment and ignore him as I reach back and unclasp my bra. I slowly let it fall down my arms, drawing this moment out. He swallows loudly at the sight of them, they've grown a lot and I know it's all thanks to pregnancy. I slowly push my panties down my legs and step out of them. I collect them off the floor and toss them to him with a wink.

"They're soaked." My tone is husky to my own ears. He balls them up in his hand and brings them to his nose, inhaling deeply and groans.

Time to show him who is the boss!

Chapter Eighteen

Cronos

I open my mouth to tell her to bring that pussy here and sit on my face, but the words die on my tongue when she widens her stance and glides her hand down her rounded belly. Her other hand tweaks her nipple, pulling a strangled sound from her. But, the moment her fingers slips through her slick folds and circle her clit, she throws her head back and cries out.

"Fuck, Nos." I grip the sheets in order to remain where I am, my mouth watering at the sight of her.

"Pinch your nipple." She does as I say and whimpers. "Push a finger inside that tight little cunt, baby." She obeys without complaint, her gaze remaining on me the entire time as she pulls her finger free and then holds it out to me. Like a dog with a bone, I press forward and wrap my lips around her finger, my eyes rolling into the back of my head at the taste of her.

She yanks her finger free. I'm about to reprimand her, but

then she climbs into my lap, resting one hand on my shoulder while the other grabs my dick and lines it up with her entrance. My breathing turns shallow when she begins to lower herself onto me. Reaching out, I grip the back of her head and force her lips to mine. I swallow each of her moans, loving how her cunt strangles my cock when I'm balls deep inside her. I've never felt so complete as I do when I'm inside her. She is perfect.

She pulls back, breaking our kiss but never her eye contact as she starts to bounce up and down on me. I grip her waist and help guide her up and down on my shaft. This time, it feels different. This isn't just fucking or having sex, this is both of us showing the other there is no more secrets, we're in this for the long haul.

"I love you," she whimpers as she slams down on my dick.

I cup her cheeks between my hands and stare into her eyes. "I love you too, angel." I kiss her without hesitation and meet her thrust for thrust, needing to be as deep inside her as I can. Her rounded belly makes it hard for her at this angle. "Get on your hands and knees." I help her off me, then wait for her to get into position. The sight of her perfect ass in the air has my cock twitching. I settle in behind her and line my cock up before slamming inside her.

"Fuck!" she screams out.

"This pussy is mine, baby. Only I know what it needs," I snarl as I grip her hips in a punishing hold and slam into her over and over again, chasing the release we both fucking need.

"Yes, just like that, Grizz, I need it."

"Who does this pussy belong to?"

"You! Only you," she vows.

"Good girl." I up the tempo and continue slamming into her dripping cunt. I feel it the second before her screams penetrate the air, her pussy clamps down on me as her orgasm slams into her with force. I tumble over the edge with her, spilling every drop of cum inside her cunt, marking her from the inside out as mine. There will never be a day in this life or any other where I don't view her as mine because Amelia Murdoch is my greatest love and it just took me a little longer to realize that than I would have liked. It still doesn't change the outcome, her and that little girl are mine. They are my redemption from the darkness and I will slaughter any cunt who tries to take my girls from me, the biological father included.

Meelz has been a nervous wreck ever since we boarded the plane. She refused to wear a sweater of her own and wanted to wear mine to hide her bump, which pissed me off and ended up with us arguing before we left, then her bent over the counter with my cock in her. She finally relaxed a little after that, but not much. When we landed in New York and she began to shut down, I relented and handed her my hoodie which seemed to ease some of her stress. After I collected our rental, she seemed to retreat further inside herself. The entire drive to her family's compound she hasn't uttered a word.

I come to a stop at the front of the gates which signals we have arrived. The guard steps forward and sees that's it me and her so he opens the gates. I drive through and head straight for Bishop's house, knowing they will all be there waiting. Sure enough, the moment we pull up out front I see King, Knight, Rook and Allison standing there. I climb out of the car and face them. King tries to take a step toward us but I shake my head, forcing him to halt his movements.

"Give me a minute, she... needs a moment."

His gaze hardens. Knight and Rook shift as if to reach for their guns but Allison steps in front of them all eyeing me warily.

"Is she hurt?" she asks.

"Not... physically." She sucks in a sharp breath at my answer, trying to peer around me but It's no use, she won't see her. I pay them no mind as I round the car and open Meelz's door, crouching down beside her. She keeps her gaze ahead and refuses to even look at me. "I am right here, I'll watch your back and be at your side the entire time. I'll be your shield and pull you out at a second's notice. I won't let this shit eat you up any longer." She slowly tilts her head toward me and her bottom lip trembles.

"I ruined him," she whispers brokenly. I snap my arm out and grip the back of her head, pulling her forward until our foreheads touch.

"No. You saved your family from falling apart, baby. You are the reason why the Murdoch family is as strong as they are. You mended your broken family the day you came into all their lives, don't let the pain of your past keep you from living."

"Don't let me go, okay," she pleads.

"Never," I vow. I help her out of the car and keep my back to her family to shield her from their sight, knowing she needs a second. When she looks up at me and nods, I interlock our fingers, then step aside so they can see her. The moment Allison and King lay eyes on their daughter they look like a weight has been lifted off their shoulders. I guide her toward them. The tension radiating between the three of them is suffocating, the front door opens and Bishop, Gage and Carlina step outside. I eye the six Murdoch siblings, something is up. They never go anywhere without their partners, especially Carlina,

Vincent is glued to her side, so the fact they are out here alone has my hackles raised.

King grips his wife's hand and leads her down the steps. Amelia pulls us to a stop and I shift subtly to block her. None of them miss my move which has King glaring at me in warning but I ignore him, his daughter is my only concern not him. They stop a couple of feet away from us. I spy Meelz out of the corner of my eye, dropping her gaze to her shoes and shifting further behind me. She unlocks her hand from mine and grips the back of my shirt as she rests her forehead against my spine.

"I don't give a fuck if you are Artemis's brother or not, I will kill you here where you stand and face London's wrath if you don't start talking now," King snarls, the warning in his tone is clear but he doesn't scare me, none of them do.

"If you hope for her to even look at you, then you will stand there and shut the hell up and wait until she is ready." His face contorts in anger. He opens his mouth ready to argue but Allison silences him when she steps forward, leaving a sliver of space between her and I.

"Your protection over *my* daughter is awe inspiring, Cronos, but here is where you are wrong. She is *my* daughter!" She shouts. I feel Amelia flinch behind me and grind my teeth in anger. "If you think my husband is the one you have to worry about, then you are mistaken. I will remove anyone in my path to get to my little girl, including you."

"Grizz?" I ignore Allison as I spin around and face my girl, she buries her face in my chest. I feel her tears wetting my shirt and wrap my arms around her, holding her close. A smirk tugs at the corner of my mouth when I feel the tip of a blade pressed against my back, I guess Allison's threats weren't empty.

"Plunge that blade into me, Mrs. Murdoch, and I guarantee your daughter will be lost to you forever." Meelz stiffens in my hold and tries to pull back but I refuse to allow her to move an inch.

She tilts her head back and peers up at me with unshed tears in her eyes. "Don't let go," she whispers.

"Never," I say with a smile as I slowly step aside and allow her to face her mother. I know this is hard for her, and I remember what it felt like having to face Costa after what happened to Aida. Allison immediately lowers her blade and sheaths it. She smiles a watery smile that Amelia doesn't return because she still won't lift her head. It takes her mother all of two seconds to take in the sight of her lowered gaze, hunched shoulders and how she is trembling before her accusing gaze lands on me.

"What the fuck did you do to her?" she screams. In an instant, King is at her side and the rest of the family is behind them. Knight has his gun drawn and aimed at me. The sight of the weapon has me pushing Amelia behind me as I face off against them. Allison moves swiftly to retrieve her blade, then has it pressed against my throat. "Answer me!" she yells.

"He didn't do anything," Allison snaps her gaze to the side of me where Amelia now stands with her head raised and shoulders back, her eyes burning with anger as she glares at her uncle for pointing a gun at me. "Your first reaction is to accuse the man who saved me... nice," she sneers sarcastically. None of them lower their weapons or move. King is the only one who looks torn which surprises me. His sole focus is on Amelia. It's now that I realize she was so wrong, if she meant it when she told him to choose between this life or her, he would always choose her.

Chapter Nineteen

Amelia

Looking at my uncles and aunt, I have a pang of longing hit me square in the chest. I didn't realize how much I had missed them all until this moment. I turn to face my mom and my breath hitches, she's not looking at me like she usually does. The intensity in which she is scrutinizing me is unsettling, it's making me feel like she can see beneath the mask I wear and is forcing me to bare all my scars.

"Everyone put your fucking weapons down, now!" The sound of my father's voice has me trembling, not with fear but with... shame. I'm a fucking coward. I can't even look at him because I know the moment I do, I'll break and I won't be able to hide from reality any longer. He will take control and force me to be strong, he won't allow me to cower and hide out with Cronos. He'll make me stand on my own two feet and take back control of the life I built for myself. He'll allow me to push him away and hate him just because he thinks it will make me happy.

"Not until I know what the fuck happened to my daughter," Mom grits out. She darts her gaze from me to Cronos and scowls at the man who has done nothing but try to be there for me and love me through all my flaws.

"Ally, put the fucking knife down, now," Dad snaps, drawing Mom's gaze back to him.

"Come again?" she grits out. My uncles step back, knowing this disagreement has nothing to do with them.

"Baby, I am telling you to get rid of the fucking blade because our daughter looks like she is about to flee if anyone threatens Cronos again." My dad isn't wrong, given the choice I would happily run with Cronos. I'm even rethinking my decision about coming here.

"King, look at her—"

"I am, Allison!" he roars. "I'm begging you to put the fucking knife away because I can't go another year without seeing my daughter." My bottom lip trembles as guilt washes over me, without me needing to say a single word Cronos is at my back rubbing his hands up and down my arms, offering me his silent support. The small gesture means more than he will ever truly know, I have never had someone stand beside me against my family.

I've never brought anyone home either.

Given who my father is and the fact I keep my true name a secret, so I can live a semi-normal life, means I lie to everyone. No one outside of my family and Cronos know who I truly am. To not have to hide that I am Amelia Murdoch is... freeing. I never expected to feel like that. I always thought it was a burden I would have to carry for the rest of my life, but turns out, I was wrong.

"Meelz?" I subtly shake my head to clear my thoughts and look at Uncle Bishop. He looks stoic and ready to pounce at a seconds notice.

"Yeah?" I ask.

"I think you need to explain what is going on before your mother resorts to her tactics of torture. I don't like the idea of my granddaughter being upset and your mother slicing her best friend would most certainly piss her off." The pleading tone he uses has me thinking my uncle may actually fear London's wrath as much as her father does.

"Cronos never hurt me. He... helped me," I answer with conviction so there is no way they can dispute it. They exchange a loaded look, which I choose to ignore, as I press back against Nos, trying to soak up some of his warmth and strength. I've never been the type of woman to need a man to hold my hand or be my rock but with him, it's different. This isn't about power or who is in charge, this is about us as equals needing the other to just be there.

"Amelia, can you explain to me why you look like you have seen a ghost then?" A whoosh of air escapes me at my mom's question. I open my mouth but no words come out, I haven't the slightest idea on how to explain this situation to them.

"Would you feel better if I wasn't here?" I slam my eyes closed at my dad's question. "I'll... leave." Before my dad can take a step, I snap my eyes open and face him for the first time since arriving. He looks... ashen and distraught—I did that to him. Just the sight of him has tears filling my eyes. My bottom lip trembles the longer we stand here staring at each other. He looks like he wants to eliminate the space between us but is scared I'll push him away like I always do.

"Daddy..." I choke out before a sob tears out of me as tears finally fall down my cheeks. It takes him a fraction of a second to clear the space between us. Nos releases me the second my dad pulls me into his embrace. I grip the back of his shirt in a vice-like hold and cling to him as horrible gut-wrenching cries claw their way out of me. Dad has an arm wrapped around my waist and the other gripping the back of my head as he holds me against his chest. I drove a wedge between us for years. Cronos is wrong, I didn't save this family I fucking destroyed it! "I'm... so... sorry," I stutter out through my tears, his hold on me tightens.

"You have nothing to be sorry for, princess." I push back and stare up at him. Shock ripples through me at the sight of his own tears wetting his cheeks.

"I blamed you for everything—"

"You had every right to blame me, Meelz. I should have tried harder, been better—"

I shake my head, denying his claim. "No, Dad. I fucked up. I broke us and I'm so sorry. Please don't hate me," I cry out. He pulls me to him again and crushes me against his chest.

"Hating you would be like hating myself, I could never do that, princess. You are the reason why I smile daily, you are everything good about me. I love you, Amelia. I never smiled until the day I found you. You give me the strength to want a better life and make sure our family never suffers like me and my siblings did. I am so fucking proud of you for wanting something different and making something of yourself. You did that, baby girl—not me or your last name. Max Kingsley gave you the freedom to be who you were meant to be." I pull back and sniff as I wipe away my tears and look up at my dad, it's like I'm seeing him for the first time in a whole new light.

"I don't want to be Max Kingsley anymore, Dad. I want to be Amelia Murdoch." His eyes widen as his mouth parts on a gasp. My mom steps forward and stands beside him, looking just as taken back as he is. I swore I would never want to accept my last name and even tried to go under my mother's maiden name but my whole family was in uproar about it.

"Honey, are you serious?" my mom asks timidly, as if she is scared I may change my mind.

"Meelz, are you sure this is what you want?" Dad cuts his gaze from me to Cronos, who just snorts.

"If you think I had anything to do with this decision, then you clearly don't know how fucking stubborn your daughter is." I scowl at my family as they all begin to mutter under their breath, even my parents are joining them. I pin each of them with a look that promises retribution. My aunt and uncles are the first to close their mouths and smile sheepishly, my parents follow suit.

"Can we maybe... go inside and talk?" I ask. Everyone begins speaking at once. I jolt backward and smack into Cronos. I look up at him to find a smile on his face.

"Still here, angel," he reassures me. Some of the panic that was rising inside me begins to ease. Nos interlocks our fingers as we follow after the others, I haven't been here since the night Uncle Bishop granted me my freedom from the family. It feels weird and kind of like a full circle. When I left here, I was adamant that I would never return and Amelia Murdoch would never see the light of day again. Now, as I enter the home I grew up in I feel... at peace. I don't need to be Max Kingsley anymore. If I'm going to raise a strong independent woman, then I need to lead by example and show my daughter that I was strong enough to face my fears and not give a fuck what the rest of the world thinks about my last name.

Chapter Twenty

Cronos

I expected the rest of her family to make themselves scarce but apparently I was wrong, we're all ushered into Bishop's office. King and Allison claim their seats on the sofa and leave the space between them open for Amelia.

Fuck that!

I tug her down onto the couch beside me and wrap my arm around her shoulders. King shoots me a glare but says nothing. Carlina, Knight, Gage and Rook claim the spare seats around the room while Bishop sits behind his desk. This doesn't feel right and I can tell from how stiff Meelz is she isn't comfortable with this setup either.

"Do all of them need to be here for this?" I say to no one in particular.

"Given the fact she made a call about an ambush, yes, they all need to be here because it was their lives and the life of my brother in law on the line that night." Meelz immediately lowers her gaze to her lap at Bishop's statement. I want to tell him to fuck off but in truth, I understand his reasoning because if that was my brothers and London I would feel the same way he does.

"Meelz, can you tell us what's going on?" Rook asks gently.

"You got something to tell us, Cronos?" King grits out. I look at him trying to decipher his meaning but when he flicks his gaze to Meelz's belly, I stiffen a fraction and shake my head trying to tell him without words not to push her on that. He looks like he wants to say more but thinks better of it when Amelia slowly lifts her head and faces him.

"I fucked up... badly," she admits. Pride swells inside my chest, she's fucking strong and courageous. Not a lot of people would be able to sit here and face a room full of powerful people like she is.

"How?" Allison asks.

"I—I think I need to start from when I left." I squeeze her shoulders gently.

"You start from wherever you are comfortable, sweetheart," Carlina adds lovingly. Meelz takes a deep breath and squares her shoulders but still keeps her gaze lowered. My anger peaks at the sight of her feeling ashamed. I reach out and grip her chin, forcing her to look at me.

"You have nothing, I mean not a goddamn fucking thing to be ashamed about, do you hear me?" She searches my gaze for a second before melting.

"Okay," she whispers. I release her and slink back into my seat, ignoring everyone's gazes on me, their opinions mean nothing. She turns back to her father, who is still glaring at me. "Colson Salvatoro found me in Chicago." At the mention of his former employee, King faces his daughter looking murderous.

"He's a dead man," King forces out through clenched teeth.

"Agreed," I mutter.

"The guy from college?" Knight asks. Meelz nods. "What does he have to do with any of this?"

"He and I were... sort of..." She exhales and closes her eyes for a beat before finally continuing. "Colson and I were an item, dating or whatever you want to call it." King's face morphs into a picture of rage like I have never seen before, his hands clenched on his lap. Allison appears to be battling to stay calm, almost like she knows exactly where this story is going. "Things went wrong a few months into the relationship and Colson... changed."

"Changed, how?" Bishop snarls. The force in which he utters those two words shows me why he is still the Don.

"He became unhinged and..." Her bottom lip trembles as she looks to me for help.

"The cunt hurt her in more ways than any of us can comprehend or want to imagine," I answer for her. She instantly huddles into my side when the room breaks out into chaos. All the males are yelling and planning ways to kill this cunt while the two females are sitting there staring at my girl with tears in their eyes. Allison ignores the men as she...

Holy fuck!

She drops to her knees in front of Amelia, grabs both her trembling hands and kisses the top of each of her knuckles. Meelz stares down at her mother as tears trail down her cheeks.

"I am so sorry, my daughter. I should have been there—"

Meelz cuts Ally off before she can continue. "Mom, no—"

"Amelia, I am your mother and I should have known!" she screams. Silence encases the room at her outburst. "I know you hate this life. I thought accepting what you wanted and letting you go would be the best thing for you. I was so fucking wrong and I will never forgive myself for that but, you also need to know that Colson signed his own death date when he laid his hands on my beautiful little girl." A sob claws its way out of her. Meelz pulls forward and drops down in front of her mother, wrapping her arms around her and holding her close as they both cry.

I cut a glance to King, who is staring at both girls on their knees crying, he looks like his heart has just been ripped out of his chest and put through a meat grinder. "I want his fucking head on a spike out front of my house," he snarls. At her father's declaration Amelia pushes back from her mother and looks at her father.

"No."

King's face turns red as if ready to argue, before this shit can turn into a battle ground between Meelz and her dad, I cut in. "He isn't yours to end, he's hers, so the choice remains with her," I declare.

"What the fuck do you have to do with any of this, Cronos?" Bishop snaps.

"He's with me and if you don't like that, then too bad!" my angel says in my defense. I know she means well, trying to speak in my defense, but given the information she has just dropped, her family won't accept my presence easily and that's okay. I'll show each of these fucking Murdoch's that I'm not temporary, I'm here for the long haul.

"Clearly my presence isn't up for negotiation, so how about we get to the part where we tell you that Colson Salvatoro knows your pick up times, the place and when for each month," I say.

"You fucking ratted us out!" Knight roars.

"You're dead, you fucking snitch!" Rook adds.

"Take him!" Bishop orders, but before any of them can move to follow the command of their don, Meelz speaks up.

"He didn't rat on anyone... I did." The looks on everyone's faces at her admission is priceless. The guys look torn between wanting to strangle her and betrayed. Carlina and Allison both stare at Meelz with understanding as if they know why she did what she did. In the eyes of the mafia, Amelia just committed the greatest act of betrayal. Most families wouldn't allow you to live. I'm banking on the Murdochs not going with that option, because if they decide that is the route they want to go, then a war will ensue because I'll never allow them to harm her.

"Why?" King whispers brokenly. "Do you hate me that much that you wanted not only me but my brothers and Vincent to get killed? Do you want your cousins to grow up without their fathers?" His questions may be valid but I know Amelia and I know she can't take much more of this shit from her family—she isn't the same girl they once knew. I rise from my seat on the couch, drawing their attention to me and off her. I keep my gaze on the males as I offer Meelz my hand blindly. She places her hand in mine and slowly rises to her feet beside me.

"Hate is a strong word, she never meant to hurt any of you!" I roar. Each of them jerk back at my harsh shout. "Did you miss the fucking part where you were told that she was beaten? How about the part where he not only physically abused her but mentally fucking destroyed the woman you once knew? Pull your fucking heads out of your ass or you will be the ones growing old without her."

"Is that a threat, you little cunt?" King snarls as he steps forward, Bishop and Gage hold him back when Amelia huddles into my side and hides her face.

"It's a promise," I say with such conviction no one can

dispute that I speak the truth. "You felt what she is hiding." King's face hardens.

"You took advantage of her—"

I cut her father off before he can continue his bullshit. "Much like her mother, I will love that little girl the same way Allison loves Amelia. There may not be an ounce of my DNA in her little veins but she is *mine*, make no fucking mistake of that, and if you or your family put either of *my* girls in harm's way, I will take them both from you. You and your family do not scare me, I've been to hell, King, and believe me, I'd go back again if it meant keeping *my family* safe."

"What the hell is he talking about?" Allison breathes out as she climbs to her feet, she looks to her daughter but Meelz keeps her face hidden in my side.

"Ally–"

"Shut the hell up, King," Allison snaps, she looks scared and that isn't a look I would have expected to see on her face. "Amelia, what are they talking about?" The pleading tone of her voice has me snapping out of my anger. I gently shift Meelz so she is in front of me with her back to my chest. Her mother runs her gaze up and down her, looking for signs of injury but the second I rest both my hands on her bump, Allison stumbles back a step and covers her mouth with her hand.

"Mom—" Meelz is silenced when her mother shakes her head. My temper flares. How dare she judge my angel.

"I'm going to be a grandmother!" At Allison's outburst I reel back, Amelia even tenses, that was not what either of us were expecting her to say.

Chapter Twenty-One

Amelia

Mom and Aunt Carlina didn't even give me a chance to utter a single word after Mom made her declaration of becoming a grandmother. They both dragged me from my uncle's office. Nos tried to follow us but my mom shoved him backward and told him that he wasn't welcome to be present for the womanly conversation we were about to have. Her and my aunt dragged me outside, then called my other aunt's, who are all sitting around the large outdoor table that we currently occupy. To say this is awkward is an understatement. I feel like a teenager who just told her mom she had sex for the first time and about to get *the talk*.

Aunt Kiara, Aunt Clare and Aunt Carlina are all sitting there staring at me with the broadest grins on their faces and it's starting to make me squirm. Aunt Anya looks as happy as my mom but my heart hurts when I look at Aunt Koby. I know she is happy for all of us kids but I also know it's hard for her to celebrate new life when she lost her son. Having Ryat and Lailani living here with her and Uncle Knight has been good for her, but it still isn't the same as having Havoc. Chaos and Cass fly out here a lot with their twins to visit and I know seeing her son helps ease some of the ache of losing his twin.

I subtly place my hand on my bump and try to force my thoughts back from that dark path, I haven't even met my daughter yet and the thought of her being taken from me or worse, dying, has me wanting to curl into a ball and cry in the corner. Now that I have this new life growing inside me I can understand why my family sometimes goes off the deep end when one of their loved ones is threatened.

"Stop looking at me like that, Meelz, I'm fine." I nibble my bottom lip, feeling like a prick that my Aunt knows I am thinking about her loss. "You having a baby is something to celebrate. I mean, I think I can speak for all of us here when I say *none* of us thought you would ever have a kid." I balk at Aunt Koby, who just shrugs her shoulders.

"Why?" I squawk out.

"Uh, are you joking?" Aunt Kiara sounds genuinely confused.

I harden my stare as I face her and nod. "Yes!" I snap.

"Because you were all about your career and never wanting to bring anyone into this family and now we find out you're pregnant and with Cronos." Aunt Kiara's assessment of the situation is black and white but it's wrong, there is gray surrounding my whole life right now.

"Yes, Cronos and I are together but he isn't..." I take a deep breath and square my shoulders. "He isn't the father to my daughter." All six of their faces slacken. I want to laugh but I refrain. I've just blown their minds. In their eyes, I am the perfect one. I never fuck up or make mistakes so hearing this news has clearly thrown them.

"He didn't need to be the one to create the life inside you to be the baby's father. His choice to stand by your side and raise that child as his own has already shown not only yourself, but the rest of the family, that he is worthy of the title *Dad*." My mom's words have me swallowing a few times to keep from crying.

"Mom–"

She cuts me off before I can finish. "Amelia Queen Murdoch, you are *mine*!" The conviction in which she says that word has tears springing to my eyes. "You may not have grown in my womb or thrived inside me but I have loved you from the moment those beautiful green eyes opened and looked at me with love. Creating life doesn't make you a parent, the love and devotion to that child is what grants you the right to call yourself a parent. I am your mother." Tears fall on their own accord down my cheeks. We have never had this conversation before. There has never been a reason to have it. Allison Murdoch is my mother and nothing and no one will ever change that. I spy my dad, uncles and Cronos out of the corner of my eye and the look on my dad's face mirrors my own. He hates hearing that Mom didn't actually give me life as much as I do.

"Ally, no one has doubted your love for Meelz," Aunt Kiara says.

"She is yours in every way that matters," Dad says as he makes his way toward us. Mom keeps her gaze on me as she continues on.

"Loving you has been the greatest joy of my life. Without you, Amelia, I had nothing. You pushed me to want more, to be more, not only for myself but for you as well." Dad comes to stand behind her chair and rests his hands on her shoulders. My uncles fan out and mimic his position behind their wives but Nos chooses to stay back and allow me the time to brave this situation by myself and I love him for knowing that I need to do this on my own. "This child you carry may be *his*—"

"He doesn't want her, Mom. He planned for this to happen so he could use me and her against..." I flick my gaze to my dad who looks hurt. "Dad."

"He's smarter than I gave him credit for," Dad growls.

"What?" I asked confused.

"Meelz, that fucker knows what you mean to me and your mother. Hurting you would make me... upset." I snort at him downplaying his anger, and my uncles and aunts even snicker but he pushes on. "But to get you pregnant, and create a life with my one and only child, he knows that shit will plague me."

"Why?" I breathe out.

Dad doesn't get a chance to answer, Cronos beats him to it. "Because he knows your father would be conflicted and hesitate to kill the father of his grandchild. Your father loves you, angel, but he also knows that your love for that little girl means more than what he wants, and him killing the father of your baby will always be in the back of your mind every time you look at him. Or, when that little girl grows up and asks what happened to her *real* father ,you would have to tell her that her grandfather killed him."

I tear my gaze from Nos to stare up at my dad and shake my head. He averts his gaze, refusing to look at me. "Dad, I-I..." The words refuse to come out of my mouth, why can't I give him permission to kill Colson?

"That is why, your father won't be the one to do it." Dread pools inside me as I slowly turn back to face the man who now owns my heart and holds it in the palm of his hand. The shadow that clouds his brown eyes has my breath hitching.

"Nos, what did you do?" I whisper brokenly.

He smiles sadly and tries to wall off his emotions, but I can see the pain in his eyes. "Colson turned you against him once, baby. I won't allow him to rob you of more time from your father." I push back from the table and stand ready to go to him but Nos holds his hand up, halting my movements. My heart is pounding inside my chest. My chest begins to burn as the anticipation starts to build inside me. "You asked me once, to choose you or my family." I swallow audibly and hate myself for ever asking him that stupid question. "This is me choosing both."

"Huh?" I breathe out.

"Amelia, you are my redemption from the pits of hell, I will always choose you." My chest expands as I suck in some much needed air. "But that baby you carry inside you is now my family as well, so I am choosing both."

"What are you trying to say?" The anguish in my own voice is easy to hear, I can feel it in my bones that what he says next is going to hurt like hell and break me.

"I'm saying that your father and uncles are too easily recognized. He will know they are coming for him and disappear again when they get close. He doesn't know me or my face." I shake my head, trying to deny what he is going to do but it's too late, he's made his mind up. "I'm going to end this so you and our little girl can be free and never look over your shoulder again."

Fuck this!

I close the space between him and I, then clutch the front of his shirt in my hands. "Don't go," I whisper brokenly.

He cups my face in his large hands and bends at his knees

so we are eye level. "Please don't hate me at the end of all of this, angel," he says quietly, then places a long kiss on my lips, unlike all the others we have shared. This one is filled with heartache and pleading, like he is begging me to not hate him and love him through all of this until he returns to us. He pulls back and rests his head against mine. We stand here for a moment just breathing each other in. "I love you, angel."

"I love you too, Grizz," I whisper through my tears.

"This is the last time I will leave either of you, I swear." Before I can say another word he pulls back and nods over my shoulder. Two arms wrap around me and I know it's my dad. Panic surges inside me when I realize what's happening.

"Cronos, no! Don't leave me, please—"

"I'll always come back for you both, angel, always. Be strong and keep that little girl safe until I get back." When he turns his back, prepared to walk away I break. Every ounce of pain I have kept hidden bursts free as I scream for him to come back. Not once does he look back as I call for him. I collapse in my dad's hold when he vanishes from view, as he heads around the side of the house.

"Cronos!" I scream his name so loud my throat turns horse. Dad's hold on me remains firm and unyielding as I try to break free and chase after him, but then a voice penetrates the fog.

"You need to calm down, none of this is good for the baby." At his words I stop struggling. His hold eases but not enough for me to escape. I slam my eyes closed when I hear the purr of the engine of the rental we arrived in.

He's leaving.

"Why did you send him away?" I ask brokenly as I collapse in my dad's hold. He lowers us to the ground gently. My back rests against his chest and his arms still remain around me.

"I didn't. I planned to be the one to do it, but he refused and told me that if I was the one to go after Colson even if you said it was okay... I would lose you for good. Call me selfish, Meelz, but I feel like I just got my daughter back and I couldn't risk losing you again. I know you hate this life and loathe the part I play in this mafia world but believe me when I tell you, I do all of this for you and your mother."

Before I can stop it the question bursts out of me. "If I asked you to choose, what would your choice be?"

"You. Always you, Amelia," he answers without hesitation.

Chapter Twenty-Two

Cronos

Eight weeks later...

"She isn't coping, Cronos. Put a bullet in the cocksucker's head and then get your ass back here!" King snarls down the phone. I roll my eyes at his dramatics.

"How the fuck do I kill this cunt when I can't fucking find him?" I snap back. Vincent, Koby, Knight, Chanel, Chaos and even Artemis have been trying to track this cunt down, hacking into every camera in the city, trying to find him. His Tech company is now nothing but ash. His security firm was to be blown to pieces, but the building was empty. No sign of life or anything inside, but a quick search told me that the fucking place is still being paid for. I've spent the past two weeks trying to track down the owner of the building to get intel from him but he's somehow vanished into thin air as well.

"Where are you?"

"Parked out front of the fucker's security building waiting for—" I'm cut off by the sound of knocking on the window. When I see who it is I growl. "Smooth," I grit out before pushing the button to unlock the doors and ending the call. King slips into the seat beside me, like this is fucking normal. "What the hell are you doing here?"

"You're taking too long and the fact we have been shot at twice collecting product and guns from the ports isn't working out well for my brothers. Be thankful it's me here and not Bishop."

I scoff. "I'm not thankful for any of you!" King pins me with a glare but I ignore it. "You should be back in New York looking after Amelia and making sure she is okay—"

"She left yesterday to go back to Minnesota."

I reel back so hard, I smack into my door. "What?" I yell.

He grinds his teeth as if this is pissing him off just as much as me. "She refused to have the baby in New York and said she wanted to return *home*." I grit my teeth so fucking hard my jaw begins to ache. I lift my phone and hit her number, it rings twice before she picks up. King and I remain in a stare off.

"Now, after all this time you want to fucking call—"

"I told you to stay the fuck in New York!"

"Yeah, well, you weren't there to stop me now, were you?" My nostrils flare in anger.

"Amelia—"

"Cronos!" Regardless of how angry I am with her, just hearing her voice and the way she is sassing me shows that she is finally starting to find her old self again and that has pride swelling inside me.

"Don't push me, angel." King's eyes narrow at my pet name for his daughter.

"I'd do a lot more to you but... oh, wait that's right, you're not here!"

A smile tugs at the corners of my mouth. "Someone seems like they chose violence when they woke up today," I tease.

"This someone can't even see their own toes or put socks on anymore, so I am violent every day!"

My anger vanishes. "I bet you still look beautiful though." King makes a disgruntled sound and tears his gaze from mine.

"I look like a house."

"A house I would love to live inside of," I answer without thought, until King snaps his head toward me and bares his teeth.

"I'll punch you in your fucking throat, asshole," he vows. I can't help the laughter that breaks free.

"Is that my dad?" The sound of her voice cuts my laughter short.

"Yup," I say, making sure to pop the '*p*' so she knows I am just as shocked about her father's arrival as I am sure she is.

"Good, he got there safely." I recoil for the second time, and this time I smack my head against the window, making my anger rise even further. King winks at me and I grind my teeth, trying to calm down enough so I don't punch my girlfriend's father in the face.

"Why is your father here?" I grit out through clenched teeth.

"Because Mom and I needed him out of the way so he wouldn't hover while we came home to set up for Kingsley's arrival and I thought if he was there to help, then that would mean you could come home sooner." I can hear the slight tremor in her voice at the mention of me coming home but all I heard was one thing.

"Kingsley?" I whisper.

She's silent for a moment as if she has only just realized what she said. "Oh, I uh... I mean I just thought that—"

"You named our baby?" I whisper. King eyes me and the look in his eyes is calculating like he is waiting for any excuse to strike out at me if I say or do the wrong thing.

"Yeah... Are you mad?" I smile and shake my head even though she can't see me.

"No, angel. I'm not mad. I think Kingsley is a perfect name for our little girl."

"Good, because Max Kingsley gave me the life I thought I wanted and that name will always be special to me so I wanted to pass that on to our baby."

"You don't want to be Max anymore?" King's eyes widen slightly and we both wait with bated breath to hear her answer.

"No. It's time I stopped hiding who I truly am. I am Amelia Murdoch and it's about time I started acting like it."

Pride swells inside me, she is fucking perfect and so strong. "God, you truly are fucking amazing, do you know that?" King scrunches his face in disgust. I wag my brows at him, earning a scathing look before he turns to look out his window.

"Stop it. I'm way too hormonal for you to be all cute and shit." It feels surreal to be on the phone with her and talking about every day shit. Her father is in the next seat beside me, with a small smile on his face like it makes him happy to hear how happy she is. "Oh my God, Cronos, I swear we need to put her in soccer because she is kicking the shit out of me."

"Angel, she is going to be a nun and live life in a church."

Amelia's laughter has warmth spreading through my chest, I didn't realize how much I have missed her until this moment. I made sure not to call or text so I wouldn't be distracted—she is a blind spot for me. Whenever she is around or on my mind,

I lose focus of everything else, she becomes my gravity, my home, my everything.

"You can't lock her away. She is going to meet a man some day and let's just hope he isn't a creep and weird."

"No men!" I growl. King shakes with silent laughter from beside me. I shoot him a glare, the asshole just pins me with a bored look.

"Coming from the dickhead on the phone to *my* daughter?" *Fuck!*

"Not the same thing!" I snarl at him and turn to look at the building in front of me. Suddenly Meelz's voice becomes white noise in the background as I watch a guy approach the front door.

"Angel, I have to go," I say, then end the call and leap out of the car with King hot on my heels. This is the first time I have seen anyone enter this building since I came here weeks ago. We both rush across the road and rather than following straight in after the guy, King and I move toward the back of the building. Once we are out of view of the public, we each pull our guns out and lean against the wall on either side of the back door.

King looks at me and holds up three fingers. I nod and wait for him to count down to zero. I maneuver and kick the door in, rushing inside with King behind covering my six. The instant we enter the main room I freeze. A young guy around my age sits on a single metal chair with a puffer jacket on and shaking like a leaf. It isn't just his shaking that makes me pause, it's the sweat that is dotting his brow and the fact he looks like he is on the verge of tears that has me tensing, King comes to stand by me and eyes the guy with the same scrutiny as me.

Something is fucking off!

"Who are you?" King asks as he continues darting his gaze around the room. I do the same, making sure to keep my head on a swivel. People think that ignoring your gut feeling is the right move but they are wrong, my gut has saved my life more times than I can count and right now, my gut is screaming at me that this is a set up.

"You're looking in all the wrong places." King and I share a look before turning back to the kid who upon closer inspection looks like he is a... teenager.

"What does that mean?" I press.

"You forget I worked with your family, I know Luka doesn't watch part of the city and know how to play in the blind spots."

"What the fuck are you talking about?" I shout.

"He's a messenger." I turn to look at King who looks... shaken. "This was a tactic we used years ago to send a message to our enemies." The weight of his words slams into me, I've heard about this type of shit before. You find some no name schmuck off the street, pay off their debt, so they can send a message without the source ever being present. Most of them speak as if they are the source but that isn't all... my blood runs cold.

"What's beneath the jacket?" I grit out.

The kid gulps, his eyes dart around the room and he looks scared, but I can tell he is trying to mask his fear by faking confidence. "You have a choice to make, your majesty."

King's jaw locks, I dart my gaze between the both of them, my gut is telling me that King's sudden appearance here in Chicago didn't go unnoticed by the fucker I have been tracking.

"I don't do well with ultimatums," King growls.

"You will have a choice to make, refuse my offer and you will lose them both."

Suddenly my own bravado begins to waiver, I swallow audibly as my mind starts to conjure horrific images.

"Lose who?" I force out through clenched teeth as I take a step forward, but still instantly when he raises his hand and I see a detonator clutched in his grip. My eyes widen, the puffer jacket makes sense now—he has a fucking bomb strapped to him!

"No sudden moves!" the kid bellows. King shifts his gun ready to fire but the kid pushes on. "The moment my heart stops beating it goes off." King waivers slightly but doesn't lower his gun, I look around the room trying to find an exit or a place to take cover but it's futile, it's a fucking concrete room and the only windows are behind the little fucker.

"Okay. I'm listening, what's your terms?" King snarls, but I can hear the slight edge of worry in his voice.

"You need to choose," the kid responds.

"Choose who?" King roars.

"The one you love most or the one who saved you from yourself." I furrow my brow confused as fuck but King seems to understand exactly what the kid is saying.

"You touch them and I will fucking slice you open and feed you your intestines, you little cunt." I turn to him and raise a brow in question but the stricken look on King's face has worry churning inside me.

Fuck no!

"Amelia and Allison," I say, barely above a whisper. King's jaw locks but he nods subtly confirming my fear.

"One may live, you get to choose which one," the soon to be dead little cocksucker says.

"You touch my wife or daughter—"

"You never gave my family a chance, I wasn't given a choice!" the kid yells. "Choose, your time is running out. Fail to make a decision and they both die." Before the little fucker can utter another word, I pull the trigger. The bullet hits him between the eyes. We have mere seconds before his heart stops. I grab King's arm and drag him after me as we rush for the exit. We manage to get out of the room and around the corner before the bomb goes off and everything comes crashing down.

The last thought I have is of my girls and praying that Allison can save them both.

Chapter Twenty-Three

Amelia

"Well, I have to say it's nice to see you smiling again after so many weeks," Mom says as she rounds the corner from the kitchen into the living room.

I drop my phone to my lap and place a hand on my bump, love for my daughter surges inside me when I feel her respond to my touch by kicking.

"I just spoke to Cronos," I tell her.

She smiles and nods, then claims her seat on the sofa next to me. "You really care about him, don't you?"

I have no idea why her question makes me feel shy but it's hard to explain what he means to me, love doesn't seem like an adequate word. "He's not just my man, he's my rest, my home, my heart and my safe place."

Mom's eyes soften, she reaches out and places her hand on top of mine, giving it a gentle pat. "All your father and I have ever wanted for you, was for you to be happy. Are you happy, baby girl?"

I mull over her words for a moment and debate how to answer. I decide to go with what I feel in my heart. "I wasn't for a long time. I thought diving into my career and burying myself in work would fill the void of loneliness but it didn't, it just masked it. I really thought Colson cared about me, Mom," I say bitterly.

"Honey, the thing about *manipulators* is when they blame you for your reaction to their toxic behavior, but never discuss their disrespect that triggered you. He used your good nature and big heart and wove a web of lies to try and turn you against your family..." She inhales sharply as if garnering the strength to continue. "For a long while he succeeded in doing that to you, but something tells me that we have Cronos Argyros to thank for showing you that we aren't monsters."

I balk at her. "Mom, I never thought you were a monster!"

She smiles sadly. "I wasn't talking about me, darling." Shame slams into me and I drop my gaze. "Your father never meant to hurt you, he thought he was doing the right thing."

"Why didn't he just tell me the truth about Colson?"

"How? He tried to talk to you after he fired Colson and banished him from the city but you wouldn't listen, Meelz. He tried for years to explain why he did what he did but you wouldn't hear him out, your anger consumed you and drove you away from us. He thought if you kept hating him then you would stay away and be safe from this life. *Max Kingsley* was created to give you freedom and a chance at a life without all of this bullshit."

"Max did give me all of those things but I was a fool for thinking I could ever escape who I truly am. If I had known who Colson really was, I would never have—"

"Yes, you would have." I narrow my eyes at her, not liking how she thinks she knows what I would have done. "I knew who your father was, knew what his family did and swore I would keep you as far away from all of them as I could, but in the end I wasn't just lying to myself, I was lying to you as well."

"What?"

"Your father is my first love, Meelz, he is it for me. No man will ever hold a candle next to him. Colson was your first love." I cringe. "If anyone had told me that loving King Murdoch would get me kidnapped and raped, I would have told them all to fuck off because I was blinded by love."

Anguish surges inside me. "Mom, I am so sorry–"

She waves me off. "I moved on from that. For a long time I blamed your father as well, Amelia. I channeled all my anger and self-loathing onto him but it wasn't fair to him or me. I didn't hate him, I was angry with myself for falling in love with him when I knew exactly who he and his family were. My point is, no one could have told you the truth about Colson because you were in love with him and would never have seen his faults, even if your father showed the proof of him stalking you and trying to use you against him."

"I don't understand why he hates Dad so much," I admit.

"We were still at war with all the families, so many men risked their lives and some innocents were lost in the crossfire. During a shootout in downtown, a family was run off the road. The woman died on impact and so did the little girl in the backseat." I gasp and widen my eyes in horror. "The man was pinned behind the wheel and had a metal beam through his chest. Your father knew he wasn't going to survive so he promised to save the man's son, then put him out of his misery. What he didn't expect was when he dropped that child off at an orphanage, that he would grow up and come back to exact his revenge."

"Dad killed his family?" I breathe out.

She shakes her head. "No. The other family we were at war with did, your father was just the one to find them."

"Oh my God. Colson's anger is misplaced, he's blaming Dad for something he didn't even do."

She nods. "Colson thinks your father was the one who killed his family. We didn't know any of this until after your father banished him. Colson was to be killed, Meelz, for breaking the rules and getting involved with you." My eyes widen to the size of dinner plates.

"Why wasn't he?"

"When he admitted to who he was, your father felt guilty, so as penance he allowed him to go free. he never expected that Colson would ever return." I cover my mouth with my hand and recline back into the sofa as I absorb everything she has just said.

"I'm the worst daughter," I mutter.

Mom chuckles and shakes her head. "Every child hates their parents at least once in their lives." I pin her with a dry stare.

"Most kids don't run away and hide for years, Mom."

She rolls her lips over her teeth to keep from smiling. "Most kids also don't return pregnant with their niece's best friend, looking at them like they are his reason for breathing." Hearing her description of Nos has butterflies taking flight inside me.

"He's... God, Mom. I'm so fucked where he is concerned."

"You are not!" she abolishes.

"Mom, he is way younger than me... he's twenty-five for God's sake and shacking up with a thirty-seven-year-old pregnant woman whose life is a mess."

"Cut that shit out right now," she scolds. I suddenly feel like a child again and sit up straight. "Cronos is smart enough to know how fucking lucky he is to have someone as amazing as you in his life, not a lot of guys his age would step up the way he has. Jesus, from what I have heard, you kicked his ass out and then a year later turned up on his doorstep—"

"Okay, Okay, I get the point, Mom. He's great, good to know." She laughs and I glare at her for a second before I join in. It feels good to laugh like this again. Her laughter dies off instantly and the look on her face has me sobering instantly. "What's wrong?"

"Go to the room and lock the door, now!" she snaps, pushes to her feet and rushes toward the front door, where she peers through the window and curses beneath her breath.

"Mom?" I call as I struggle to my feet and wince when the pain in my lower back makes itself known again.

"Go, now and don't fucking open that door!"

Fear takes hold of me. "Mom, what the hell is going on?"

She turns away from the window and races to her purse on the counter to retrieve two guns. My eyes widen when her fear filled gaze lands on me. "Call your father, lock the bedroom and stay there. You don't come out no matter what, Amelia." A memory of when I was child and how she hid me beneath her bed while she faced off against the men who kidnapped her slams into me.

"No, I am not leaving you again!" I yell. She rushes over to me and cups my face between her hands, her eyes hard and unyielding.

"Go to your room, call your father and wait for him and the other's to get here—"

"Who is out there, Mom?"

"He found you, baby," she says quietly. I try to pull back

but she doesn't allow it. "Let me protect you and my grand-daughter the only way I know how."

Tears fill my eyes. "Mom, no I won't lose you—"

"You protect that baby with everything you have, do what-ever you have to in order to survive, do you understand me?" Gooseflesh dots my skin as tears fall down my cheeks.

"Mom, please—"

"Hush. Go now, there isn't time to debate this, baby girl. Your father won't get here in time, so you need to be prepared for that. If you can escape out the back, you do that. Now go, Amelia!" She releases me with a gentle shove. I feel like a coward, the scum of the fucking earth as I turn my back on my mother. I peer back over my shoulder to see her standing there with a forced smile on her face and nodding at me encour-agingly.

"I love you, Mom."

Her shoulders deflate. "And I love you, Amelia, more than you ever know. When you hold that little girl for the first time, you will understand then just how much I love you." A pit is forming in my gut, this is so fucking wrong. My family is the most powerful in the fucking world and my stupid decision to leave the safety and protection of my family's compound to return here so I can prepare for the arrival of my daughter, has put us all in danger. "Go!" she snaps.

"Mom—" I sob.

"Amelia, that little girl inside you is the priority, you protect her and fucking run. Don't you dare look back or try to come out. You find an exit and you take it."

Chapter Twenty-Four

Cronos

I groan as I slowly blink my eyes open, my ears are ringing and my vision is hazy as I look around and see people running through the cloud of smoke and dust. I turn and hiss in pain, a large chunk of concrete is pinning my ankle. Suddenly King appears, limping toward me, cut up and bleeding. If he hadn't tackled me out the front door we would both be dead right now.

"Can you move?" he shouts, his loud voice can be heard over the ringing in my ears. I nod my head, bending down, he grits his teeth as he flips the chunk off my ankle. I bite down on my lip to keep from screaming out. King doesn't give me a chance to recover, he grabs my arm and hauls me to my feet. Wrapping my arm around his shoulder, he helps me hobble across the road to my car. I feel like a fucking bitch, he has to help me inside the car but I draw the line at him trying to put my seatbelt on.

"Just get in the fucking car!" I snap. He growls but does as I say and rounds the front of the car to climb behind the wheel. The sound of sirens can be heard in the distance as King drives like a mad man through the streets.

"Where's your phone?" he demands. I grab it from the console and hand it to him. He scrolls through the contact list and then hits dial before tossing it back to me. It rings through the car's Bluetooth system, I peer down to see he has called Allison. "Come on baby, pick up!" he mutters to himself.

"The man himself." My heart stops for a second at the sound of his voice, my worst fears are coming to light and from the way King is gripping the steering wheel—he is as fucked up inside as I am.

"Colson," King snarls. The sound of a woman screaming in the background has the both of us tensing.

"Don't be rude, Ally, I'm on the phone!" The sarcasm in Colson's tone is thick.

"You fucking take me, you cunt! You let my family go—"

"You don't make the fucking rules, King!" Instantly he snaps his mouth closed, his breaths are coming in fast pants as he tries to control his anger. Allison can be heard whimpering and I can only imagine how that sound is killing him inside.

"What do you want?" King's tone is even and calm, he is faking the hell out of his calmness.

"I want you to suffer the same way I did. You took my family from me and now I will take yours from you." King turns the car hard left and the tires squeal but he never lets off the gas.

"You want me to suffer, then take me, I'll come willingly, just let them go and you can have me."

Colson tsks him, clearly loving having the upper hand. My stomach is in my throat as worry for my girl and our baby takes hold of me. "You wouldn't suffer enough but this way, I know it will hurt so much more. You're too far away to save them. I'll do you a solid though, okay? I'll let you say goodbye to her." Before King can utter a word Colson presses on. "Say hi, Ally."

"Suck my dick, you little cunt, my husband is going to slaughter all of you fuckers—Argh!" Allison screams.

"Don't fucking hurt her!" King yells so loud I recoil.

"Say your goodbyes, Ally," Colson grits out.

"Baby?" King whispers brokenly.

"You keep that shit bottled up, you save our girl and end this," Ally gasps out. I can hear the pain in her voice but my mind is reeling, she said to save Amelia so she is still alive!

"I'm coming for you, baby, just hang on, okay?" King's tone is filled with pain like I have never heard before, I can see him fighting back his own tears.

"Love them both enough for the both of us, I'll always love you." Before King can reply, the call ends.

"Allison?" he screams. "Ally?" I drop my gaze to my lap as I fight to keep my own emotions in check. "Allison, baby?"

"King—"

"Call her back now!" he roars. Knowing he won't listen to reason, I try to call her back but it goes to voicemail. "Call again!" I do as he asks and continue to do it three more times before an incoming call stops me. I hit answer.

"Is my brother with you?" Bishop's deep voice fills the car.

"B?" King whispers brokenly. I peer over at him to see tears cascading down his cheeks.

"Where are you, brother?" Bishop's tone softens slightly but not much, he knows he needs to be strong for his brother.

When King doesn't answer, I do it for him. "Heading to the airport."

"I have a plane there waiting to take you both to Minnesota. We're enroute there now."

"How did you know?" I ask.

"My niece alerted us, we're all coming, King, I'll be there, brother," Bishop vows.

"B, I can't—"

Bishop cuts his brother off before he can continue. "Don't! You just get the fuck here and then we go to war. They are your wife and daughter but they are also our nieces and sister. We protect our own." Bishop ends the call without another word. I place another call, it rings twice before she answers.

"I'm coming, Nos!" London says, her voice is laced with rage.

"He has them," I mutter.

"Not for long, the Murdochs, *Memento Mori* and Godfather's are all coming, Cronos. My Dad has called Knox and Waverly, both of them have locked their borders. The Re Della Strada is coming but Taylan is leading them. Knox can't leave his wife and nor can Xander, Trey and Wave." I had heard that Lakeland wasn't doing well with this pregnancy and is high risk. Taylan coming means he is no doubt bringing his girl with him, he won't leave her at college unprotected.

"Lon—"

"No. This is not the same thing as before. Unlike last time, you and Artemis aren't on your own, you have me and the rest of my family with you. We will save them. Do you hear me?"

"I hear you," I whisper.

"Is Royal with you?" King cuts in and asks.

"No, him, Mom, Uncle Chaos, Aunt Sin and Uncle Kacey will be the first to arrive. They were only a couple of hours away on business. Aunt Cass is still in Miami with the twins," she answers. How she can lock her emotions down so well I will never understand.

The entire plane ride is agony. King and I are both antsy and trying not to jump out of our skin. Every minute feels like a fucking hour. The second we land, we don't even wait for the plane to stop moving down the tarmac before we both leap out of our seats and wait at the fucking door for the hostess to open it. The local airport here is tiny as fuck, and barely has any flights coming in or out of it.

We may be injured but neither of us can feel a lick of pain through the adrenaline coursing through our veins. There is a driver waiting for us. King shoulders the guy out of the way and climbs behind the wheel of the Hellcat Durango. I barely make it inside the car before he is planting his foot on the gas.

"Tell me where the fuck to go!" he snarls over the roar of the powerful engine. This fucking car is a beast and is eating up the road like a bat out of hell.

"Keep heading straight for a few miles then you're gonna turn left into the town." King drives like he is fucking Mad Max. I grab the *oh shit* handle and hang on for dear fucking life as he takes each turn, the SUV handling the beating he is putting it through like a fucking champ. The closer we get to the town the more I grow anxious, no one has called since I spoke to London. A part of me thinks it may be a good thing and they arrived in time but then another part is scared that they don't want to deliver the news over the phone. "Left!"

King jerks the wheel and the ass end of the SUV skids out behind us, gravel flicking up around us but neither of us care as he plants his foot—at this time the town is usually quiet so no one should be on the road, hopefully.

"Take a right, here," I bark out.

"How far?"

"A mile."

"You couldn't choose anywhere further fucking out, could you?" he growls.

"Fuck you, King!" I snap.

"If anything has happened to them, I'll fucking kill you," he declares.

"You can fucking try," I force out through clenched teeth. When he finally turns into my driveway, my stomach sinks. There are cars everywhere. At the sound of our arrival everyone turns toward us with guns raised. King doesn't let off the gas until we are near the front of the cabin. I lock my knees, expecting him to plough through his family and my house, until he slams on the brakes and sends us both propelling forward only to be jerked back by our belts. He and I both leap out of the car and rush toward Bishop and the rest of his brother's. London and Artemis stand by her father, aunt and uncle. She breaks away from the others and runs to me. I embrace her quickly before pushing her back and darting my gaze around.

"Where are they?" I ask.

"Where the fuck is my wife?" King roars so loud that everyone goes silent, no one even dares move.

"King—"

"Where is she, Bishop?" he yells right in the Don's face. Bishop purses his lips and steps aside. The rest of the family follows his lead and the sight has me stumbling back a step. Blood coats my porch, ropes hang from the rafters as if they had someone tied there. "Noooooooo!" King screams as he drops to his knees. My mouth parts on a gasp at the sight of a human heart sitting there in the center of the porch. "Ahhh-hhh, no, no, not my girls!" he screams, everyone feeling his pain.

My chest feels like it's cracking open.

I expected this to be like a movie, you know how you think the hero won't make it in time but something happens and then they do and they save the day, but this isn't a fucking movie and that is a real heart.

Chapter Twenty-Five

Amelia

I managed to escape through the bedroom window. I didn't make it more than a few hundred meters before I was captured. I tried to fight the bastard off but the threat of him punching my stomach had me stopping my struggle and allowing him to lead me toward the front of the house where Colson and all his men stood facing off against my mom.

She looks like a badass with both her guns raised and aimed at the fucker that tried to break me, but the instant she spots me she falters. Fear enters her eyes when Colson steps toward me and runs the back of his knuckles against my cheek. I shudder in revulsion.

"Drop the guns and I promise I won't hurt your daughter," the bastard says as he comes to stand in front of me, giving my mom his back like he knows she won't refuse or shoot him.

"Touch her and I'll kill you," Mom promises.

Colson's eyes darken as he smiles at me. I press back into

the fucker holding me, trying to get as far from him as I can. "Do that and my men have orders to cut that baby out of the bitch and slit its throat in front of your husband." My eyes widen and my jaw unhinges.

"You are fucking sick!" I seethe.

He ignores me as he speaks to my mother. "Now, Allison, or she dies." As if to prove his point he pulls a gun from the holster under his jacket and presses it against my forehead. I refuse to cower under the pressure of his gaze or the barrel pressed against my head.

"Pull the trigger and do us both a favor," I sneer.

"Amelia!" Mom shouts but I ignore her as I push on.

"You don't scare me. You are nothing but a sad little boy who is trying to play dress up and act like he is someone impor-tant, but let's be real. You don't hate my father because he killed your family, you hate Daddy because you know you will never be half the man he is." The moment a shadow falls over his face I brace for him to strike me, but what I don't expect is for him to punch me in the stomach, endangering the child he created with me. I fall to my knees, gasping and clutching my stomach.

"Leave her alone!" Mom screams. I flick my gaze to her to see her toss her guns away. I try to speak through the pain to tell her to run but pain is exploding in my stomach. I cry out when a wave of intense pain tears through me.

"Take her and throw her ass in the back of the van." Two men lift me by my arms at Colson's orders. I cry out when they haul me to my feet.

"Don't fucking hurt her!" Mom screams. I can't even push through the pain to look back at her. I have never experienced pain like this before. Don't get me wrong, I have fought in the ring and have been trained from a young age to fight so I have taken some hits, but this feels different—I can tell something is wrong. The bastards toss me into the van. I manage to twist at the last second to land on my side. I curl into a ball and grit my teeth as another wave of pain rushes through me.

Through the haze of pain, I feel something prick the side of my neck. I peer out of the corner of my eye to a man smirking down at me. I flinch when he yanks the needle out of the side of my neck.

"Sleep tight, bitch, we'll play with you after we kill your mommy." I open my mouth to curse him out but no words come. I begin to feel sluggish and that's when I realize the fucker just gave me a sedative.

Please don't let my mom or baby die, Dad, is the last thought I have before everything goes black and I pray everyone got my messages.

Chapter Twenty-Six

Cronos

Mayhem.
Madness.
Pain.

Those are the emotions running rampant through everyone who surrounds King Murdoch—a man as powerful as him has been brought to his knees by a punk street kid. Colson Salvatoro managed to stay in the blind spots of all the Murdoch's surveillance. I thought he was some chumped up fool trying to play at the big boys table by owning his own tech company and security team.

"We are right here with you, uncle," Chaos says firmly as he steps forward with Royal and Sin at his side. King pushes to his feet, waivers slightly but Gage and Bishop are right there, gripping each of his arms to hold him steady. The grief coursing through his veins is clear in his eyes. He pulls free of his brother's hold and stumbles forward, his legs give out at the edge of the porch where the blood is thickest.

"No one touched it, Grandpa wouldn't let anyone near it," London says quietly from beside me. Artemis makes his way over to us and claps me on the shoulder as we all wait with bated breath to see what King does. As if he is in slow motion he reaches out but leaves his arm suspended mid-air, unable to touch the lone heart. His chin drops to his chest as he begins to shake with silent tears. Unable to stomach the sight any longer, I turn away, only for my eyes to widen at the sight of Beth standing there in the darkness looking pale and like she has seen a ghost. Pulling away from my brother and London, I rush to her side. Gripping her arms, I give her a gentle shake to snap her out of the trance-like state she is in.

"Beth, what's wrong?" She looks up at me but her eyes aren't focused.

"He told me to take her." I furrow my brow and peer over my shoulder to see I have the attention of everyone. I shift subtly to block Beth from their sights.

"Beth, where is Bill? Why are you out here alone?" She blinks a couple of times and this time when she looks at me, it's as if she is seeing me clearly for the first time.

"You need to come with me." She grips my hand and turns to leave, but I pull back forcing her to a stop.

"Beth, I can't leave, I have to—"

"You will come with me!" she screams. Tears gather in her eyes and this sinking feeling starts to take root inside me. I have never seen Beth so out of sorts like she is now. "I lost him for her, so you will come with me!" I swallow audibly and nod. I shoot a look over my shoulder to London who nods and signals they will follow us. Beth climbs inside her beat-up car, I have to practically fold in half to fit in beside her. To say the silence stretches between us is an understatement. I have no idea what to say or even do. I'm too fucked up in the head right now to even form a coherent thought let alone think about what my next steps are. Allison is dead. Amelia is... I slam my eyes closed and pray to any fucking cunt that is listening that her and Kingsley are okay. When Beth bypasses the street to her house, I grow more confused but when she takes the next right I start to panic.

"Beth, why are we going to the morgue?" She remains silent and pulls into the carpark. This place brought me peace for a year of my life and every morning I woke, I found myself eager to get to work and help the dead. Unlike the living, they never pester, annoy or use you. The dead expect nothing and that is a trait I resonate with. She parks the car and climbs out, leaving me no choice but to follow. When she reaches for the front door, I dart in front and block her path. "What the fuck is going on?" I snap. The others begin to pile out of their own cars, I didn't expect for them *all* to follow after me, maybe just London and Artemis.

"He told me to save her, I did and now he's gone." I reel back.

"Where is Bill?" I speak to her as if she is a child. Her bottom lip trembles as she pats me on the chest.

"Come now, boy, you will see." She pushes me aside and I allow it. I follow her inside, feeling hopeful but wary, she said she saved her but who is the her? As we near the back of the building my breaths become shallow. I pause a couple of steps back from the swinging doors, just needing a minute to gather myself because the second I step through the doors and see what lays beyond it makes it real, I won't be able to fool myself into thinking my girl is safe and just hiding somewhere. I feel a hand slip into my own. I look to my left to see my best friend staring directly at me.

"I have your back, side and front if need be. I got you always." London's words have me swallowing. I force myself to move and push through the doors the instant I do I see a sight I wish I never did.

I've only ever felt loss like this once before and I barely recovered the first time, I don't know how I will overcome this one.

They were innocent!

I stumble further into the room, until I am gripping the edge of the metal slab, staring down into those eyes that held so much love and saw through the bullshit walls I had built to surround myself to keep everyone out so they couldn't hurt me. I don't let people get close because of this very fucking reason. London was different, she forced her way into my life and didn't give me a choice but to love her. But, this right here, this was a choice. I allowed myself to care and now here I am staring into soulless eyes that will haunt me each time I close my eyes.

"What the fuck is this?" I close my eyes and ignore Rook's question as I tighten my grip on the slab.

"Cronos?" I hear my brother calling out to me but I can't move, I'm frozen in place.

This is my fault!

"Someone explain to me what the fuck is happening!" King screams. It's the sound of the pain in his voice that has me strengthening my resolve and locking down the tears that threaten to spill. I take a deep breath and slowly lift my gaze to Beth's who stands on the opposite side of the slab with tears trailing down her cheeks. I reach out without thought and cup her cheek in my hand, her bottom lip quivers at my touch.

"He saved her, didn't he?" She pushes her lips to the side to fight back a sob as she nods. "My girl called him, didn't she?" I ask gently.

"Amelia?" King breathes out as he comes to stand beside me.

"He said to save her, *no matter what Bethy, you don't come back for me.* That's what he said to me, I couldn't drive away," she chokes out. I nod, understanding why she couldn't leave him behind. "There were only three of them there, he shot two but the third, he got him and my Bill went down. I wanted to go to him but I... I couldn't... I—"

"You did the right thing, Bethy," I say. King reaches out and lifts the white sheet from Bill and pulls it back to reveal his chest that has a gaping hole right where his heart should be.

"It wasn't Allison's heart," King breathes out but Beth ignores him.

"I watched him carve his chest open and toss his heart on the porch—"

King cuts Beth off before she can finish. "Where is my wife?"

I glare at King. "She's in shock, shut the hell up or she will shut down and we'll never find her." King's eyes blaze with anger, but he does as I say and clamps his mouth closed.

"I just sat in the car hidden by the trees and watched them take the life of the only man I have ever loved." The raw unfiltered pain in her eyes is what caves my chest in. I push King aside as I round the slab and pull Beth into me. Her cries bounce off the walls and force each of us to feel her loss—her and Bill were high school sweethearts.

"The old man would never have wanted it any other way," I say trying to ease some of her pain.

"I waited. When they left, I drove the hearse up and placed

him in the back. I couldn't leave him, boy! I couldn't leave him there!" she screams. I pull back and cup her face between my hands, bending at the knees, making us eye level, so she can see the truth in my eyes.

"You did the right thing, Bethany. I would never have left... Amelia either." Hearing my girl's name seems to be what brings her out of her grief for a moment.

"There was a woman—"

King cuts in again. "Where is she?" he begs.

"She was strung up, we thought she was your angel." I force myself to remain calm and not react. "She's in a bad way." I see King open his mouth out of the corner of my eye, and before he can utter a single word. I snap my head toward him.

"Push her again and I'll throw your fucking ass out of here!" I snarl. Bishop, Gage, Vincent and the twins step forward, ready to defend their brother if need be. Royal, Kacey, Sin, Chaos, London and my brother subtly move toward my side as if they are preparing to take on their own family for me.

"I cut her down," Beth whispers. Hope surges inside King's eyes.

"Please, I am begging you, please tell me where she is?" Beth keeps her gaze on me as she answers King.

"Chiller," she rasps out. I smile and place a kiss to her forehead, then turn to London ignoring the curious stares of the other's.

"Comfort her." London looks horrified and about to argue but I push on. "She's important to me, Lon." My words have her tampering down her disgust at having to console someone but to my surprise, Artemis cuts in front of London and comes to stand before me.

"Go, I got her, brother." I pat him on the shoulder before I round the table. I shoulder past the Murdochs and grab the scruff of King's shirt, pulling him along with me. He protests and tries to break free. I whirl around on him and get right in his face.

"Quit your bitching if you want to see your fucking wife!" My words have his face paling and his eyes widening. I don't have the capacity to deal with his emotional damage right now. I continue onto the chiller, then gripping the handle I yank the door open. I have a second to lay eyes on Allison before King shoulders me out of the way and rushes inside.

"Ally!" he cries out as he reaches her side. In an instant, the chiller is filled with his brothers and Vincent. None of them look like they know what they are doing, so I push forward and hold two fingers against her throat feeling for her pulse. King holds his breath as he waits for me to announce if the love of his life still lives.

I meet his gaze and nod. He deflates and drops down beside her battered body, her face busted and her pulse weak. I peel the red blanket back from her body and hiss at the sight of two knives sticking out of her stomach.

"Fuck, Luka get me a chopper!" Bishop roars as he moves forward to catch King before he falls to his knees. Rook and Knight shift to try and grab the gurney but I pin them with a look that has them halting. Vin and Gage move in closer.

"Before she can be moved we need to stabilize the knives."

"You think you're a fucking doctor now?" Rook bites out.

"I'm an undertaker, dumbass, I'm also about to marry a doctor, one who may have taught me some fucking things so you can either listen or kill your sister-in-law, choose?" The twins' faces slacken, Gage and Vin both cut them out as they come to stand opposite me. Bishop enlists the help of Knight to drag King out of the room, he's fighting with everything he has to get back to his wife's side.

"You do whatever you have to, just save her," Gage implores me.

"We save her and then all of you are going to help me find my girls," I grit out.

"You have our word, our services are at your disposal, Cronos," Vincent answers without missing a beat.

Chapter Twenty-Seven

Cronos

I managed to wrap the knives to keep them stable with the help of Gage and Vincent. The three of us are wheeling her out front where the medivac chopper is waiting, clearly the Murdochs have forgone the no hospital rule. Before we can exit the building, King darts in front of us, forcing the three of us to a stop. He rounds the side of the gurney and gently lifts his wife's hand and places a kiss to the back of it.

"This isn't how our story ends, Ally," he whispers. "I'm gonna find our daughter and bring her home, then we're all going to disappear for a while. I'm so sorry I couldn't keep my promise, baby. I failed you and I just hope you can forgive me because I can't live in a world where you don't exist, Allison." I feel like I'm intruding on a private moment, I can see King is torn between going with his wife and helping track down his daughter.

"Go with her, we'll go after Amelia," Gage offers but King shakes his head, keeping his gaze on his wife.

"If she finds out I didn't go after our baby girl, she'll murder me herself," he answers, then places a kiss on her lips. "I got it, kid," he mutters as he pushes me back and takes my spot, the three of them wheeling her out front to meet the chopper.

"Nos?" I spin around to see London standing there looking uncomfortable.

"What's wrong?"

"She keeps crying and I don't know what to do. Artemis is trying to console her but she knows he isn't you."

"Let me guess, she said he was too sweet to be me." London rolls her lips over her teeth and nods, trying to hide her smile. I sigh and make my way back to Beth. She still remains at Bill's side, I need to deal with this first before I can help the others. I ignore Beth's cries as I close Bill's eyes for the last time. I've done this hundreds of times but this time, I actually feel something other than peace and numbness. "Beth, I need to move him to the chiller," I say out of courtesy. I don't wait for an answer as I retrieve the other gurney, ignoring all the others and focusing on my task.

As I reach for Bill to move him, Chaos, Kacey and Royal all come forward and help without saying a word, I know everyone can tell that Bill and Beth are important to me. I fix the white sheet and then pull the red throw blanket over him, stopping just beneath his chin.

"I'm going to live with the guilt of this for the rest of my life, old man. Thank you for saving my angel's mother, you are a true hero," I say quietly. "I don't know how I'll find my fight anymore, I'm tired and just want to live in peace but this life doesn't offer that." Bitterness coats my words but I feel no remorse for the others hearing them, they all know that much like Meelz I didn't want or choose this life, I was forced into it and have been trapped since Aida died.

"You don't have to live with shit! You just need to find a reason to fight, find something that gives you the strength you need for change and I promise you, boy, it will be the most frightening and exhilarating feeling in this world." I stare at Beth in utter shock. Her husband said something similar to me once, her voice is firm and unyielding. "That man there," she says, pointing to Bill. "He fought for me. When my daddy said he was no good, he fought. He proved everybody wrong and showed them he was good enough. The stupid fool didn't realize the only person he had to prove anything to was me. That girl will be your strength. That baby will be the second chance you both need. Don't you dare let my Bill's sacrifice be for nothing, you go on now and get that angel back."

Determination flows through me at her words. I give her a subtle nod as the doors swing open. I look back to see King, Gage, Vincent and Taylan enter with Destiny at his side. The Re Della Strada has arrived. I grip the gurney, preparing to place Bill in the chiller until I return, but King grips my arm, drawing my attention to him. He releases me as he stands by Bill's side and pulls a dagger with a solid gold handle from his side and lays it atop Bill's chest.

"Your bravery today is unmatched, you saved the life of a woman you didn't even know and in doing so, you have earned the respect of my family which in turn extends to your wife. I cannot offer you anything in the afterlife but what I can give you is peace of mind. That blade has served me well over the years and it will remain with you in the next life so you may protect yourself until your beloved finds you again. Your wife will have the protection of the Murdoch mafia, *Memento*

Mori, Re Della Strada and The Godfathers Of The Night. Rest easy, Wild Bill." My mouth pops open in awe at King's words.

"To Wild Bill!" Vincent calls out. Every person in the room mimics his call, and a lump forms in my throat when everyone forms a line on either side, drawing a path to the chiller for Bill —showing their respect for the man that saved one of their own, but what they don't know is this man also saved me. Artemis leads Beth over to me. I shift so she is at her husband's head. Art and I grip the sides of the gurney and slowly walk toward the chiller. Each person places a closed fist over their hearts and bow their heads. To see Royal and Bishop as the Don's of each of their families bow their heads in respect for my... friend has me fighting back my own tears.

I help Beth secure Bill in the chiller, then wrap my arm around her shoulders, pulling her into my side and placing a kiss on the top of her head.

"You have been thanked for saving Allison but I have something else to thank you for." Artemis cuts a glance to me as he continues to speak. "Thank you for bringing my brother back to me, Bill." I stare at my twin in surprise. "He was lost for a long time but now he is found, thanks to you." My phone's shrill ring pierces the air, shattering the moment. I release Beth and pull it from my back pocket, nearly dropping the fucking thing when I see Amelia's name. I answer and bring it to my ear as I exit the chiller, garnering everyone's attention.

"Angel?" King is in front of me in the next second, mouthing to put it on speaker. I do as he says and wait to hear her voice.

"Cronos?" My shoulders deflate at the sound of her voice, King shudders as if relieved to know his daughter is alive. She sounds a bit dazed but I try not to focus on that.

"I'm here, baby, are you hurt? Where are you—"

"I can't do this with you anymore." My brows slant as I stare down at the phone confused.

"What?" I rasp out.

"I want a real family and I can't have that with you. Colson showing up and... proving to me that he does love me showed me I need to be with my real family." The slight hitch in her voice is a clear sign she is being coerced into saying this shit. so I play along.

"Is that so?" I growl. I shut down all my emotions and force those fuckers to stay buried so I can keep a clear head.

"Y-yeah. Don't try to find me, go chase my niece and see if she will finally notice you, maybe take her to the place where I first met the Devil and see if she falls for you there."

King shifts as if to grab the phone, I strike out with my free hand and grip his throat. The others rush in but don't make a sound. I shake my head at him urging him to keep his fucking mouth shut so I can figure this shit out. I release him as I speak, not caring about the fact he pulls his gun and presses it against my chest. Artemis pulls his own gun and aims it at King forcing the others to all draw their guns, I roll my eyes.

Idiots!

"Angel, I warned you not to fuck with me and what I would do if you ever tried to leave, didn't I?"

"Your threats mean nothing, Aida isn't your baby!" I suck in a sharp inhale but not for the reason everyone else thinks.

"Okay, baby, you want to run off into the sunset and live in that big old castle with that little bitch who is living on borrowed time?"

"Aida and I will be happy with Colson, tell my family not to try to track me down." I hear her hiss and worry gnaws at me but I remain calm, not wanting to alert the fucker who I know is beside her listening to her every word. "Go after London, take her from your brother and maybe then you will stop being a weak ass bitch." The call ends, and chaos erupts.

"You son of a bitch!" King roars as he punches me across the jaw.

"Touch my brother again and you'll be next in the chiller!" Artemis roars as he cuts in front of me and aims his gun at King.

"Think carefully, dipshit, you pull that trigger and I can't save you," Royal warns. London ignores everyone as she stands in front of Artemis, putting herself in the line of fire of everyone.

"Drop your fucking guns!" Bishop yells. They may all be pissed but no one will risk hurting the princess or inciting Bishop and Royal's wrath if they hurt her.

"Art, I swear I never did anything with Nos, you know I love your brother but—" Before London can continue I cut in.

"She used your name to tell me where she is going." All their gazes swing to me.

"What?" Chaos snaps.

"You better start explaining shit now, asshole!" King bellows.

"Get a plane ready to fly to Switzerland."

"Why, Cronos?" Knight asks.

"Amelia is going to Switzerland," I answer.

"How do you know that for sure?" Sin presses.

"The first place she met the Devil was at Blackwood Academy. She knows I told London about Aida there, that's why she called Kingsley Aida, so I would piece it together," I announce.

"Who the fuck is Kingsley?" Rook asks no one in particular.

"My daughter," I say with conviction, daring any of them to argue with me.

"She's going to Blackwood?" King mutters.

"No, she's going to Switzerland. It was the only way she knew I would get what she was putting down. He's taking her to Switzerland because he thinks that's still neutral turf, but he doesn't know that you all control the majority of the table." I turn to Taylan next, knowing he is the only one here with the power to help me. "I need you to garner Knox and Waverly's consent to shed blood there." Taylan sighs but nods and leaves the room to place a call. I look to Royal next. "You need to get Ian's permission to start a war there, and just so we are all clear, I don't a give a fuck if those three agree or not. I will go there and shed as much fucking blood as it takes to get *my* girls back." I don't stick around to hear what they say, I grab Beth's hand and lead her out of the room so I can take her home before I go after what is mine.

Chapter Twenty-Eight

Amelia

The pains are frequent and closer together, sweat is beading down my brow. I've nearly bitten through my bottom lip to keep from crying out, I refuse to allow this bastard to know I am in pain and give him the satisfaction of knowing he will be here when I give birth to the child he doesn't want.

When Colson told me I had to call Cronos and break his heart I tried to refuse but a swift backhand and the threat of him kicking my stomach had me complying. I don't know if Cronos understood what I was saying. I am praying with every ounce of my being that he got it, I feel horrible for using Aida's name against him but I didn't have a choice. He sounded so cold and detached on the phone.

When another wave of pain robs me of breath I arch forward in my seat and slam my eyes closed as I tighten my arms around myself.

Please, Kingsley, not now, sweet girl!

The only bonus to the constant pain is that it keeps my mind off my mom. I haven't been able to stop the tears from flowing since I woke up on the plane. The sight of her standing there looking utterly broken and torn in half will haunt me, when I asked Colson where she was he smiled wide, placed a kiss on my lips and said *dead*. I screamed and wailed until he punched me in the face, dazing me, my cheek still aches from the hit but it's nothing compared to the pain in my heart and the contractions.

I can't have this baby without my mom!

A sob claws its way out of me and I bite down on my bruised lip to remain silent but Colson hears and he looks pissed.

"You want something to fucking cry about?" he snarls from his seat across from me. I shake my head.

"No."

"No, what?" he screams at me, I flinch in fear.

"No, sir," I say shakily.

He smiles triumphantly. "You're a fucking pathetic waste of space. Soon as that kid is out of you, you'll join your mother." My eyes widen as fear grips me in its clutches.

"Colson, please, don't take her from me—" Before another word can be spoken, he leans forward and slaps me. I cry out, which only angers him further. He hates when I make a sound as he beats me. My head is yanked back by his grip on my hair, I look up in time to see his fist coming. I can't even protect myself, on the second punch, I black out.

I'm woken by a sharp pain in my lower back. I groan as I try to open my eyes but only one does, the other is swollen shut. I whimper but quickly quiet myself so no one hears. I fight through the pain and push myself into a sitting position. I gasp as I look around to see I'm in a bed in a room with four white walls. The beeping coming from my left draws my attention and my eyes widen at the sight of a heart monitor. An IV is set up and I see the cannula in my hand, I'm even wearing a yellow hospital type gown.

My ankles are chained to the end of the makeshift hospital bed. This cannot be happening! He knows Kingsley is coming and there is nothing I can do to stop it! It's too early, I'm only thirty-four weeks, without the proper facilities to help a premature baby she won't make it. A lump forms in my throat as more tears gather in my eyes, I can't lose my mom and daughter!

The door opens and a nurse enters with a tray, she looks at me without an ounce of remorse. I inhale through my nose and compose myself as I draw on every ounce of training I have received throughout my life.

Pain won't last.

Take the beating and never let them see they are under your skin.

Don't let them in your head.

Your body can be broken and used but your mind is your safe haven.

I remain still as the nurse wheels a table over and places the tray on it. When she reaches for my wrist, I jerk away, Her lips thin and eyes narrow in warning but I scowl back. Something about her seems familiar but I'm putting that down to the amount of pain I'm in. I have been weak for too fucking long and I will not allow these cowardly bastards to take away my free will. I will fight until my dying breath to save my daughter from these monsters like my mom saved me all those years ago!

"If you don't allow me to check your pulse, I will be forced to bring in some men to restrain you while I do it, then check to see how far you have dilated while they watch." I grind my teeth in anger. I relent to her demand and give her my wrist. She checks my pulse and then notes it down on the chart I didn't see earlier on the table. "Easiest way to do this is heels together and then drop your knees open."

"You took a vow, you promised to help people and here you are trying to help monsters—"

"Coming from the woman who ran off and stole a man's child and refused to allow him to be a part of his child's life?" I balk at her.

"What?" I squawk out.

She scoffs. "Open now or I will call for help." My anger peaks. Colson, the lying son of a bitch, has fed this woman lies and she ate them up like a fucking addict. I watch her glove up then do as she instructed. She perches on the edge of the bed and lifts my gown right as another wave of pain tears through me. "Breathe through it, don't fight it."

"It's too soon," I grit out through clenched teeth.

"She is coming whether you are ready or not." I whimper when she pushes her fingers inside me, breathing through my nose to keep from crying out. The whole ordeal lasts about a minute before she is crossing the room and dumping her gloves in a small trash can. "You're about seven centimeters dilated." My eyes widen.

"How long was I out?" I breathe out, that's too far along for me to have been out for a few minutes. She doesn't get the chance to answer, because the door opens and Colson walks in.

I close my legs and push my gown down to cover myself as best as I can.

"I'll be back to check on her in an hour," the nurse says as she leaves me alone with the monster. Colson looks clean and showered, he even looks rested, the fucking bastard. When he looks at me, I feel nothing but deep hatred for him. I can't believe I fooled myself into thinking I could actually love a piece of shit like him. Colson remains silent as he crosses to the far side of the room and gazes out the window, keeping his back to me.

"As a courtesy to you, I will make your death swift and painless."

I snort, he whirls around and looks at me with utter contempt. "A courtesy to me would be you blowing your own fucking brains out!"

"You like pushing me. Don't you?"

I stare at him for a second trying to understand why he would want to hurt me. My dad did his father a mercy and yet here he is using me and trying to hurt my father by killing his daughter and taking his grandchild.

"You know my family won't stop," I grit out through clenched teeth as another wave of pain slams into me. Colson smiles at the sight of me in pain, he loves seeing me writhe in agony. "Kill me, do whatever the fuck you want but you will never be able to stop running. They will chase you to the ends of the earth and never give up until they find you and take back what is theirs!"

"That fucking cunt of a kid is mine!" I recoil on instinct. I guess my mind thinks we are past the trauma but my body is still reacting to muscle memory.

"How can you call her that?" I ask quietly, utterly stumped by the fact he could possibly despise his own flesh and blood.

"Because you're it's mother, that's why I hate it."

"You are a fucking disgrace and I can't wait for the day my father and Cronos find you. They will drag your death out for years so you can feel every ounce of fucking pain you have caused me and my family!" I scream. "I want them to cut out your fucking tongue and pull your eyes from their sockets with a fucking spoon and make you eat them before they cut off your ears so you can go to the afterlife deaf, dumb and blind!" I slump forward and drag in lungfuls of air, just in time for another contraction to hit, this one more painful than the last, forcing me to arch my back and breathe in through my nose.

I whimper when Colson rips my head back by the hair, the contraction is still pulsing through me, the pain making me delirious. "For that comment, you dumb bitch, I'll make your death slow and painful. Hurry the fuck up and have that kid so I can get rid of you." He releases me with a hard shove.

Before he can leave the room I call out. "I can't wait for the Devil to arrive and drag your worthless ass back to fucking hell!"

"Fucking you was hell, so going anywhere else would be better than touching that wretched cunt again." Indignation burns inside me as he slams the door closed behind him.

Chapter Twenty-Nine

Cronos

It's early hours in the morning by the time we land in Switzerland. Bishop got the green light from Ian, Knox and Waverly both agreed that the Da Luca Family and the Re Della Strada would stand behind us on our hunt to bring Amelia home. King had Allison flown back to New York where his sister and sister-in-laws will remain at her side until we all return. Bishop has the whole floor Allison is on blocked off and thirty men standing guard with Luka leading them—they have orders to shoot to kill.

"Nos?" I shake my head and turn to look at London, who is sitting between me and Artemis while King drives and Vincent rides shotgun. King says he won't leave my side in case Meelz calls again. I know it's fucking with his head that she called me and not him. Truth is, I know she only called me because that fucker wanted to hurt her more than he already had by forcing her to end things with me.

"Yeah?" I croak out.

"Whatever it takes, no matter how long, I swear Artemis and I will be by your side. We'll destroy that fucker and tear him apart limb by fucking limb and feed him to our dogs."

"Baby, we don't have dogs," Art interjects. London just shrugs.

"We'll get some dogs then, whatever. My point is, we'll kill every single one of them and make them pay for hurting your feelings."

"Lon, you know that fucker hurt Amelia, right?" I ask. London doesn't do emotions so this is a subject we need to tend to gently or she will clam up and go on a rampage just to prove she has bigger balls than any man.

"Yeah, well, she hurt you too." I sigh and scrub a hand down my face.

"You know she's your aunt, right?" King growls.

"Not by choice." London mutters.

Before anyone can butt in I push on. "London, I love you. You are my best fucking friend but you have to let this shit with Amelia go." Her eyes narrow. "She is important to me and as much as you love me, you love Artemis more, right?"

I can see she doesn't want to answer but when my twin clears his throat she has no choice. "Yes," she grits out.

"Well, I feel the same way about her, Lon. Her and Kingsley are the most important people in this world to me and I will do whatever it takes to get them both back. I need you to let go of the past and accept what this is because she is my future, and I want you to be in my life, but not if you keep hating her. I won't raise Kingsley like that."

Her gaze waivers slightly, which is the only sign I get that my words have hurt her and I feel like a dick for doing it, but she has to know that Amelia is it for me and I won't allow anyone to shame her or make her feel anything less than the fucking queen she is.

"Fine. But if she ever hurts you again, kid or not, I am going to beat her ass." Both King and Vin snort.

"You do know she has years of training on you and put my daughter on her ass, right?" Vincent says. London scrunches her face and shoots him a sour look. Artemis being the pussy pleaser he is, wraps his arm around her shoulders and pulls her in close.

"I think you could take her, babe," my twin says.

"And I think you could take a bullet from Royal but I guess we both know the outcome of either of those situations for sure," King adds, earning a cough laugh from Vin while I mask my own laughter. My brother may be marrying the heiress, but he still cops shit from her family daily. It doesn't matter if he is the Don of the Greeks, or the reason London is alive today and stepping up to take over when the time comes. He will always take shit from them because that is just the relationship he has with his future in-laws and I guess... they will also be mine someday too.

It's strange to think like that. I never once thought I would put a ring on anyone's finger after Aida and yet with Meelz, it feels like the right next step to take. She isn't like most girls and I know the age gap between us puts me years behind her, but it has never bothered me. At the start it was her that tried to push me away and told me to find someone my own age, but what she didn't realize was age is nothing but a number. I plan to spend the rest of my years showing her how much I love her and will never allow her to see herself as anything less than perfect.

It's been too long since her and I spent a night tangled up in the sheets and fucking like wild animals. She may tease me about my age but she fucking loves how my stamina rivals anyone else she has been with before.

My thoughts are halted when we pull up in front of one of Costa's old houses. We chose to stay here rather than buying a new house and drawing suspicion, in case Colson is monitoring the market. Artemis and I haven't been back here since we left Switzerland, this home holds no good memories for us or any memories really. I spent as little time here as I possibly could. That fucker was never my father, he just happened to be the human whose nut sack I came from.

Artemis lets us out and the others fan out to make sure the house is clear, not trusting my brother or his men who already went ahead and scouted the place out. I smile to myself, knowing Royal is only doing this to fuck with him but I can tell it pisses my twin off to constantly be under minded.

I head into the kitchen to wait for the others, I'm itching to get the fuck out there and start tracking. I know a lot of this mission is resting on Chaos, Sin and Vincent. They are the best trackers the Murdochs have and Vincent's skills are unmatched by anyone except his own daughter, who managed to evade him and earn the name Hellhound. No one around the world knows Vincent Murelo's true identity, except for those in his close circle. To the rest of the world he is known as the Blood-hound, he is the man you send in when everyone and everything else fails to take down your enemy.

"Where can I set up?" Vin asks.

I wave my arms around the room. "Wherever the fuck you want, this place is at your disposal." He nods and waves over two guards, who carry bags and suitcases, then lines them up on the giant size dining table. He pulls out wires, cords, screens and so much other shit I lose track. Sin and Chaos come to lend a hand while the rest of us stand around the room—it's fucking infuriating having to wait for someone else. I hate not having control and being the one knowing everything.

"Okay, I'll narrow down the feeds for the airport and any private airstrip, you two take the northern and southern routes and I'll take the eastern and—"

"Give me the north." My brows raise in surprise at London's declaration, she lifts her head and shoots me a wink. Vincent hands her the other laptop as she takes a seat between Chaos and Sin. I watch them with rapt attention as they push so many keys on the keyboard I lose track.

"Do you mean what you said?" I look to the side and raise a brow at Royal.

"About?"

"London told me what you said about Meelz in the car." Bishop comes to stand behind his son, I get the feeling he is only here to try and intimidate me, so I nip that shit right in the ass before they can continue.

"I meant every word. You know I love London, always have and always will, I'll protect her with my life."

"I was talking about what you said about Amelia."

"My relationship with her is none of your concern, Royal."

"It may not be his but it is mine. We all helped raise that girl. She will always be special to my family as the first child. You break her heart and I'll break your fucking neck," Bishop threatens.

"I got a positive ID!" Sin calls out, ending our conversation as we all rush to her and fight to peer over her shoulder.

"Unless all you dumbasses want her to shoot you, back the fuck up and give her some space!" Kacey shouts. Given how well everyone knows Chanel and how short her fuse is, we all take a step back and allow Kacey to move forward and stand behind her. "Do you, Sin."

A hush falls over the room as we all listen to Sin and Kacey calling out details to London, Vincent and Chaos. My brother stands behind London and speaks quietly so none of us can hear what he says.

"If you are anything like your brother, you won't have a problem with my family," Royal says low enough so only I can hear.

"If that was the case, why do you keep putting him through the shit you do?" I volley back.

"Because Artemis constantly needs to be tested, unlike you when he marries, he inherits two of the most powerful families in the world as well as his own. Your brother will be the most untouchable man on the earth when he takes over for me and my dad. That power can cause some men to alter who they truly are. I won't allow my daughter to be married to a man who succumbs to power. He needs to show us all that he can keep a level head and block out all the noise to rule fairly."

"Has he proven that to you?"

Royal lulls his head to the side and pins me with a dry stare. "If I didn't think he could handle it, I wouldn't allow the little shit to be marrying my daughter, no matter what my wife said."

"Artemis isn't like me, he will always rise to the challenge and prove anyone wrong who doubts him. Make no mistake, I love my brother but I also love your daughter. If I thought for a second that he was using her, I would end their relationship myself."

"Why didn't you take her from him when you had the opportunity?" he queries. My upper lip twitches. I know this is his way of testing me, to see if I am good enough to be with his cousin so I decide to surprise him by answering.

"Because she was never mine to take. I allowed the demons

of my past to cloud my judgment for a short time, that is why I would never be able to lead. Unlike me, my brother is not ruled by his emotions, his only blind spot is London. Nothing else in this world matters to him. He would walk away from all the power in the world to be with her."

"And you wouldn't do that for Amelia?"

"No. Having all that power would mean I could protect her and keep her safe, but it would weigh too heavily on me and given both mine and Amelia's pasts, it would crush us both and I can't allow that to happen."

"If your brother ever falls, what becomes of the Greeks then?"

Ah, there it is, the real question he wants an answer to.

"He would be married to London by then. She can have it all, so long as myself and the triplets are never called back to serve. I would walk away and allow her to have our birthright. You and I both know she was born to lead, she has every characteristic of a true leader. You don't really care about what is happening between me and Amelia." A sly smirk tugs at the corner of his mouth. "You just wanted me to validate what you already suspect about my brother and confirm your faith in your daughter."

"We got a location, let's roll out!" Chanel shouts, every single one of us rush into the entryway to arm ourselves.

I'm coming for you, angel.

Chapter Thirty

Amelia

"Her contractions are a minute apart, she's nine and a half centimeters dilated now, she's about to have this baby," the nurse from earlier announces to Colson, who is standing at my side. Another two nurses have been brought on to assist with the birth. They wheeled in an incubator and everything, which has eased some of my worries about Kingsley's safety. He may hate me, but he needs my daughter alive to torture my dad, so I know he will do everything in his power to save her.

"What do you need?" Colson snaps.

"I need to prep and get her ready for the birth. The moment the baby is out we will need to move fast. These cuffs on her ankles need to be removed for better access. We need to get her on a ventilator because her lungs will most likely not be fully formed, which is the biggest worry here about her going into labor."

"I don't give a fuck, get the fucking kid out now!" Colson roars. The nurse reels back, but before she can respond, the door opens and one of his men sticks their head inside. "What is it?"

"We have a situation," the man replies. Colson scrubs a hand down his face, clearly annoyed at how long this process is taking. I'm exhausted, sore and clinging to my sanity by a string.

"Get that fucking baby out, now!" he snarls before tossing some keys to Kim and storming out of the room, slamming the door closed behind him. The other two nurses are busy setting everything up on the other side of the room, leaving me to tend with the nurse from earlier. She leans in close as if she is checking my pulse.

"You weren't keeping the baby from him out of spite, were you?" I shake my head, my bottom lip begins to tremble when regret swims in her deep brown eyes. "You weren't beaten by your drug addict boyfriend either, huh?" Again, I shake my head. A whoosh of air escapes her as she rounds the bed and keeps her back to the other nurses who speak quietly between themselves, effectively ignoring us. "I will do whatever I can to save your baby and help you." I'm unable to speak as another contraction rips through me. I cry out in agony. "Breathe through it, it's nearly over. I'll help you through this, Amelia. My name is Kim." I nod my head, unable to utter a single word through the pain. As a doctor, we are taught that all women can endure childbirth but until you have experienced it yourself, you will never know what the definition of bringing life into this world means.

"We're all set for the arrival," one of the other two says to Kim.

"Once this contraction has passed I am going to check you,

is that okay?" she asks the last part quietly. I take a deep breath after the pain subsides.

"Yes." My voice is hoarse to my own ears.

"Crap, we need to head out to the rig, we're missing the tubes." Kim turns to the other two women.

"Hurry," she snaps in an angry tone. The second the nurses are out of the door and we are alone, she faces me again. "Is there someone I can call?" Tears fill my eyes, I nod as she hands me the phone. I manage to enter Nos's number before the next contraction hits. Kim takes the phone from me and makes the call. She is risking a lot to help me and that shows she is a good person, I am grateful to have her on my side.

"Who the fuck is this?" I hear Cronos growl. Kim doesn't place the call on speaker but I can hear his voice just fine from how close she is to me.

"My name is Kim and I am with Amelia," she says quietly.

"If you fucking hurt her, I will slaughter everyone you love—"

"I'm the one helping her deliver her baby, we don't have long before they come back."

"She's in labor?" I hear the hurt and worry in his tone. I know he wanted to be here for our baby's arrival.

"She's nearly ready to deliver. Colson plans to take the baby and kill her. I don't know who you are but you need to hurry, trace my number if you can. We must go—"

"Wait!"

"What is it?" Kim asks.

"Can you just... just tell her I love her and I'm coming for them both. I won't let history repeat itself." A lone tear treks down my cheek. He understood my message and is coming for me! Kim ends the call and places her phone in her pocket just

in time as the other two nurses return with Colson who looks...
stressed.

"Is she having it yet?" His tone is laced with annoyance and
that shit pisses me off.

"I'm about to check," Kim replies as she gloves up and
resumes her position at the foot of the bed. Unlike the first
time, she doesn't lift my gown. She inserts her fingers right as
another contraction hits. My back arches off the bed as a pain-
filled scream tears out of me. "She's still at nine and a half."

"Fuck it, we need to move," he snaps.

"We can't move her, everything is in place—"

"I don't give a fuck, you're here to keep that baby alive. Do
your fucking job and you may just survive the night." Kim
swallows audibly and nods. "Pack your shit, I want her ready to
move in three minutes." Colson rushes out of the room. The
other nurses begin packing their things as Kim does the same. I
breathe in and out trying to rest as much as I can between
contractions.

"After you deliver, I am going to give you a shot which will
stop you contracting and make it so you are unable to pass the
placenta, buying us more time for your rescue party to arrive."
She begins to undo the cuffs on my ankles.

"Thank you," I croak out.

"Don't thank me, I should have tried to stop your labor
when I arrived but I misjudged you." I understand her
reasoning and why she did this but I'm not sure my family will
feel the same. Just as the two nurses return ready to wheel me
out, a strange cramp forms in my lower belly and the urge to
push overcomes me. I cry out.

"She's coming!" I grit out through clenched teeth. Kim's
eyes widen and she darts between my legs and lifts my gown.

"Shit. She's crowning, get all the gear back in here now,"

she barks at the other two. I become dizzy as the pain starts to consume me. I feel light headed and nausea becomes a new kind of torture as I gag continuously but unable to throw up. I can hear shouts and feel hands touching me but my mind is hazy. I can't make out any words as I scrunch my eyes closed and scream out in pain.

Chapter Thirty-One

Cronos

"How far out are we, Chaos?" King asks as he yanks the steering wheel left. I slam into the door but make no complaint, silently willing him to go faster. Ever since we got that call from Kim no one has spoken a word till now.

"Two minutes tops, security cameras in the area have been tracking our convoy. He knows we're coming," Chaos tells us.

"Good, unlike him we aren't bitches who do a sneak attack. I want him to know that we are coming and his time to die is near," I say.

"Someone forgot to take their happy pills today," London teases from her place between my brother and Chaos in the back.

"Baby, not the best time to joke around," Artemis coos.

"Why the hell not? I like Nos better when he's unhinged and blood thirsty." I hear Artemis groan and smile, London has always had a flare for the dramatics.

"Next right and then it's the building at the end of the street." At Chaos's words, I sit taller and check the magazine of my gun. As we careen down the street, I look at King who is practically bouncing in his seat.

"You find her! Don't hang back, don't fuck around, you find my daughter and you get her and that baby the fuck out, do you understand?" I don't argue with him.

"You have my word, King." He nods. Gunshots begin to spray the front of the car. King yanks the wheel to the side and slams on the brakes, we all duck and climb out through mine and Artemis's side and duck down as the other cars join us and form a wall.

"London?" Royal calls out.

"I'm fine, Dad. Jesus, it's just some bullets." Royal crouches down low and runs to his daughter's side.

"Why the fuck couldn't you like dolls and pony's?" he growls.

"I do like riding *a* pony–" Artemis covers her mouth with his hand and shoots her father a sheepish smile, as I lean around the front of our SUV and fire off four rounds, managing to hit one of those cunts in the chest.

"Taylan has taken Gage, Vin, Chanel and his men around the back. We need to take these fuckers out and move in," Bishop announces to all of us. King taps me on the shoulder and motions to follow him. I leave Artemis to stay with London as King and I push the back seat forward and drag the case of guns out. King and I begin passing out guns and magazines while arming ourselves. Knight and Rook have their cases out and are arming their men, there are at least eighty men total here—we have to outnumber this cocksucker.

"You two, find a way in and take it. We'll cover you both," Bishop says, then darts away to order his men to fan out. Royal tells us that Sin and Vincent are taking positions on the rooftop on the building next to us—they are the best snipers in the fucking world.

"We wait five minutes for them to take some of them out then move," King says as he flicks the safety off his gun. I strap my vest and stuff three mags in my pocket, then press in close behind him against the SUV, waiting for him to give the signal. The instant our side begins firing back, King rushes forward, using the cover of darkness and anything we can along the way as cover. It's fucking risky moving around in the open like this but we don't have a choice. I am not letting my girl give birth without me at her side. "We need to find a way inside the fence." I peer around King as we hide behind some scrap metal, trying to see through the darkness as best as I can but it's hard with the dim lighting.

"I can't see shit!" I snarl as I duck back down when more bullets begin to fly past. King looks around and comes to the same conclusion as me. We are going to have to go Rambo style and shoot our way in.

"We don't have time to sit here and hold our dicks, we move in five!" King shouts over the gun fire. I nod my agreement and pull the rifle forward that is strapped to my back. Us rushing in like this is going to get us filled with lead but much like him, I can't just sit here and do nothing! "Five... Four... Three... Two... O–"

"Fire in the hole!" I snap my head to the side. My eyes widen in horror at the sight of London with a fucking Missile Launcher.

"London, no!" Royal screams.

"Baby!" Artemis screams as they both take off running for her with Bishop on their heels but it's too late, she steps out from behind the SUV in the middle and pulls the trigger,

Artemis tackles her to the ground too late taking a bullet to the back. I attempt to push to my feet to check my brother but then an explosion goes off sending me face planting into the concrete.

Fuck!

I groan at the sound of ringing in my ears yet again! I'm getting really sick and tired of nearly getting blown up. My ankle is still fucked from the first one, but I don't have time to worry about that or the pain in my arm as King drags me to my feet by my vest.

"Move!" he screams. I shake my head to clear it and follow after him with my rifle raised and the scope at my eye ready to shoot whoever fucking survived, I just hope like hell the building isn't fucked up and putting my girls in danger. "Two at three O'clock." I turn and fire two shots, putting two fuckers down. I tap King on the back letting him know to keep moving forward.

"On our six!" I clip out as I turn and fire four shots hitting my target with the last, I'm fucking rusty at best. Four shots to hit one person is disgusting, Costa would be rolling in his grave.

"Move out," King snaps. I veer around him and take the lead as Royal, Knight and Rook lead some of their men forward to clear a path for us to get inside the building, which looks to be faring well after taking a fucking bomb!

London and I are going to have a long fucking chat after this shit is over!

"Approaching door one," I say quietly. I press my back against the wall and wait for King to do the same on the other side. We exchange a look before he nods. "Three, two, one." I whirl around and kick the fucker open, instantly we are met with gunfire. I jump back and resume my position from a second ago.

"How many?" King yells as he and I return fire.

"Dozen," I bite back as I hit one of the cunts hiding beside the stairs.

"Grenade!" he roars.

Not again!

I crouch down and cover my tender ears as King throws a fucking grenade inside the building his daughter is currently giving birth in. We hear shouts from inside but it doesn't matter because a moment later the grenade goes off and we move in, with Royal and the others on our asses. Any survivors are shot in the head.

"Fan out, find my daughter!" King barks. Knight, Rook and Royal each take a team of men and split up as King and I take the staircase in the middle, waiting for no one as we take the steps two at a time. We may be inside the building but I still feel so far away from her and I can feel it in the pit of my gut that the worst is yet to come. We keep climbing the stairs until we reach the top floor, knowing there is no way he would have hidden her on the lower levels. The fact we haven't encountered anyone or a single shot doesn't bode well in filling me with confidence.

Something isn't right.

"Argggh!" King and I freeze at the sound of a scream. "No!" Neither of us say a word as we both run as fast as we can toward the sound coming from the far corridor. There are two doors at the end. If we enter the wrong room, we give them the advantage of knowing we're here. I place my hand on his chest, drawing his gaze to me. I place a finger to my lips, praying he listens to me and waits. I know this is hard but we can't fuck up, we're too close and I won't lose her when she is right within my grasp.

Chapter Thirty-Two

Amelia

"You're doing great. On the next contraction, I need you to push as hard as you can," Kim says.

"No!" I scream. "I can't do this without them, I won't!" I choke out. The fact Colson isn't here and it's only me and the three nurses doesn't ease my anxiety.

"You need to push, she is right there and you are doing her more harm than good fighting it," Kim snaps, clearly annoyed at my refusal to give birth. I need my mom! Just the thought of her has me crying harder. I choke on my own spit in fright when the door is kicked open. My heart stops, thinking it's Colson coming to kill me because I'm taking too long.

"Angel." At the sight of him and my dad standing there looking utterly spent and distraught, I cry.

"Cronos." At the sound of my cry they both rush forward and look angry at the state of the bruises on my face and try to touch me but another contraction hits, making them halt as my back arches off the bed and I scream out.

"Push!" Kim barks. Dad grips my hand in his and squeezes.

"I'm right here, Meelz, I got you both," He reassures me.

"Come on, angel, bring our girl into this world so we can get you both home," Nos coos as he places a kiss on my forehead. Just as I bear down to push, gunfire can be heard outside the room.

"Shit, stay with her!" Dad barks. I reach for him but it's too late, he's already across the room and rushing out to fight the enemy I brought to my family's door step. For the first time in my life I can't blame my family for this horror story. I concocted this all on my own and breathed life back into this hate Colson has toward my father because I was desperate for a bit of attention. Cronos snaps me out of my thoughts when he dumps his guns on the ground, then pushes me forward so he can climb on the bed behind me.

I rest back against him as he wraps his arms around me and holds me tight. Kim doesn't look pleased about this new position but fuck her, I need him close.

"Come on, baby, you can do this," he encourages as another contraction hits. I dig my nails into his forearms, scrunch my eyes closed and push with every ounce of strength I have left. I am exhausted and could sleep for a week, but not until I bring our daughter into this world and make sure she is safe.

"Ahh," I cry out in frustration when the contraction passes.

"Next one, I need you to push harder and get her out, she is starting to stress," Kim says as she flicks her gaze to the heart monitor that is attached to the band around my stomach. I look over and see her heartbeat is dropping.

"Oh my God," I breathe out. "Please—"

"Shhhh, angel, you're doing great. One more push and then the pain will be gone and we can go home." I shake my head as tears falls faster down my cheeks.

"I can't do this, I need my mom," I cry out.

He brushes the hair back from my face and looks down at me with a loving smile but I can see the fear in his eyes. "Then we'll be stopping by the hospital with Kingsley to surprise your mom." Before I can ask what he means another contraction hits. His lips brush the shell of my ear. "She's alive, angel, now push." Something about hearing that news has a renewed sense of strength flowing through me. I grit my teeth and meet Kim's stare as I growl loudly and push harder than I have before.

"Just like that, when I say stop, stop or you will tear." If she thinks she is getting an answer from me, then she is out of her fucking mind, I can barely breathe let alone talk right now. "The heads out, stop!" Instantly, I obey her command. I can feel Nos shifting behind to try and get a better look but he can't see over my gown. "On the next one, I need you to give me one last big push, then she will be out." I nod. Normally I get nearly a minute break between contractions but not this time, this one comes hard and fast.

I push and feel it the instant my baby is out. It's a relief to know she is here and we can finally meet her but I feel so... empty without her presence inside me. I can no longer protect my little girl from the horrors of this world, she was safer inside me. Before she even entered this world, she had a man wanting to hurt her, people who will come for her because of who her mother is—because of who our family is—and now suddenly, I understand why my father was the way he was. So over the top and always checking in or making sure I would send him a message when my plans would change. It all makes sense now.

"Can I see her?" I ask as Kim starts clamping the cord,

Kingsley's cry finally rents the air and I begin sobbing at the sound of my baby.

"You did it, baby, you did so fucking good." I look up at Nos to see tears in his own eyes. All we can see is our baby's back, I just want to see her face and look into those beautiful eyes.

"Take her now and get her on the ventilator," Kim barks at the other two nurses. They rush over and take Kingsley. I start to panic.

"I want to see her!" I shout.

Kim lifts her gaze to me. "Her lungs aren't formed, Amelia, let us get her on some oxygen and then get this placenta out so we can move you and her, you will have all the time in the world to see your baby when we get the hell out of here." I purse my lips and choose to remain silent when Nos tightens his hold around me. Now that I can think clearly for a moment, I start to worry again.

"Where's my dad?" I feel him tense behind me. "Go find him," I grit out.

"I'm not leaving you, I'm staying right here," he argues.

"Cronos, I can't move until this placenta is out, we aren't going anywhere for a while." The argument dies in my throat when Kim stands and removes her gloves, dropping them to the floor. I open my mouth to ask what's going on, but the second she bends and collects the rifle from the ground and kicks the other two guns to the side, her intentions are made clear. I feel Nos stiffen behind me.

"Think very carefully about this choice, Kim," Cronos grits out, fear gripping me but not for myself, for my baby who is currently being held captive in an incubator across the room.

"Oh, I have thought long and hard and this is the outcome I have been praying for," she replies, sounding evil and unlike the woman who tried to help me earlier. She pulls her gaze from him to look at me, I see so much loathing and hate in the depths of her eyes. "You don't remember me, do you?" I recoil and flinch when a sudden cramp hits me. I breathe through the pain of the contraction. It's nothing like the last ones, thank God.

"Should I?" I force out through clenched teeth as the urge to push overwhelms me again.

"Considering we worked together, I would have thought so." Earlier I thought she looked familiar but I just put it down to the pain I was in, clearly my first instinct was correct. I study her for a minute trying to recall a memory or anything but I keep coming up blank until I don't. My eyes widen in horror.

"You were there that night at the pub with Amara, Lisa, Devon and Kevin." I remember her now, at the time I was too focused on keeping Colson calm and trying to hide the fact I was pregnant that I didn't even pay her much attention.

"Ding, ding and the award for the world's dumbest bitch goes to you!" I fight to keep the pain of the contraction from splaying over my face.

"Why are you doing this?" I snarl through the pain.

"If you had paid closer attention, you would have seen the signs."

"What fucking signs?" I scream.

"How did he know when you worked late? When you changed your shifts? When you were somewhere you weren't supposed to be?" My jaw unhinges as her implications sink in.

"You were his spy?" I mumble.

"No, not a spy, just a big sister helping her little brother out." My brows raise in surprise. "You see, the day my family died, I was at my friend's so I wasn't in the car. It took me years to find Colson through the foster system. When I did find him, we promised we would do whatever it took to avenge our family and now we are finally about to fulfill that promise." She flicks her gaze to the two nurses. "Take the kid, meet me at the elevator."

"Take that baby and I swear your ending will not be swift or painless," Cronos vows.

"Fucking hell," Kim snaps, then shoots the blonde one in the center of her eyes, the raven-haired one screams and begins to plead for her life.

"Take the fucking kid now or you join your friend." She shoots us a regretful look, before shakily wheeling the incubator out.

"Please!" I scream. "Take me, she means nothing to my father. If you kill me—"

"Angel, no!" I ignore Cronos as I push on.

"You will destroy King Murdoch if you kill me. You already killed his wife, he doesn't care about that baby." I'm taking a calculated risk here, I have no idea if they know my mom survived or not, but the fact Nos only told me about it, I suspect I am right when Kim purses her lips. She doesn't get a chance to respond as the pain returns tenfold and rips through me, forcing me to push.

Labor fucking sucks!

"Nice try," Kim snickers. "Follow us and I put a bullet in the kids head, if your father hadn't killed my family things may have been different." As the two of them rush out of the room, I push with everything I have to get this fucking thing out of me so I can go after my baby. I just hope I don't have a sticky placenta and it gets stuck. The second they exit the room, Nos moves from behind and retrieves both his Glock's from the corner,

"Go!" I grit out as I feel the placenta pass, the pain I'm in is minimal compared to the worry churning inside me over the safety of my daughter. It's only now I register that gun fire is still happening outside. I swing my legs over the edge of the bed and cringe at the sight of the placenta and all the blood on the bed. My yellow gown is instantly soaked in my own blood as I stand shakily. Cronos is at my side in an instant, wrapping an arm around my waist as blood trickles down my thighs.

"Can you walk?"

"Yes, just leave me and go after Kingsley," I beg.

"I can't leave you, Amelia, please don't ask me to choose between you both right now." I hate that I understand his fear, I don't waste time fighting. I limp beside him as he leads me to the door. Before we can exit, he hands me one of his guns. I take it without hesitation.

"You know how to shoot—"

"I'm a Murdoch, of course I know how to fucking shoot!" He pulls the door open and then we move. I have my gun raised and ready to kill any son of a bitch that gets between me and my daughter. This bloodlust is new for me, I have never wanted to harm anyone like this in my life. Maybe I was scared to embrace who I truly am because deep down inside, I always knew there was darkness inside me begging to be released. We round a corner and Cronos fires a shot. Before I can even blink, a man falls to the ground. "How did you know he wasn't one of ours?"

"I didn't but I'm not taking any chances with your safety." I balk up at him.

"You're kidding, right?" I snap as we move forward.

"Yes, Bishop instructed all his men to have green on their vests and he didn't." Relief washes over me, I would fucking hate for him to have been serious and accidentally shoot one of my cousins or something. My eyes widen when I see Kim push the incubator with my screaming baby into the elevator. I raise my gun ready to shoot the cunt but she shifts and ducks inside. Nos smacks my gun just as I pull the trigger.

"You do not take an uncalculated risk when it concerns Kingsley's safety. Do not take a shot without a guarantee, am I clear?" This is the first time he has ever spoken to me like this. I nod my head, unable to form words as he drags me toward the elevators.

Chapter Thirty-Three

Cronos

I help Meelz into the metal box and press the basement level. I push her into the corner near the front, making sure she is shielded and then hand her my spare mag. I look down and curse beneath my breath at the sight of the blood pooling between her legs. Without thinking I grip her face between my hands and kiss her. She melts into me instantly. I pull back and stare deep into her green eyes.

"No matter what happens, you stay the fuck alive, okay?" She nods. "I need the words."

"I'll stay alive," she whispers as I pull away and mimic her position on the other side, we have three floors to go. I shoot a quick text to Royal and Bishop telling them to get to the basement.

"When those doors open—"

"I know what I'm doing, Nos. I may not have liked being a Murdoch, but it doesn't mean I don't know how to be one."

Just as the ding sounds out announcing our arrival, she calls out, "I got left." Bullets whizz past us and pierce the back of the metal box. I press in closer to the wall and wait for them to reload, then shoot her a nod as we both step out and prepare to fire, but both freeze at the sight of King on his knees with Rook and Knight on either side of him. Colson stands behind King with a gun pressed to the back of his head. I look them over and wince at the sight of Rook clutching his stomach, blood seeping through his fingers. Knight looks just as bad as his twin with blood soaking through his shirt. King on the other hand, his lip, nose and brow are all split and bleeding.

"Drop the gun, Amelia, now." She cranes her neck to see Kim with the help of two of Colson's men lifting Kingsley and her plastic crib into the Ambulance that is parked behind that fucker. She takes too long to comply, so he shifts his gun and shoots King through the shoulder. He cries out and hunches forward. Amelia screams and tosses her gun forward so it rests in the middle of us and them. I do the same. Colson pulls King up by his hair, the poor fucker winces and grinds his teeth, putting on a brave face for his daughter.

"I'm gonna slit your fucking throat and fuck the wound for that, you cunt," Rook hisses.

"Rook, stop taunting the little man, I've told you about picking on weaker men!" Knight scolds his brother, who smirks through his pain. I'll never understand how these men can resort to humor whenever they are in situations like this.

"Shut the fuck up or the next one goes in her head!" Colson yells as he points his gun at my girl. On instinct, I leap in front of Amelia and become her shield. At my protective move he laughs. I use this moment to count the number of men he has down here. On a quick count I tally at least twenty. The bastard was smart. He kept most of his men with him and used the ones out front as a distraction while he moved everyone else down here to wait for Kingsley. Getting his sister to call me was smart, we never expected her to be working with him because she led us to believe she was helping Meelz at the risk of her own safety.

"Let my dad, uncles and Nos go and you can have me." I reach for Amelia when she darts out from behind me with her hands raised. When I try to shift to cover her again, she darts forward out of my reach.

"Why the fuck would I take a useless whore like you?" I grind my teeth in anger.

"Well, she must be a good whore if she has you doing all of this for her," Rook taunts. He gets pistol whipped by one of Colson's guys and flops forward—he's knocked out.

"Touch my brother again, you son of a bitch, and I'll have your mom and sister working my block," Knight grits out— he's lying but the threat sounds good.

"Amelia, don't—"

Meelz cuts her dad off. "You want to destroy him and make him feel half the pain you do, then taking me is the answer. You killed his... wife, if you take me, he has nothing."

"You mean your mom?" The mirth in his voice pisses me off. My girl squares her shoulders and lifts her head.

"Allison Murdoch is my..." she drops her chin to meet her father's gaze, "... aunt, my mother died giving birth to me." King's eyes widen and his mouth pops open. "Take me, I'll never fight. You know I will be good." It makes me sick to hear her speaking about herself like this. "I will follow all your orders and keep you... satisfied." Colson and his men snicker and laugh at her innuendo, Knight and King both shudder at the image she is painting. I will die before I ever let her go back to that cocksucker. "Colson, take me. Do whatever you want to me but don't leave me behind while you take our... daughter." Pain vibrates inside my chest at her words.

"You lie," he snarls. She slowly inches forward, taking small steps and when she is a foot away from King, he cocks his gun forcing her to a stop. "You mean nothing to me."

"I know. You know I love you and I will do whatever you want if you just please take me with you. I swear it. I will be good and do whatever you ask but please let me come, our daughter needs her mother."

"Either kill the bitch or bring her with us, she's wasting time for the rest of them to get here!" Kim screams from inside the rig.

"I'm not, I swear." A reflection out of the corner of my eye snags my attention. I only move my eyes so I don't alert the rest of them. Taylan pops his head up from behind a car parked across the space and nods, then flicks his gaze to the other side. I shift my sight to see Gage behind a van. I need to cause a distraction so they can move in.

Please forgive me, angel!

"You lying bitch!" I roar, garnering the attention of everyone just like I hoped. King scowls and Meelz spins around, trying to implore me with her eyes to understand she doesn't mean what she says.

"Cronos—"

"No. You fucking lied to me, Amelia!" I force all the pain I can muster into my tone so Colson believes what I am saying. "You said you were over that piece of shit. I told you not to fuck with me if you were still hung up on him." Her face contorts and I try to communicate without words to play along. There's a slight glint in her eyes and I weep with joy internally.

"I just needed somewhere to lay low until he found me like

I knew he would—" A shot rents the air when Colson fires his gun. My world stops spinning as a scream tears out of my angel. King and Knight both scream out as we all watch her fall to the ground. All hell breaks loose when Gage, Taylan and the others all start firing back. I move without thought as I dive for my gun and roll once I have it in my hand and aim at Colson, but the fucker jumps in the rig and it starts to drive away.

"Go after her!" King roars. I don't hesitate or even look at Amelia, knowing the sight of her laying there will cripple me and drag me back into that dark pit of nothingness. I push off the ground and run as fast as I fucking can, chasing that fucking rig like my life depends on it, and in a way I guess it does—inside that rig holds my hearts greatest desire that I was too afraid to hope for. When the driver breaks to round one of the pillars, I release a loud roar as I jump and pray I make it inside. A shot rings out, but I pay it no mind as I go straight for the guard at the end. I toss him out the open back doors and then move to Colson. He tries to lift his gun but I'm faster.

I hit him with a right hook, He shakes it off, then rams me back into the other side of the ambulance. Kim is screaming and trying to get a clear shot but she won't risk hitting her brother. I grunt when he lands a fucking good hit to my ribs. But unlike him, I have lived in a constant state of pain my whole life so it isn't something new to me if anything, it helps me focus better.

"Kill him!" that bitch yells. Kingsley is screaming her little head off and I hate that the first time she is seeing me is like this, but I will spend every day trying to erase this first memory she has of me from her mind. Colson is stronger than I expected, he is giving me a run for my money. I try to lift my gun but he bats it away as we slide sideways when the driver takes another turn. I can't let them get out of the parking lot—

if they hit the main road, we could lose that little girl for good and I won't let that happen.

He wraps his hands around my throat and tries to crush my windpipe. My vision turns hazy when he bangs my head against the metal wall of the rig. I strike out and punch him in the ribs over and over again as I fight not to give into the blackness dotting my vision. When we round another turn the momentum from the turn propels me forward, knocking Colson off his feet. I use the moment his grip weakens to my advantage and slam him into the other side of the rig, he shouts out in pain but his cries only fuel the beast inside me. I want to draw this out and carve his skin from his bones and turn it into a rug so I can fuck Amelia on top of it, but Kingsley needs me.

"I'll be back for you," I shout right in his face as I use every bit of strength I have left to throw him out of the rig. The crunch of his bones cracking against the concrete has a shiver of pleasure rushing down my spine.

"Stop!" Kim screams to driver, who slams on the brakes. I drop to a crouch and brace for the kick back of the ambulance coming to a stop and scramble to find my gun, but the bitch is right there, pressing the barrel of her gun into the side of my head. Being on my knees isn't something new to me but she isn't the woman I want to be kneeling for. "Look at me," she screams. I slowly lift my arms and tilt my head back to stare up the deranged bitch. "You will pay for what you did to my brother." I take a shuddering breath as failure washes over me. I couldn't save Aida, I couldn't even save Amelia when I was given a chance and now, I will lose the little girl I have fallen in love with that I haven't even met. I'm doomed to always fail those that I love.

"Not before you watch him die!" The sound of London's voice has my eyes widening. Kim pales, then grabs the scruff of my shirt, forcing me to my feet. She spins me around so my back is to her. The sight of London, Royal, Chanel and Chaos standing there with Colson on his knees, bleeding and clutching his arm while blood trickles down the side of his head, is euphoric.

"Release him now or I kill this bastard." I gulp audibly when all emotion vanishes from London's face, even Royal looks worried at the sight of his daughter. I know what that look on her face means, someone is about to die and I just fucking hope it isn't me!

"You touch a hair on his head and I'll tear your brother limb from limb while you watch. I swear it," London promises. As if to taunt the unhinged woman before us, Kim presses her gun into my side and then ruffles my hair with her free hand. Before anyone can blink, pain explodes in my shoulder, the pressure of the gun pressed into my side vanishes as Colson's anguished screams penetrate the air when his sister falls to the ground behind me, crying out. "I told you not to touch his hair," London snarks as I spin around and kick her gun out of the rig. I ignore the bitch, knowing the others will deal with her as I rush to Kingsley's side.

Chapter Thirty-Four

Amelia

"Meelz!" I whimper and blink my eyes open at the sound of my dad's voice. I slam my eyes closed as pain vibrates throughout my body. "Thank fuck. Stay still, baby, you've been shot and have lost a lot of blood already."

"Kingsley?" I croak out. Dad's face falls and a sob claws out of me. "No!" I cry out.

"Cronos went after her, we have cars coming to move us all. Rook needs to get seen to ASAP, he's not in a good way," he says somberly. Guilt over putting my entire family in this position fills me.

"Dad, I'm so sorry—"

"Shhhh, we'll worry about everything else later. I need to get you out of here and to a hospital—"

"Mom?" I rush to ask.

His face fills with pain. "I need to get back to her as well, I had her airlifted to New York and I haven't... heard anything since." I swallow and nod my head, we'll deal with that later as well I guess. When cars begin to pull up, Dad helps me to my feet and I stagger. Uncle Knight and Uncle Gage each help Uncle Rook to the first SUV that takes off the instant he is inside with Uncle Knight. "We're next," Dad says as we both limp toward the second car. Before he can help me in, I pull back and shake my head. "Meelz—"

"I can't just leave my daughter, Dad. I need to find her—"

"You've been shot!" he argues.

"I don't care, I need to find her and Cronos—"

"He's already on his way to the local hospital with your daughter, Meelz." I spin around and stumble back, but Dad is there to catch me before I slip in my own blood. "London is with him, Artemis will be there as well."

Tears prick my eyes at Royal's words. "They're both okay?"

He nods. "You guys get out of here, we'll clean up and meet you all back at Dad's." Before he can leave I ask.

"Where is *he*?" He doesn't have to ask which *he* I am referring to, he can tell from the hatred in my tone.

"Him and his bitch of a sister have been patched up so they don't die on their flight back to New York. We'll deal with them when we—"

"No." Royal frowns and looks to my dad. Before either of them can say a word I cut in. "No one touches them but me. The human body can survive three days without water, give them enough water to keep them alive and food every six days until I get there. I want them to suffer from the moment they land until I can deal with them."

"Meelz—" I look at my dad and whatever he sees in my eyes has him clamping his mouth closed.

"It's my decision. You wanted me to embrace who I am, this is me doing that." I turn back to my cousin. "No one is to touch them. Keep them separated. Find some recordings of a woman screaming and play it to him every so often so he thinks his sister is being tortured. Do the same to her, I want their minds broken before I break their bodies."

"Jesus, you sound exactly like my fucking daughter," Royal says with a shudder as I turn away from him and climb into the car.

I'm about to rip my nurse's throat out if she doesn't hurry the fuck up. We were taken to a private hospital and they refused to allow me to see Kingsley until I was cleaned and checked out. I went to reach for my dad's sidearm and shoot the bitch, but when they reminded me of the risk of spreading infection to my preemie baby, I resisted.

Artemis, Dad, Uncle Knight and Uncle Rook are all in the ER with me, it's no surprise that my family had the local hospital locked down so only our people can be treated. I make no comment because a part of me is extremely grateful for that, it means my daughter is safe. The only reason I have been able to remain this calm is because I know Cronos is with her and he won't let anything happen to our daughter.

"I have some clean clothes, pads and some toiletries in the shower for you. I can assist if you need?" Given the fact I'm in a fucking sling, I have no choice but to accept her offer. She helps me off the bed. I see my dad begin to panic across from me but I reassure him I am just showering, then I'll return. I'm way past caring about who the fuck sees my body, I'm a doctor and know how desensitized these nurses are to seeing a naked body. The woman is careful in helping me remove my sling and removes the shower head from the wall and holds it at stomach level, so I don't wet my bandages.

By the time I have changed and exit the bathroom in a fresh set of clothes and my hair in a messy bun, I feel ten times better but exhaustion is weighing on me now. Dad and Artemis wait at the edge of the bed I was occupying. I raise a brow at him.

"We'll come with you. Knight will stay with Rook, he needs surgery. When he is well enough to travel we'll have him flown back home." I nod my head in understanding, I know my family hates being separated, which is why they all live together pretty much. Artemis looks like he is about to jump out of his skin if he doesn't set eyes on London soon. I can't blame him, my own skin is crawling with the need to see my daughter and Nos.

"Follow me." The three of us follow behind the nurse, nerves wracking my body the entire way. I can't seem to control the urge to tell her to hurry the hell up, but I know what it's like being in her position so I refrain. As we draw near to where we see the signs for the NICU, my dad grips my hand in his and gives it a squeeze. I relax at the feeling of his comfort.

When she swipes her badge and the large doors open automatically, my breath hitches. As we enter the NICU, I immediately dart my gaze around and spot London across the large room. Artemis practically runs to her, and at the sight of him, she smiles and stands as he embraces her. Dad and I stand back and give them a minute, I'm fighting not to tap my fucking foot.

"Excuse me?" a new nurse asks from beside us.

"What?" I snap and cringe, I shoot her an apologetic smile that she ignores.

"It's parents only allowed in here."

'What?" I snap.

"I may have kind of told them I was the mom so I could stay with her and Nos." I shoot London a wide eyed stare, she doesn't look remorseful and I can't blame her. I push away my annoyance and smile at my niece.

"Thank you for staying with them," I say to her before turning to the nurse. "I'm the mother, where is my daughter?"

"Angel?" I spin around at the sound of Cronos's voice. He looks at me like he's seen a ghost, which has me cocking my head to the side in confusion. He shakes his head and blinks twice. "You're alive?" he mutters. I recoil as he steps out of the room in the corner and eats up the space between us. Much like me, his arm is in a sling and he even looks like he has showered as well. With his free hand he reaches out and shakily places it against my cheek. When he feels my skin beneath his palm, he deflates and leans his forehead against mine, closing his eyes as he breathes me in. "You're here," he whispers.

"I'm right here, Grizz," I answer as I clutch his shirt with my good hand. "I need to see her now." He pulls back and smiles wide, the look of unreserved love in his eyes steals my breath.

"She's perfect, angel. God, she is fucking beautiful." The love and awe in his tone has a watery smile stretching across my own face. "Come on, come meet the owner of both our hearts." He interlocks his fingers with mine and leads me toward the room, but at the last second I pull him to a stop and look over my shoulder to see my dad standing there with his head down. I know he is torn up inside, wanting to be here for me but always needing to be back home with my mom.

"Dad?" he snaps his head up.

"Yeah?"

"Want to meet your granddaughter?" I ask.

He swallows and blinks his eyes a couple of times to rid

himself of those pesky tears. "More than anything." I flick my head motioning for him to follow us. The moment Cronos pushes the door open, my heart skips a beat. He gently tugs me inside the room where I see an incubator resting in the middle of it. I freeze. I just stand here staring at the bundle of pink blankets. I can see a pink beanie on her head but I'm scared to get any closer. Nos pivots and stands in front of me with a look of concern on his handsome face.

"What's wrong, angel?" he asks gently. I step back and look at both him and my dad, they both look worried.

"Promise me, no one will ever harm her. Whatever it takes, we all keep her safe and never allow the horrors of this world to taint her or tarnish her innocence." They both nod firmly with looks of pure dominance in their gazes.

"I swear to you, she will come to no harm as long as I live," Dad vows.

"I accepted my position as Artemis's underboss so I would have the power to keep you both safe." My face falls at Nos's admission.

"Why would you do that? You were happy being an undertaker," I say.

"You make me happy, she makes me happy," he says, pointing behind him. "I will do whatever I have to in order to protect you both—"

"What if I can give you your wish of staying out of the mafia and still protecting your daughter?" my dad asks as he faces Nos.

"How?"

"We need an undertaker. I'll fund everything if you come to New York and work with us. Not in a capacity that would require you to work for us in the way you think."

"What does that mean?" Nos pushes.

"We need an undertaker for when our men fall. Rather than paying everyone off, it would be easier if we had someone of our own running it." Nos turns and looks to me as if seeking my reaction. I smile encouragingly. Being in New York means I get to be close to my family who will help protect Kingsley, but it also means Nos gets his dream of continuing to work with the dead and not having to return to Greece. "Think about it, my offer stands until you give me an answer." Nos nods his head, he looks utterly speechless. I leave him with his thoughts and step around them both as I move toward my baby. The closer I get, the more I begin to feel tingles down my spine.

Warmth spreads throughout my entire body the moment I lay my eyes on her beautiful face for the first time. Tears instantly blur my vision. I try to blink them away but it's no use, they fall regardless of my efforts.

"She's perfect," I whisper.

"She looks exactly like you," Dad breathes out.

"She has a hint of the Devil in her eyes and that's all me," Cronos adds. I look over at him to see him smiling down at our little girl, my love for him growing daily. I'll never have to wonder my worth where he is concerned. I know he will always do what is right by me and Kingsley. They say that every person has someone out there for them and I found mine. I found the happy ending I was always searching for within him. He says I am his redemption but the truth is, he was the shot of adrenaline I needed to wake me up and force me to see the world as it is instead of through rose colored glasses.

Chapter Thirty-Five

Cronos

One week later...

Today is the day we can finally transport Kingsley back to the States. King tried to fast track things but even he wouldn't put his own kin's life at risk when Meelz explained the complications. Many tests have been run to check the development of her lungs. We have to fly back with a team of nurses who will keep her stable and make sure she is fine until we arrive at the hospital in New York. I know King was happy that Knight and Rook were still here with us, they will fly back today alongside us as well. Artemis and London refused to leave until we did, it's been great having them both here and I know Amelia has loved it as well. Her and London seem to be getting along better, but Lon still refuses to touch Kingsley.

When she first saw her, she scrunched her face up and

looked my brother dead in the eyes and said, "I will never push one of those aliens out of my vagina for you." Needless to say, I don't think London plans to become a mother anytime soon or if ever.

"Okay, we're set," Knight says from the doorway. I nod and move to Meelz, who is standing by Kingsley's travel incubator. I hate that the moment we land and get Kingsley settled that I have to leave. I promised Beth I would be the one to organize everything for Bill and I plan to keep my word. Artemis is flying back to Minnesota with me, the plan to be gone three days tops.

"Angel, it's time to go." She nods and steps aside to allow the nurses to do what they have to do. We follow them out of the room and remain beside our daughter the entire way. We're all nervous about this trip but I would be lying if I said I wasn't happy to get the fuck out of Switzerland and never step foot back in this place again.

Once we get Kingsley sorted on the plane, Meelz and I take our seats while Knight helps Rook board. He looks like shit but I know he is just as eager to get home to his wife. His daughters even flew home from Rome to be there when he arrives. Unlike the others, Rook's daughters are princesses and are spending time overseas with their boyfriends. I hear one of them is wanting to break into the fashion world and make a name for herself that way.

"Kingsley Billie Argyros." I lull my head to the side and frown at my girl.

"Huh?" She smiles up at me. I'll never tire of the sight of her looking at me like I hung the fucking moon.

"Her name. I want that to be her name." My mouth pops open in surprise.

"Y-you want her to have *my* last name?" I rasp out.

She smirks. "I mean, her daddy better pop the question and make her momma an honest woman soon, or I'll be the odd man out with a different last name—"

"Marry me?" She throws her head back and laughs. "I'm serious," I grit out.

She shakes her head and pats me on the chest with her good arm. "Nice try, Grizz. If you seriously think I would say yes to that half-assed proposal, then you are out of your fucking mind."

"You best be asking my brother first or you won't live long enough to buy your tux for the big day," Knight calls out, causing Amelia to laugh again and me to huff out my annoyance, game on.

You'll be an Argyros soon enough, angel, just watch.

It was fucking hard saying goodbye to my girls, I hate leaving them. The doctors gave Kingsley the all clear and requested she stay with them for another two weeks to monitor her little lungs. I wanted to argue but refrained, knowing this is the best place for her and the fact her mom is a doctor is also a bonus. Before I left though, I took Meelz to visit her mom. Fuck, Allison looks weak and a wreck. We were informed she died twice while they were operating, she said it wasn't her time and refused to leave King behind to help raise her granddaughter on his own. That broke the tension and had everyone laughing.

Before I left, King promised to have Allison moved upstairs into the NICU unit so he could watch over all three of them, which eased some of my worries. Rook, of course, is being moved there as well, so the whole family will be on the same floor.

"You two really are identical." I lull my head to the side to look at London, who is smiling at me and Artemis. He and I both frown.

"Are not!" we both say in unison, then glare at each other, which makes the evil she-devil laugh.

"You both have slings on and are wearing black," she says.

"But I have a bigger cock," Artemis says with a wink, which has me rolling my eyes.

"The fuck you do, asshole. I can prove we aren't identical," I say cockily, my brother's face falls.

"If you pull your dick out in front of my girl I'll shoot you!" he growls.

"Calm down, bitch face," I snap.

"How can you prove it?" London asks.

I smile wickedly. "He has a scar that I don't."

Art scoffs. "Where is this scar you speak of dumbass?"

I snort. "Your back is covered in them." His face falls again and London looks like she is about to stab me for teasing him about those but I push on. "But, I was referring to the one your darling girl gave you when she ran a knife through your chest." His face turns red with anger but the sound of London's laughter draws his attention to her.

"Something funny to you?" my brother grits out.

She waves him off. "You have to let that go, both of you," she scolds.

"You fucking stabbed me!" he shouts.

She rolls her eyes. "It was barely a prick—"

"I nearly died, London!"

"But you didn't, did you?" I tune out their bickering,

knowing this is their form of foreplay and I refuse to watch that shit unfold.

Seeing Bill again brought feelings back to light that I thought I had overcome—I guess grief hits you in stages and you can't control when it happens. Embalming him wasn't easy, he was someone I cared for deeply and having to pump his body full of chemicals sucked, but I did it. Beth helped me dress him and chose a casket, I refused to allow him to be buried in a standard pine box.

I had a custom one made for him while I was still in Switzerland, it's solid black with silver handles and a mural painted on the front. When Beth saw the lid of the coffin, she broke down in tears. I had it airbrushed with a picture of Bill with angel wings on his back and a portrait of their daughter, with her baby in her arms, and they are both looking down on the portrait of Beth.

I may not have been able to express my feelings for him in life but I fucking hope I can show him in death that everything he taught me, gave me and showed me will live inside me until I see him again. I've been here longer than I had planned, it's been nearly a fucking week because the police were notified that Bill was murdered by a random source. I had a lot of red tape to cut through but I managed to line the right pockets and got it all stowed away.

Beth sits beside me in the hearse as we drive to the local cemetery. I have been trying to work up the courage to speak to her since I arrived and I know now might not be the right time but I won't get another chance.

"Beth, I want you to come live with us," I blurt out. She chuckles, I peer at her out of the corner of my eye. "What?"

"I was wondering when you would ask." My face contorts. "What?"

"Boy, I have had my bags packed since you left, the only thing that was keeping me in this town is in that box behind us. I never got the chance to love on my own grandbaby, so I would love the chance to share some of my love with my adopted granddaughter." Hearing her speak about Kingsley like she is her own means more than she will ever know.

"Thank you."

"Thank you for giving us something to live for. Bill and I were living day to day until you showed up. You saved us both. I hadn't seen my husband smile in a really long time until you came into his life, so it's me who should be thanking you." I don't respond as we pull into the cemetery. Cars line either side of the road. Beth sits up in her seat and looks just as surprised as I do. When we finally clear the vehicles and I see dozens of men in suits, then it hits me.

"Angel," I breathe out just as she comes into view at the edge of the road with our baby tucked close against her chest. I see her sling is gone, much like my own. Her mother and father stand on either side of her with the rest of their family, sans Rook, standing close behind.

"They your in-laws?' Beth asks.

"Soon to be," I rasp out as I park the hearse and climb out, heading straight for my girls. Meelz smiles up at me when I'm close.

"Surprise." I don't respond to her. Instead I grab her face between my hands and kiss her, ignoring the growls coming from her father. I pull back and shoot her wink when I see the lustful look in her eyes.

Yeah, baby, I'm horny as fuck for you too!

I gently stroke the backs of my knuckles along Kingsley's cheek and place a feather light kiss on her forehead.

"Move boy, I want to see that baby!" I bite down on my lip to keep from laughing and step aside so Beth can meet Kingsley. Just the sight of her has the old woman beaming from ear to ear. "She's beautiful." Meelz melts at the compliment.

"Beth, I want you to meet our daughter, Kingsley Billie Argyros," Meelz says quietly, waiting to see Beth's reaction. "We wanted to name her after the hero that saved her other grandma." Beth swallows a few times and looks away as she swipes the tears from her eyes. Everyone around acts like they don't see her crying out of respect.

"T-that's a fine name she has, my Bill would be mighty pleased with that." I release a breath I didn't know I was holding at her acceptance to our baby's name.

"I never got the chance to say thank you, Beth," Allison says, drawing Beth's gaze to her, the two women share a long look and I begin to feel nervous. Bill sacrificed his life saving Allison and I don't know how Beth is going to react to that. I see King subtly shift behind Meelz to be closer to his wife if need be.

"My Bill did the right thing," Beth says, breaking the tense silence.

"My family and I owe you a debt we can never repay for what your husband did for me, it is because of him why I am standing here today."

"You can repay me by allowing me to watch that little one grow until the good Lord calls me home." Allison smiles warmly and places her hand on Beth's shoulder.

"It would be my honor to have you in our lives," she says.

"And mine," Meelz adds. I leave the girls to talk as I move

to the back of the hearse to assist Bill on his final walk. Respect flows through me when Royal, Bishop, Chaos, Knight and even King come to help me carry him. Most of the town is here to bid farewell to Bill. We place him on top of the ropes that will lower him to the ground. I've never led a service before. I normally leave this part to the family's priest but Beth asked me to do it, so I will out of respect for her and Bill. I drew the fucking line at holding a Bible though, if I touched one of those things I'd go up in flames.

I clear my throat before I begin and lock eyes with Amelia. "Everybody's talking about heaven like they just can't wait to go, but I can because I have my angel here on earth. Bill found his angel in Beth, the love of his life. Her daddy thought Bill was no good for his little girl." I smirk when King rolls his eyes, unlike Beth's father he knows no matter what he does or tries to do I would never stay away from Amelia. "Bill didn't need to win her daddy's approval though, because he already had hers. They lived a life filled with love that many envied... they faced a horror no family should." Beth lowers her gaze. "Yet, they both pulled through that tragedy because they loved each other enough to remain here on earth and not follow after their own daughter. For that, I am grateful." I turn to Beth next and wait for her to meet my gaze. "I never had a mother, the father I did have wasn't... nice. I found a mother and father figure in the both of you and for that I am eternally grateful. Bill saved me from my own demons and never gave up when I pushed him away."

"He loved you, boy," Beth croaks out. I nod and smile.

"The feeling was mutual, because of Bill I didn't allow my heart to be crippled by the vein that I kept on closing. I let it beat again in the hopes he was right and to my horror... he was." Everyone laughs. "I found my family thanks to him and with that, I want to say to you, old man." I focus on his casket and lay my hand on the portrait of him as I speak. "Thank you for loving me when I didn't think I could ever be loved. Thank you for forcing your way inside my own heart and forcing me to see that love doesn't have to be jaded and dark. I'm going to miss you and our lunch times together. Fly fucking high, Wild Bill, and give them all hell for me."

Chapter Thirty-Six

Amelia

Two weeks later...

"Are you sure you don't mind watching her?" I ask Beth who shoots me an eye roll that has me thinning my lips.

"Get out of here, me and my grandbaby have a bath time to get to." She shoos me out of Kingsley's nursery.

"I expressed some milk for her and Mr. Snaggles is in her crib if you need him!" I call back. When we returned back to New York, Cronos and I moved into my parent's house with Beth. Mom and Dad are staying at Uncle Bishop and Aunt Kiara's until I overcome my fear of being away from the safety of the compound. Mom and Dad said we could build a house here, but the horrified look on Nos's face told me that wasn't an option.

Last week Dad came over and dropped off my old bear that

I couldn't sleep without as a child. I was shocked he still had the old thing. He told me some nights he would cuddle that bear and pretend it was me, that shit ate me up inside. He and I are trying to repair the damage I did to our relationship and we are taking a huge step in doing that tonight. I smile at my dark angel when I step out onto the porch. Cronos looks like a fucking snack in his jeans, Chucks and black hoodie with the hood pulled over his forehead.

God, I want you!

My pussy flutters but I force that bitch to remain calm, Nos refuses to touch me because the stupid fucking doctor said to wait six weeks after giving birth. I reminded him multiple fucking times that *I* am in fact a doctor myself! It's pure torture being near him daily and sleeping next to him every night without being able to feel him inside me.

"Stop looking at me like that, angel," he scolds gently. I bat my lashes and step into him, resting my palms flat against his chest as I peer up at him.

"Like what?" I hear the husky lilt to my own voice and can't find it within myself to give a shit, he knows how bad I want him and I won't feel ashamed for wanting my man.

He groans and tilts his head back staring up at the sky. "Lucifer, give me fucking strength," he growls.

"No. Don't give him strength!" I shout.

"You guys are weird!" I snap my head to the side to see London staring at us like we are a circus act, while Artemis stands there shaking with silent laughter.

"Don't you have a country to run or some shit?" I snap as Cronos wraps an arm around my shoulders and tucks me into his side.

"Someone is grouchy." London snickers.

"You would be too if you weren't getting dicked!" My eyes

widen the instant the words fly out of my mouth, Cronos and Artemis both laugh at my expense, I bury my face in Nos's side.

"That is fucking nasty, you're old and he's my best friend!" I reel back and stare at London with my mouth hanging open in stupor.

"Time to go, baby!" Artemis quickly drags London after him toward Uncle Bishop's house, with me and Cronos following after them at a slower pace.

"I am not that fucking old," I growl under my breath.

"Age is nothing but a number, baby. She's just angry because my brother is spending so much time with Kingsley and she's worried he's gonna want a kid of his own."

"I should spite her and poke holes in his condoms!" Cronos laughs.

"I like seeing you petty," he coos.

"Give me your dick and you won't have to deal with my bitchy moods."

"Amelia!" I freeze on the spot and cringe as I slowly turn to see my Dad, Uncle Gage, Uncle Rook and Uncle Vincent standing at the edge of the porch of Uncle Bishop's house. My dad looks like he wants to flay me alive but when he turns his angry glare to Cronos it darkens. "I will slice you into little fucking pieces—"

"If you heard what she said properly, then you would know I am the one being molested, not the other way around." I balk at Cronos.

"You fucking traitor!" I shout as I shove him away from me. The fucker just laughs when I stomp away from him. I don't make it more than five steps before his arm bands around my waist and I'm hoisted off my feet with a huff. The asshole places a kiss on my neck, sending a shiver down my spine.

"Don't be mad," he begs.

"I am so mad at you right now," I growl.

"The doctor said I couldn't penetrate you but he never said I couldn't eat your pretty cunt." He keeps his voice low enough so that only I can hear, making fire burn inside my veins.

"Don't tease me," I growl as he places me on my feet and turns me to face him.

"There is no way I will be able to resist you after you claim your vengeance, baby. Be a good girl and I promise I will have you quivering and screaming my name before the night is out." His promise spurs me into action, I tear out of his hold and practically run to the bunker out back where the others are waiting, I don't even glance at them as I make my way inside. The promise of coming on Cronos's face has me wanting this to be over quickly.

Luka pulls the final door open for me and I'm instantly hit by the scent of urine. Working in a hospital has made me accustomed to the scent so it doesn't bother me like it does the others. The sight of Colson strung up with his arms above his head and the tips of his toes touching the ground brings a sense of joy to me. He had planned to ruin my family and take my baby from me. I could have moved on from him hurting me and overcome that trauma, but he chose to come after me and hurt me worse.

I feel Nos at my back when Colson lazily lifts his head, the sight of me has his eyes widening in surprise.

"You're alive." His voice is hoarse and riddled with pain.

"You're the second person who has said that to me in a month. Contrary to what you think, dick, I'm not that easy to kill." My dad grumbles behind me but I ignore him as I step forward, leaving a couple of feet of space between me and my tormentor. Looking at him now, I feel like a fool for ever living in fear of this piece of shit. "Want to know a secret?" I don't give him a chance to answer. "I wholeheartedly believed that if I didn't escape you the night that I did that you would kill me." The entirety of my family growls and begins spewing threats behind me.

"I should have done it when I had the chance," he spits. I shrug and nod.

"Yeah, it would have saved you a lot of pain but we can't live with should of, could of, would of now, can we?" I don't wait for him to answer as I shrug off my jacket and toss it to Cronos. It surprises me to see London, Artemis, Royal, Sin, Kacey, Erika, Chaos, Cass, Dad, Mom, and all my aunts and uncles here. It means a lot having them here, they're showing me they have my back no matter what and we protect our own. "As a doctor, I know which places to cut to inflict the most amount of pain and damage without killing you."

Colson sneers at me. "Do your worst, bitch." Cronos steps forward but I hold him back with a hand to his chest.

"Oh, you silly, I'm not going to hurt you." His brow dips in confusion. "Luka, bring her in." Everyone makes room for Luka as he drags Kim in. At the sight of his sister, Colson begins to fight and starts spewing useless threats that fall on deaf ears. Chaos and Royal help Luka string Kim up by her hands in front of Colson but far enough away. I slap her face to wake her up. She begins thrashing and darting her gaze around the room until she sees her brother—her face pales.

"Colson," she breathes out.

"I'm here," he replies, earning an eye roll from me.

"Once upon a time I would have rebelled against my family for doing this to another human but given what you two tried to take from me, I will enjoy this so much."

"Don't fucking touch her! Do it to me—" I spin around and shush Colson.

"I recall begging you to not take my daughter from me and did you listen?" He clamps his mouth closed.

"I don't believe he did, I think he shot you and then ran like a little bitch with our daughter," Cronos snarls.

"My daughter!" he screams. My anger takes control. I snatch a blade from the table beside Kim and plunge it into her thigh. She throws her head back and screams.

"You fucking bitch—"

"She isn't your daughter!" I scream. "She is nothing of yours, do you hear me? She will never know your face, never know your name or who the fuck you are. You are going to learn tonight why no one crosses my family."

"Kill me, not her!" Colson pleads.

"I'm not going to kill you... tonight. You are going to witness my wrath—tonight you are the victim and I'm the big bad bully. All those times I begged you to stop hitting me and you didn't listen, remember that while you watch me make your sister my bitch and if you're a good boy, I might just let her say goodbye to you before I slit her throat." Colson's pleas fall on deaf ears as I block everything out. I get tunnel vision as I picture all the ways I am going to make Kim wish she never tried to take my baby from me. Nothing else matters to me as I pull my earphones from my pocket and place them in my ears, then press play on my playlist. I close my eyes and bob my head to the beat for a second as I shake my arms out, this is a ritual I do before every shift and that is how I am treating this. I get in my zone and blank my mind, I close off all my emotions and feel nothing but sweet numbness.

"Angel?" I shake my head and frown at Cronos, he holds one of my ear phones in his hands.

"What? I'm about to start," I grit out, his brows form a deep groove on his face.

"Baby, you have been at this for hours." I jolt and turn to Kim, my eyes widen at the sight. The skin on her cheek is gone, her ears have been removed along with her nose. Fingers and toes litter the ground beneath her, slice wounds line her abdomen but the sight that holds my attention is her intestines wrapped around her neck.

"I did that?" I breathe out in... horror.

"Come on, you're done and you'll never be coming back here again." I drop the scalpel to the floor and allow him to grab my hand.

"Why? Why Amelia?" Colson screams. I flinch at the sound of his voice, I had forgotten all about him. I slowly turn to face him, and the haze from earlier starts to return and my need to inflict pain on him starts to drag me under until Cronos speaks.

"Stay with me, angel," he whispers.

Colson's eyes are bloodshot from shedding tears. "Because you tried to break me, you tried to use me to hurt those I love but the final push was you calling my daughter a mistake and a cunt." Nos's grip on my hand tightens as his own anger rides him. "Had you not tried to hurt my beautiful little girl, I would never have taken the person you clearly love most in the world from you. I hope you rot in fucking hell."

"See you when you get there, bitch!" he spits back.

"I run hell, motherfucker, I'll find you when *I* get there," Cronos grits out. I let him lead me out of there, ignoring all the wide eyed stares my family throws my way. Years ago I had my ribs tattooed with a saying, *η ελευθερία είναι δική μου* it's Greek for *Freedom is mine to take*. I just took that shit back tonight and it feels fucking amazing to finally be truly free. "I believe I have a debt to pay, angel," he says as we cross Uncle Bishop's back lawn.

"What debt?"

"I owe you a ride on my face and I plan to pay up as soon as I get your sexy ass in the shower."

Fuck, playing on the dark side just might be more fun.

Epilogue

Cronos

Three weeks later...

King wasn't joking when he said he wanted me to run a funeral home. Two weeks ago he handed me the keys to this place on the condition I keep Amelia from ever stepping foot in the bunker again. I agreed without argument. He has chosen to take over the torture of Colson, he and Allison refused to allow me a turn and that shit pissed me off but I understood why they wanted to do it—he nearly took his wife from him and in turn nearly killed his daughter and Kingsley.

Unlike the one back in Minnesota this one is double the size—three chillers, a separate part of the building is for the embalming and there is even a legit office for me in the back. Since opening the doors eight days ago it has been nonstop, you wouldn't believe the number of people that drop dead every day in New York.

"Don't you look cozy." I look up from the stack of papers on my desk to my angel standing there in a pair of heels and a navy colored trench coat. My brows raise on their own accord and all the blood rushes to my cock when she locks the door, and makes a show of twirling the string that is holding the coat closed as she walks toward me. I swallow audibly when she rounds my desk and pushes my chair back so she perches on the edge of my desk. I slide in closer and trap her legs between mine.

"Angel," I warn, keeping my hands off her is getting fucking harder and harder. Every night she taunts me with her body and I'm forced to endure the sounds she makes as she comes on my tongue or fingers. My cock is so hard it's painful.

"Shhhhh," she coos as she places her finger against my lips. I dart my tongue out, tasting her skin, her eyes blaze. "You got your wish."

"My wish is to be balls deep inside you," I mutter bitterly, bringing a smirk to her face.

"Well, I just happened to come from my final checkup." I shove my chair back and stand, she leans back and places her palms flat against my desk and stares up at me. "Six weeks, Grizz."

"Don't play with me, angel," I growl.

"Kingsley is spending the night with my parents, I have Vance coming over at nine." My nostrils flare. "I'm afraid I can't wait till then, so why don't you unwrap your present before we have to go pick our daughter up from Beth." Reaching out, I tug the coat open and groan at the sight of her in a blood-red lace set, her tits so full they nearly spill over the cups of her bra. She opens her legs wider and I nearly whimper at the sight of her pussy. "Crotchless panties make for easier access," she says huskily.

"Fuck, baby, I'm so hard." She pushes forward and grips the hem of my shirt, pulling it over my head. She smiles at the sight of my ink. I had angel wings inked on the front of my neck with *AQA* tattooed beneath it. It seemed only fitting I get something different to represent her now since my daughter's name is already inked on my abs. She says it's presumptuous of me to assume that she will marry me but she and I both know she will have my last name, it's just a matter of time. I slide my fingers between her folds, loving the way her eyes burn with want. "So wet for me," I growl as I lean and bite her bottom lip, relishing in the sound of her whimper.

"Cronos, don't tease me. I need to feel you inside me now." I pull back and plunge two fingers inside her greedy cunt. She throws her head back but I grip her neck with my free hand and force her gaze back to me. She knows it gets me off when she holds my gaze and comes, I love all the faces she makes as she chases her release.

"You're gonna come on my fingers, then I'm fucking this pussy so you remember exactly who the fuck it belongs to."

"Oh, fuck yes," she breathes out as I stroke that sweet spot inside her. I want to drag this out and torture her like she has done to me for the past few weeks but my need to be inside her refuses to allow me to do that. The pace in which I finger fuck her is ruthless, she won't last no matter how hard she tries to fight it.

"Keep trying to hold it off, baby, you know I always get what I want." She opens her mouth to sass me back, so I curl my fingers at just the right angle that has her crying out.

"Fuck, yes, Grizz—" I tighten my hold on her neck and shake her as I growl in her face, earning a devilish smirk from her. "Make me come and I'll scream your name."

"With pleasure," I grit out. It takes five more pumps of my

fingers before she's arching forward and dragging her nails down my naked chest, leaving her mark behind as she comes screaming my name. Pride swells inside me at the sight of her blissed out and rocking her hips to ride the last of her orgasm out. Just to be a prick, I yank my fingers free, earning a pout from her. I push the coat down her shoulders and then tug the string free of its loops, before helping her to her feet. "Fuck those tits are begging for me to bite them." She moans and stomps her foot.

"I want you to but they are so fucking sore because Kingsley can't seem to stay off them," she pouts.

"I never thought I would be jealous of my own daughter," I mutter bitterly, earning a chuckle from my girl.

"Turn around and bend over the desk, baby." She eagerly obeys. I grab her wrists and tie them behind her back with the cord from her coat, then kick her legs apart. "Fuck, I can see your cum coating your thighs, baby."

"Lick it," she demands. Like a feign searching for his next hit, I drop to my knees and grip the globes of her ass in my hands, then spread her cheeks, licking her hole, drawing a heady moan from her as I trail my tongue down through her pussy, loving the way she shakes when I suck her clit into my mouth. I release it and lick her inner thighs clean. She tries to push back to redirect me to her greedy little cunt so I smack her ass and stand.

"You get what I give you, angel."

"Nos, please, I need to feel you inside me, it's been too long."

"Watch." She looks back over her shoulder and watches me pop the button on my slacks. She darts her tongue out to moisten her lips as I tug the zipper down and push them down, freeing my cock.

"Fuck, I miss that!" she whines. I grip my shaft and groan when I pump myself. "Please, let me taste it or fuck me." I slap my cock against her ass.

"You don't get to taste this until Vance is fucking this pussy, then you can blow me while he makes you come." The thrill of what's to come tonight has me rubbing my dick through her slick folds. "I'm gonna fuck you so good, baby," I promise as I prod her entrance and slowly push inside her.

"Oh fuck," she cries out when I'm halfway inside her. "I want all of it," she begs. I grip her hips in a punishing hold and slam the rest of the way inside her. Both of us cry out at the feeling of being joined again—fuck, this is as close to heaven as I'm ever gonna get.

"Marry me?" I breathe out.

"No." I pull out leaving only the tip inside her. "Cronos!" she warns.

"Say *yes*," I growl as I slam back inside her hard and the desk shifts forward.

"Again."

"Marry me?" I ask again as I repeat the same move.

"Fuck me!" she snaps, tired of me constantly stopping just to keep her on edge.

"Say *yes* and I'll make you come so fucking hard, angel." I thrust inside her again driving my point home, I'm about to ask her again when the intercom on my office phone goes off.

"Mr. Argyros, your two O'clock is here." My eyes widen, shit the sight of my girl in that coat made me forget. I'm about to tell her to cancel when an idea hits me, Meelz looks back over her shoulder at me in horror when I press the button on my side.

I hold her gaze as I answer my secretary. "Tell *King* I will be out in five minutes." Amelia's eyes widen. She tries to move and push me away with her hands, but I'm not having it. I clamp my hand down on the back of her neck holding her in place as I thrust inside her again.

"Cronos," she moans.

"Marry me, angel?"

"Oh fuck," she grits out when I hit that spot inside her. "My dad is going to hear," she warns but I don't give a fuck. I'm gonna give him another grandchild soon enough. Meelz and I both agreed we wanted another baby and we don't want a big age gap between Kingsley and the baby, so no more protection and fuck it feels amazing to fuck her raw.

"Say yes or I'll make you scream so loud your father busts through that door and sees you being fucked by the Devil himself." She doesn't get a chance to answer as I draw back and thrust inside her again, making her bite down on her lip to keep quiet. I smirk, loving the challenge. I repeat the move over and over, knowing it's only a matter of time before she either gives in or screams out. Amelia couldn't stay quiet while being fucked if her life depended on it. I begin to doubt my decision when she starts to turn red in the face, my balls are tightening and it's coming down to a battle of wills right now, and I refuse to lose. I pull her up so her back is against my chest. When I pinch her clit between my fingers, her eyes widen in horror, she knows she's about to come and in turn, she'll scream. "Say yes, angel, and he'll never know I was fucking his baby girl like an animal."

"Yes!" she snarls. I smash my lips to hers, swallowing her cries as she comes all over my cock. The second her pussy clamps down on my dick, I come, groaning into her mouth. Shudders tear through me, that orgasm has me weak in the fucking knees. "Get. Out. Of. Me." I smile and kiss her cheek as I ease out of her. I know she's mad I forced her hand but I'll make it up to her.

We both dress quickly, but before she can escape, I grab her hand. She opens her mouth to argue but snaps it closed when I tell Linda to send King in, forcing a frown to her face. When my office door opens, I drop to one knee. Her face slackens and her mouth pops open.

"Cronos—"

"I asked your father for your hand five weeks ago." Meelz turns to her dad who doesn't look happy but nods. "Even without his permission, I would still be asking you this because I want forever with you and our daughter. I want to wake up every day next to you, I want to raise babies with you and grow old together. Make me the happiest fucking man in the world and say yes because if you don't, we will have to repeat what just—" She smacks her hand over my mouth, I can't help the laughter that bursts out of me. I bat her hand away and wipe the smile from my face. "I love you, Amelia. Please give me the honor of making you Amelia Queen Argyros so you can share the same last name as our daughter." Tears shine in her eyes.

"Now that's how you ask a woman to marry you," she says through tear-filled laughter. "No ring?" she jokes. I reach into my pocket and pull out the black Carbonado ring I had made for her. Her jaw unhinges at the sight of it. "Nos."

"I had to find the perfect ring for the perfect girl but turns out there wasn't one good enough for my queen so I had to have it made. It's black because it matches my soul which you own. Put the ring on, baby, so I can scream from the rooftops that I finally got the queen."

Happily ever afters are what you make of them and I made mine, I found my queen and princess, this is how my story ends and I couldn't be happier.

SAMANTHA BARRETT

The End

THANK YOU

To say this moment is bittersweet is an understatement. This book is the end of the Murdochs, Memento Mori, Godfathers and Re Della Strada. There will be no more books in their world... maybe... Never say never I guess. I miss each of these characters already. I have no idea what is next for me but I am excited to take a break from mafia and try something new. I hope you follow me on that journey.

Acknowledgments

There are so many I have to thank really, this mafia world has created some of the most amazing friendships and the support I have gotten from them while writing this series is the reason why I was able to write so many books in this world.

Marcus, without you none of this would have been possible. Well... maybe I could have done it alone but it feels weird saying that when I'm supposed to thank you for something so I guess I'll just say thank you for all the dick appointments and making me scream your name.

My children, you have sacrificed so much for me to be able to follow my dreams and for that, I am forever grateful to you both. You have no idea how much you both mean to me and how your understanding and constant encouragement to write helps give me the strength to delve deeper into these dark books. I love you, babies!

Leah, woman, thank you isn't the right word. I would not be where I am without you, babe. I couldn't have dreamed of finding a friend like you. You always being there to call and bounce ideas off of helps me so fucking much. All these graphics and covers are what makes these books sell, thank you for making them fucking epic, my Wednesday. I love you!

Jaye Pratt, thank you for all the formatting and holding my hand as I wrote most of these books. Your opinion wasn't really that great but hey, you kind of helped so I thought I better say thanks for nothing.

My alpha's, Debbie, Clare and Sarah, the three of you have held my hand through all of this. I don't know what I would have done without the three of you. Truly, these books are what they are because of you amazing as fuck ladies I get to call friends. From the bottom of my black heart, thank you for being on this journey with me.

My beta & ARC army girls, thank you beautiful souls so fucking much for always sticking by me and trusting me to mend those hearts that I break.

Lizz, my friend, you have been with me from the start. Bishop went far beyond our expectations and I am honored to have had you believing in me from the start. You always said I had a winner in that book and I guess it just took me longer to realize that. I am so grateful to be able to call you my friend. Thank you, Lizz, I appreciate you so fucking much.

My darling dark delicious readers, thank you again for following me and reading each of these books. I know I break your hearts and leave you mad when I end a book on a cliffy but I love that you trust me enough to heal those hearts and come back for more, I love you.

Sam xxx

Also By Samantha Barrett

Mafia Romance

Murdoch Mafia Series

Played By The Bishop

Tormented By The King

Tortured By The Knight

Tempted By The Queen

Turned By The Pawn

Ruined By The Rook

Murdoch Mafia Novella

Stalemate

Memento Mori Series

Reign Of Royal

Broken By Sin

In Havoc Lays Chaos

Godfathers of the night

London has Fallen

Damned By His Angel

Re Della Strada

Shattered Soul

Fractured Heart

Tainted Essence

Fairytales With A Twist

Condemned Beast

Secret Society/ Bully

Filthy Few

Forever Filthy

Filthiest Of Them All

Sports Romance

Playing For Keeps

Offside

Touchdown

End Game

Hail Mary

Blindside

RH Sports

Hate Us Like You Mean It

MM

Love Me Like You Mean It

Paranormal Romance

The Dream Series

A Beautiful Dream

A Twisted Fate

A Beautiful Nightmare

Redemption

Anarchy

Brutal Savages

Savage Lies

Brutal Truth

Savage Beast

Brutal Beauty

About the Author

Samantha Barrett is originally from Auckland, New Zealand but living in Brisbane, Australia.

Sam writes all things dirty dark and delicious with a side of twisted mind fuck.

She is a lover of all things red flags and an anti-hero is a must.

www.ingramcontent.com/pod-product-compliance
Lightning Source LLC
Chambersburg PA
CBHW030618170726
48283CB00002B/657